I0631147

KAIKŌURA RENDEZVOUS

A SPOTLIGHT MYSTERY

Stephen Johnson

Clan Destine
PRESS

First published by Clan Destine Press in 2023

Clan Destine Press
PO Box 121, Bittern
Victoria, 3918 Australia

Copyright © Author 2023

All rights reserved. No part of this book may be reproduced or transmitted in any form or by any means, including internet search engines and retailers, electronic or mechanical, photocopying (except under the provisions of the Australian Copyright Act 1968), recording or by any information storage and retrieval system, without prior permission in writing from the publisher.

National Library of Australia Cataloguing-In-Publication data:

Johnson, Stephen

Kaikōura Rendezvous

ISBN: 978-1-922904-45-4 (paperback)
ISBN: 978-1-922904-46-1 (eBook)

Cover Design by © Willsin Rowe
Design & Typesetting by Clan Destine Press

Clan Destine
P R E S S

www.clandestinepress.net

Cyclone Gita in this story was real.

Thank you to Rotorua Noir,
Lindy Cameron and Fin J. Ross
for inspiring the fiction.

FEBRUARY 3

Gita was born in the traditional manner of her South Pacific predecessors: alone, unloved, unwanted, feared. No howling was heard from the newborn, although the lungs would soon demonstrate their capacity. But Gita's first mewls did not go unnoticed; they were monitored safely from a distance.

It was Gita's location which made Semesa Bari take a keener interest. The first stirrings were 435 km southeast of the Solomon Islands. The projected easterly track could put his islands in danger. The 37-year-old scratched his thick beard as he ruminated about the possible lifespan and impact of this new tropical depression. It was cyclone season, a time to be wary at the Fiji Meteorological Service.

Gita showed no indication from the early data that she would escalate to headline-grabbing attention. Yet, Semesa had an uneasy feeling that Gita might develop into a wild child like Cyclone Fehi. His shift started with television news reports of the remnants of that cyclone pounding the South Island in New Zealand.

Gale force winds and heavy rain caused major flooding; dozens of homes on the West Coast were damaged. The storm surge coincided with a king tide in Nelson. Semesa watched in horror as spectators on the shore were swamped by waves. They were lucky not to be swept out to sea. Semesa could not prevent that foolishness. His job was to warn Pacific nations about approaching threats. He could only hope that information was used wisely.

He stretched arms, back and legs. It needed to be done more frequently than in his days as a rugby prop. Semesa looked at his empty mug, time for another herbal tea. There were still three hours on his shift; he would check the data several times before logging out.

Roughly 2,000 km west of Nadi, the 29-degree ocean was playing its role in encouraging Gita's development. The rising warm air was evaporating and spinning. Next would come the cooling process and towering cumulonimbus clouds, the mass always expanding. Perfect conditions for Gita to grow from a newborn into a monster.

FEBRUARY 4

KAIKŌURA, NEW ZEALAND

Gordie Tulloch eyed his former cellmate sceptically as condensation dripped from his beer bottle. No hospitality had been offered to the unexpected visitor, Mutton Kineen.

'Mate,' Mutton said. 'This could be the start of something big. The Australians want a reliable guy with a sea-going boat in North Canterbury. Someone who won't run off with the goods.'

'How big is the shipment – and how soon?' Gordie had automatically assumed it involved drugs. Mutton was sent down for five years for dealing and possession. The trade was too lucrative for Mutton to change careers.

'The pick up is in a couple of weeks. I dunno about the weight. They said the stuff will be in an airtight container just below the surface, but attached to a buoy. They can drop it away from the whale and charter fishing boats. You just need to be on standby and swoop as soon as the ship goes past.'

'I can haul it in by myself?'

'I guess so. The Sydney guys said they want a one-man band for security. If you're in, they'll send a contact to meet you in a few days. He'll confirm the pay, where to hand over the stuff.'

Mutton eyed the beer and licked his lips. The fridge door remained shut.

'The gangs pay well for reliable service and loyalty, mate. They hinted it could be the start of a new run for them.' Mutton looked around the decrepit villa. 'I reckon the money would be regular enough for you to fix up this dump – or get rid of it.'

Gordie ignored the slight. It could be the payday he had always dreamed about. Do a good job, keep his sticky fingers off the merchandise and there might be more. Kaikōura was a tourist hub: all eyes were on the whales, dolphins and feathered fuckers. Gordie could slide under the radar. But there were some elements of the plan that didn't sound right.

'If they're an Australian mob – why the fuck are they getting their shit dropped in New Zealand?'

Mutton shrugged. 'Who said it's for the Aussie market? A lot of Kiwis are being booted because of the *bad character* law. If they dealt drugs in Australia, they'll be doing it here.'

That made sense to Gordie. He was in debt with few prospects of earning money from his only asset, a battered fishing vessel.

'Okay. Set up a meeting at the pub.'

FEBRUARY 5

Kim Prescott stood with arms folded, chin tucked. The TV current affairs reporter trembled in her black shorts and shirt. It was not cold; she was embarrassed – and in trouble. Other emotions sought attention: anger, remorse, anxiety. What to deal with first? How to deal with any of them? Or the problem that had her under police scrutiny – again.

Of all the people Kim could choose to whack, it had to be an off duty policeman. Not that Kim knew he was a constable when she lashed out on the Yarra River jogging track. A few moments ago, he was a potential killer. Kim was running for her life; the pounding footsteps on the path was the assassin about to pounce. She was breathless, alone, no weapon to protect herself. Death moments away. Just like in the bush at Mount Macedon last May.

That assailant had a gun. One bullet sent a chunk of gum tree slicing into her scalp, the next round struck her in the shoulder. Luck saved her from the killer's *coup de grâce*. The repercussions from that attack had made her life a misery, especially since Christmas. It led to her current conflict with the law, not that the stubborn 25-year-old journalist would admit it.

'Look, Constable. I'm sorry I hit you.'

Kim's right hand stung. No bones were broken, although she wasn't sure about the policeman's nose. Blood trickled from his left nostril. His spattered white running shirt resembled a butcher's apron.

'I … I had a panic attack. I honestly thought you were going to hurt me.'

Kim hugged herself tighter; shuffled her feet. It was the first time she had publicly admitted her fears. She woke up stressed by the latest nightmare – another flashback to the day she almost died in the bush. The terrifying dreams were happening too frequently.

A jog before work was supposed to be calming. Instead, the heavy breathing of the overtaking 95-kilogram copper had triggered terror. Kim swung an arm in fear, to ward off the threat. The poor plod's nose was in the wrong place at the wrong time.

A vindictive Kim wanted to blame Sexy Rexy. Her loyal companion was absent; the greyhound recovering at home from a sprained ligament. That injury had occurred during a fox hunt through the Botanic Gardens on Friday night. If Rex had been with her, the runner would not have come close. Rex would have warned her about any danger. Guilt quickly quashed that silly notion. *I'm an awful bitch!*

Guilt had been a constant companion since the shooting. Kim knew it was reckless behaviour that put her life in danger. Not just her own. Jo Trescowthick and Nathan Potter could have been shot as well. One was a work colleague; the other a detective sergeant and – at that time – a potential new boyfriend. It was Nathan who saved their lives.

Blood dripped from the wounded runner's nose. 'You can't hit a policeman – or anyone – and expect to walk away, miss.'

His next words were directed to the police communications centre.

'A homicide car? I'm not bloody dead.'

Kim paled. It was a slap, not attempted murder. The cop was six foot of muscle and bone that could swat her in a second if he wanted payback. Why were they sending out the heavies to arrest her?

'I need transport back to Prahran for processing.'

Kim looked at her mobile. Did she need her own cavalry? The television studio was closer than the cop shop. But she didn't want to worry her program producer, David McKenzie. Mac didn't know about her previous altercation with police on New Year's Eve.

Kim was a tall, slender brunette whose communication skills had forged a successful media path many of her compatriots envied. That couldn't be derailed. *Patience Kim. You can talk your way out of this.*

'Okay, okay.' The constable sighed. 'Tell them I'm not in danger. The accused is with me on Alexandra Avenue at the bottom of Caroline Street.'

'Will they arrive full noise – sirens and lights?' Kim glared at the bloodied constable. 'Maybe call out the cameras to record your heroic rescue from the crazy woman jogger?'

'Sarcasm won't help you, miss. They sent the message as an officer in trouble – the homicide car was closest.'

The flashing grill lights of a Commodore raced towards the crime scene a few seconds later. As it approached, Kim saw the driver was the last person she wanted to speak to: Detective Sergeant Nathan Potter. Her ex-boyfriend – as of Saturday night.

'Shit!'

KAIKŌURA

Lachlan Naismith's stomach rumbled as his patrol car passed the barbecue van at Jimmy Armers Beach. The windows were sealed for the air conditioning. The seafood aromas could penetrate any glass or steel.

Two dozen tourists were scoffing crayfish, seafood platters, whitebait fritters, chips and a smattering of salad. Another dozen waited for their orders and a spare seat at the picnic tables. It was multinational communal dining with Kaikōura's renowned crayfish the *lingua franca*. Lachlan wiped his lips to avoid drooling on his stab-proof vest.

The price made it a rare treat on a policeman's pay. Not one he would enjoy on the current posting at the local station. His girlfriend – still in Nelson – kept an eye on his spending during secondments.

The Tasman police district covered the upper South Island and much of the West Coast. His semi-bachelor status made it easier to slot into various stations to cover leave or illness. The Kaikōura duty was for six weeks. Even with travel allowances, the seafood chowder at $6 was the most he could hope for. Maybe he would stop after a loop of the car park at the Peninsula Seal Colony.

February was peak seal-viewing season; occasionally skirmishes flared over the right to park closest to the slumbering mammals. Some tourists were too keen to get a selfie with the star attractions. It was Department of Conservation turf, but Lachlan's boss advised him that drive throughs helped keep the peace.

Motorhomes, camper vans, SUVs, utes and cars were bumper to bumper on the road edge. Most vehicles were in some sort of order, not hindering traffic, no need for tickets. Lachlan grew up in Auckland which nourished a lasting bitterness for parking wardens. He estimated a quarter of his first-year university student allowance was gobbled by parking infringements. Penury was avoided by joining the cops instead of completing the Bachelor of Arts. Lachlan would never intervene unless a motorist was blocking traffic.

Five cars waited at the park entrance. A driver was trying to navigate into a tight space behind the trees. Lachlan waited a minute, then two as another 10 cars were lined up behind him. Tempers would soon fray in the heat so Lachlan grabbed his cap and got out to find the source of the obstruction. He stretched his back, always necessary after several hours on patrol and 15 years as a blindside flanker. Sometimes his 32-year-old muscles felt like they were borrowed from a pensioner.

A few metres from the vehicle Lachlan was greeted by The Witch.

'Ah! Constable Naismith. Just in time to save a tourist from further embarrassment.'

Saffron Fernsby wasn't riding a broomstick or waving a wand. The 70-year-old's wispy grey hair couldn't be described as tell-tale signs of a sorceress. She was a jovial, compact woman in a light, ankle-length dress intent on a good deed.

'A large motorhome is trying to squeeze into a bay that wouldn't hold a Mini.' She pointed at the growing line of cars. 'I think your intervention is required.'

'Thanks, Professor. Any other dramas to worry about?'

Saffron chortled. Lachlan knew she preferred the academic title to the local nickname. A four-decade career in Ancient and Modern History at Oxford University had earned Saffron world-wide respect. A retirement quest for more knowledge had brought her to Kaikōura.

It was over an introductory sherry at the pub that Saffron had declared an interest in the natural world and the Wiccan community. Saffron swiftly became The Witch to the patrons. It was meant in jest, although the epithet swept through the community within days. It was an education for Saffron in South Pacific humour.

Saffron's coastal rambles included the seal colony when the weather was fine. Lachlan would often see her surrounded by a dozen tourists, freely sharing her knowledge of history, nature, life. Several times the policeman had been grateful for her multi-lingual skills when assisting European tourists. The woman was a welcome addition to the community, as far as he was concerned.

'No seal rustlers to worry about – just a German driver to send on his way.'

Lachlan tapped his cap in salute and turned towards the source of the traffic jam.

'Oh, there is one other matter constable. Not immediate, but it will require planning by town officials. There's another cyclone on the way.'

'I haven't read anything about that, Professor. Where's it coming from? New Caledonia again? Vanuatu?'

'It's a bit further east.'

'Christ! Another one – Cyclone Fehi was just a few days ago.'

Kaikōura had escaped the deluge of that one, but not the winds which reached more than 110 km/h. Lachlan had arrived for his secondment just before State Highway 1 was closed north of the town. He was glad to be away from Nelson where beachfront suburbs were swamped.

Saffron did not offer reassurance. 'I fear this one could be worse.'

Lachlan nodded. The seafood chowder might have to wait. He needed to move the tourist and check the forecast about the projected cyclone track.

He looked at the sky: it was overcast, mild, about 20 degrees. No hint of a tropical storm about to descend. The light layer of icy snow on the alps was a reminder of the diverse nature of the local climate. Who knew what was brewing behind those distant rocky crags? Would the cyclone spare Kaikōura again? How far away was it? Strange that he had not seen any reports about weather threats.

'What's it called, Professor?'

'I don't know. It's just an infant.'

Saffron smiled and walked away from the confused policeman. Perhaps there was more to The Witch moniker than Mainlanders really knew.

MELBOURNE

Mac twirled an empty Collingwood Football Club mug on his desk as he listened to the landline.

'No. I didn't know that.'

His two-metre frame was hunched over the command post for *Melbourne Spotlight* at Channel 5's South Melbourne studios. He was surrounded by the mid-afternoon bustle of a television current affairs program: reporters wrestling scripts, editors assembling stories, camera operators lounging. The frenzy came on late-breaking stories in the last half hour before broadcast. The noise would horrify compliance officers. Not that anyone could hear them in the bowels of the mid-20ᵗʰ century building.

'That is concerning.'

Mac pushed aside his second new mug of the year – they kept disappearing – and scanned "the dungeon", as it was more commonly known. He ran fingers through his wavy ginger mane and beard as he observed Dugal Cameron and Ken Withers fiddle with a drone-mounted camera. Reporters Pete Benson and Stephanie Grant were assaulting their keyboards; first to finish could claim the next available edit suite. Mac watched their lips moving as they typed. That was normal; delivery is important to visual storytellers. They wrote for the voice, not the pages of dailies that used to wrap his fish and chips.

'The second time? Tell me more.'

To his left, production assistant Jo Trescowthick worked at her computer. The office Svengali was eavesdropping; the tell was her keyboard limping along at 30 words per minute, well below the usual clatter of 80. He wasn't worried; Mac considered the *Spotlight* crew an extended family and a wayward child needed help. He pivoted slowly to face the rear wall.

'Yes, I agree. We need to be more proactive.'

Mac's gaze settled on Kim. Her desk faced Mac's right-hand man, senior producer Christopher Rogers; better known as Curly for his sparsely populated cranium. They would be staring into each other's eyes, except for the desktop screens between. Curly's fingers worked at warp speed; Kim's barely moved. She had been subdued all day.

That was attributed to her weekend breakup with Nathan Potter. Jo had whispered the juicy tidbit moments before the planning meeting. The crew understood why the morning's banter washed over Kim. Everyone went through dating blues. Mac's latest marriage frequently navigated stormy seas. Kim was given distance and a light workload. But now a phone call suggested Mac's youngest and bravest reporter was in more turbulent waters.

He swung the chair back to the monitors above the desk as a news promo played. There was no breaking story to concern him. Mac lowered his voice. 'Thanks Nathan. I appreciate your help keeping Kim out of the lockup. She's been off the boil since we came back from the Christmas break, but I didn't know she was battling demons from Mount Macedon. We'll get her help.'

His hand explored his red beard more intently, always an indication of imminent action.

'Yep. I'll keep you posted, mate. She's stubborn – but we'll find a way to sort her out.'

The phone was barely in the cradle before Jo's death chariot rolled to within millimetres of his ankle. No flesh was gouged; Mac understood that she wanted the gossip.

'What's happened? Tell me.'

Mac glanced over his shoulder. Curly was still going ten to the dozen; Kim was down to one finger typing. Her other hand was probing the scar above her ear; a nervous action that was more pronounced in recent weeks. Curly should be party to Mac's confab with Jo. It would have to wait until he finished the script, or whatever was being pounded into the computer.

'A coffee I think, young Josephine.'

Jo glared. 'You live dangerously Mac.'

'Let me enjoy a moment without fear – I have information you want; my shins are safe. Join me in the kitchen.'

Jo silently pedalled her chair behind the stocky producer. The tearoom was a few metres away, but Jo never walked when she could roll and always a speed that crushed the toes of slower traffic.

Jo swiftly prepared two espressos. Station management provided a large supermarket-brand coffee tin for departments every week. *Spotlight's* first delivery had never been opened. Standards had to be maintained; the crew bought their own machine and blends after much bullying from Jo.

She inhaled the aroma. 'Right, that's two coffees I've made you today. You're in extreme debt – talk.'

Mac sipped. *Knowledge is power!*

Jo's patience wasn't elastic.

'That was Nathan. Kim was almost arrested this morning for belting a copper.'

'Shit. Not again.'

'You know about the first incident?'

Jo waved away Mac's incredulity. 'What happened today?'

'She was running beside the Yarra. Another jogger got too close; she lashed out. Gave a Prahran plod a bloody nose.'

'What did Kim say?'

'She said it was a panic attack. The heavy footsteps reminded her of Mount Macedon – she thought Beacham was gunning for her again.'

'Well, that's understandable. We got chased through the bush by a nutcase. She was wounded twice. No surprise if she might have a flashback.'

Mac towered over his petite 29-year-old PA.

'Oh, don't give me that look,' she said.

'I thought she was doing fine after the extra surgery and rehab. There was no indication of post-traumatic stress by Christmas. I took that as a good sign because it often starts within a month or two of a shooting. You came through it okay.'

'I got a thump to the head, not a bullet in the back.'

Mac suppressed a shiver as he thought about almost losing two members of his media family.

It started with *Spotlight* receiving a tip off about live-baiting in greyhound racing. Kim got her teeth into the story and uncovered two dead dog trainers, a captive woman and a snake-loving killer who settled grievances with a chain saw. The trail led his adventurous colleagues to a property north of Melbourne where they almost died. Their lives were saved by homicide detective Nathan Potter, better known now as Kim's ex-boyfriend.

'Why didn't you tell me about the New Year incident? She's smacked two cops in five weeks.'

Jo rolled her eyes. 'That was valid – everyone at Berwick agreed. We went to a New Year party with Nathan. A dickhead lit homemade fireworks at midnight. The first cracker landed behind Kim.' Jo lowered her voice. 'She went troppo. Flew at the guy – thumping and kicking him. It was wild. Nathan had to drag her away.'

'Lucky she wasn't charged.'

'The noise was humungous; the idiot used too much powder. A few detective mates of Nathan wanted to belt the constable as well.'

Mac finished his coffee and put the empty in the sink. 'Two indications that Kim's not coping.'

Jo retrieved his cup and stacked it beside hers in the dishwasher.

'It seemed justifiable at the time. With hindsight – yeah, she must be struggling. Did the cop accept her explanation about a panic attack today?'

'With a bit of persuading from a detective sergeant. Kim got lucky – he was close when they put out an alert about a cop in trouble. He talked the underling out of laying charges.'

'Good old Nathan.'

'What about Nathan?' Kim stood in the kitchen doorway; eyes narrowed. 'What's he been telling you Mac?'

'Um – he called me. About this morning. He's worried about you.'

A mobile phone tune at the command post was Jo's escape from Kim's wrath. Mac was left to fend for himself.

Jo flinched at the caller display: Dad. Sterling Trescowthick rarely called before the broadcast – unless it was critical. She propelled her chair to the empty hallway outside the dungeon.

'Hey Dad. What's up?'

'Sorry to bug you before the show. But I had to tell you – Melissa's torn up the plane tickets to New Zealand.'

'Shit!' Jo rubbed her brow. 'Too many emotions to deal with?'

'Yeah. She'll never get over Byron's death.'

Tears welled. Her stepbrother had been struck by a hit-and-run driver in Kaikōura two years ago. Byron died at a lonely beach a few hundred metres from the campervan rental where his girlfriend slept.

'You still there Jo?'

'Yeah, just trying to process things.' The tears were swiftly blotted before a curious colleague walked past. 'I thought Melissa was ready to forgive the Kiwis.'

'She doesn't hate New Zealanders, but she can't set foot in the Shaky Isles. The dread finally exploded an hour ago.'

Jo dabbed her eyes with a tissue.

'New Zealand's a stunning country.' Sterling said. 'I thought a motorhome holiday before the anniversary would reduce the anguish. I was being too optimistic.'

Jo snorted. 'A bloody lunatic. We should have known that it would be more like a pilgrimage than a holiday for her.'

'That's my Jo. Don't sugar coat anything.'

They laughed.

'I'm always the practical one, Dad.' A final tear was absorbed by the tissue. 'Can we get a refund on the airfares and motorhome?'

'Well, that's why I called before the program. Mel tore up *our* tickets. Not yours. Do you still want to go?'

'What, me drive the motorhome?'

'You don't fly until Saturday. Can you find a friend to share the driving.'

'You mean someone who can reach the accelerator?'

'I was being diplomatic. I'd rather someone who might use the brake pedal too.'

Their laughter was curtailed by the dungeon door slamming. Kim stomped down the hallway.

'Was that an earthquake?'

'No, the station's not collapsing. Just the usual mayhem.' She watched the grumpy reporter boot a rubbish bin. 'Well, not so usual – Kim's had a meltdown with Mac. She punched a copper this morning.'

'Jeezus Jo! Was she arrested?

'No. The ex-boyfriend happened to be the next copper on the scene. He outranked the plod she thumped for getting too close while jogging.' Jo giggled. 'Wish I had been there to see that.'

'You lead a crazy life. Look, have a think about the motorhome. But you've only got a few hours. I'll need to ring the owner tonight. We were supposed to hand it over to American tourists in Queenstown on February 23. If you can find a mate, I won't have to feel guilty about leaving him in the lurch.'

Jo felt a different pang of guilt. There might be someone to share the journey, but was it wise to tell her father about that contender?

'Okay. I'll call you after the program. It would be a shame to waste a holiday.' She paused a beat. 'Plus, I need to visit Jimmy Armers Beach.'

'A tribute to your stepbrother would be nice. Mel would appreciate that.'

Jo wiped a final tear, then spent half a minute thumbing an international text before rolling back into the office.

KAIKŌURA

Constable Lachlan Naismith checked the MetService website at the end of his shift. It displayed sunny icons from Kaitaia in the far north to Christchurch, two and half hours south of his desk. Less than two, if he put the lights and siren on for an emergency. The West Coast forecast showed clouds and the deep south could expect rain. No cause for concern; cyclones never appeared from beneath New Zealand. The bottom of the world was expecting a mild summer to continue.

Station boss, Senior Sergeant Barry McCullers, groaned as he released his utility belt. The vest thudded onto his desk. It was a ritual pleasure for the stocky 43-year-old at the end of every shift.

'You checking the surf reports Lachie? I saw some good waves at Hapuku this afternoon. The water was pure turquoise, almost like Fiji – but 15 degrees colder!'

'Nah. Last time I tried to ride a Malibu was at Piha, near Auckland.' Lachlan clicked on the link for tropical cyclone activity. 'It was a two-metre swell. Sliced my leg open with the fin. Twenty stitches convinced me to stick with boogie boards. Foam can't disembowel you.'

'You northerners are bloody pussies.' McCullers stretched arms and legs cramped from a day in a patrol car. 'I bet you were wearing a wetsuit as well.'

'Of course, Baz. It was January. The water was only 22 degrees.'

McCullers laughed as he lugged his kit to a locker. Lachlan checked the whole weather site: no warnings to batten down the hatches.

'Hey Baz.'

'Yo!'

'You heard anything about a cyclone heading our way?'

A head and hairy chest appeared around the locker door. 'Shit! No – nothing. We were lucky to miss Cyclone Fehi. That would have stuffed all the quake repair work.'

Lachlan often wondered if the South Island was cursed because of the frequency of natural disasters. Christchurch was devastated by two earthquakes in five months; the second struck at lunchtime, killing 185 people. A few years later it was Kaikōura's turn to get smashed. A 7.8 magnitude quake tossed residents from their beds. Two people died and almost 100 km of coast was changed forever.

'We should have got a warning from HQ and Civil Defence.' McCullers was puzzled. 'Where did you hear about it?'

'You know Professor Fernsby?'

'The Witch?'

'The eminent Oxford academic.'

'Have you heard her talk about Wiccans and paganism? "The divine character of the natural world." She's nuttier than a fruitcake, Lachie. I reckon it's that sherry she drinks. Rots the brain.'

The locker slammed. McCullers emerged in a dark blue polo shirt.

'Christ Baz, you make rednecks sound like choir boys.'

'Guilty your honour. But don't tell the white supremacists, I get enough of their recruitment letters.'

Kaikōura was a small office and camaraderie was important, especially for the occasional blow-in like Lachlan. He knew McCullers was joking, most of the time.

'Why does The Witc … Um, why does the nutty professor believe there's a cyclone brewing?' McCullers scooped his Holden keys from the other desk. The V8 power eclipsed the patrol car.

Lachlan scratched his neck. 'She said … she … felt the birth.'

McCullers stared at his colleague for five seconds before the grin emerged. He shook his head. 'Wait till they hear about that at the boozer – the earth mother is delivering us a cyclone.'

Lachlan smiled ruefully. The community banter would engulf him as well; he was boarding at the pub.

MELBOURNE

'You two want another beer?' Jo didn't wait for an answer.

Mac and Curly had their feet on the command post desk, chairs at full tilt. Kim's tantrum had sent the rest of the crew scurrying from the dungeon after duties were completed. Bad vibes in the *Spotlight* office were unfamiliar.

Executive producer and presenter Richard Templeton was also absent; he had been summoned by a higher authority. Channel 5 chief executive Reg Bradley heard about Kim's backhander to the cop and wanted an explanation. The consensus was that Kim had PTSD and required professional help.

Jo checked her phone. *Finally, a text!*

Can only spare a night when you pass through

Damn you Julian. She sighed, collected the lagers and wine and tuned back into the amateur psychologists. 'Kim won't do counselling. She's in denial – she thinks I didn't have problems after the shootout, so she shouldn't either. It would be showing weakness.'

Curly flipped the caps on the desk edge. 'How did you deal with the trauma?'

Jo raised her glass. 'Vino. Lots of vino. And vodka. Some gin as well. Even some leftover bourbon when the booze cupboard was bare. Kim shared a few sessions. We talked. She seemed all right – but there must have been more guilt.'

'She blamed herself for almost getting you killed?'

'And Nathan. He only had a tyre lever to rescue us from a gunman. It must be eating away at her.'

'Has she said anything about nightmares,' Curly asked.

'Nope. Obviously, she doesn't share everything.'

'The station will pay for a shrink,' Mac said.

'Christ!' Jo's death chariot pivoted. 'Don't ever say that word to Kim. You'll never get her to therapy.'

'What about a holiday?' Curly suggested. 'She had two operations, then a lot of physio work to fix her shoulder. It was a long time off work – but it wasn't relaxing. She came back like a bull at a gate. She only had a few days leave over Christmas. I don't know why she volunteered for extra duties on the News.'

'That I can explain,' Jo said. 'Stephanie Grant.'

Mac paused with the bottle at his lips. 'But Steph's with *Spotlight* full time.'

'Despite being a media seer, you do miss the obvious. Who ended up with all the big stories while Kim was off work?'

'Stephanie,' Curly said.

'Kim's paranoid that she'll get squeezed out of the reporting roster by the new *Spotlight* star.'

Mac was perplexed. 'But I told her the job was safe for life – no station would ever dump a reporter wounded in the line of action.'

'Unless they develop a habit of hitting cops,' Curly said. 'So, I come back to my point – she's had time off work – but not a proper holiday. Would that help? If she won't listen to the professionals, do we give her some space?'

Jo sighed. 'Come on Curly. Spit it out. You want Kim to join me in the motorhome.'

Curly shrugged; Mac nodded. 'Now why didn't I think of that?'

'What if I wanted a few days of solitude – me and a cute Kiwi guy. And a few bottles of Marlborough's finest wines?'

'Think of the problems the last Kiwi guy caused you.' Mac said. 'Have you heard from Julian Oliver since he fled Australia?'

'That's none of your bloody business.' Jo gulped too much wine and sputtered.

'Have you found anyone to share the driving?

Jo groaned. It had been a mistake to share the holiday hiccup. 'Not yet.'

'What are the chances you'll find someone in a few days?'

'Not great.'

'You told us you're on a deadline.' Mac looked at his watch. 'Your father needs to decide about the motorhome booking. If he cancels – you'll be stuck here treading on eggshells with Kim like the rest of us.'

'Oh joy. What a fabulous choice.' A sip, no choking.

'Taking Kim would solve a few problems,' Curly said. 'You get your holiday, Kim might destress – and you would have a designated driver for every vineyard in New Zealand.'

'Okay that's settled.' Mac beamed. 'Jo's taking one for the team. Curly, it's your job to tell our grumpy reporter that she's off to New Zealand.'

'Why me? You're the boss.'

'She's not talking to me.'

'Brilliant. Couldn't it be something simpler – like predicting the grand final winner in September?'

'That's easy – Collingwood. Look, Kim and Jo might get lucky. Nature's always crapping on the Shaky Isles. The news guys had dramatic vision of a cyclone in the South Island a few days ago. Tell Kim she could be *Spotlight's* foreign correspondent for their next natural disaster.'

FEBRUARY 6

KAIKŌURA

A fit person could run from the railway bridge at the start of Kaikōura's main street to the tourist information office at the other end in a minute. Most of the commerce happened between these landmarks, and the town's most distinctive building was a feature. The district council, library, museum and other civic operations were housed in a giant craypot. It was really a curved wooden façade, a suitable tribute to the sea which had sustained Kaikōura.

The vibe dipped a few heartbeats beyond the tourism HQ where the road curved with the rocky coast. A memorial park to the war dead, a stand of Norfolk pines, motels, beach homes, the pub, wharves and the food caravans at Jimmy Armers Beach lined the road until the terminus at the seal colony.

Saffron Fernsby was a rambler, not a runner. The retired academic saw no need to hasten through life: observing, listening, chatting were more rewarding. She nursed a herbal tea while nibbling at a typically frugal blueberry muffin. The location was a favourite; a small square formed by tourist shops in revamped shipping containers.

An endless procession of motorhomes, campervans and cars crawled past a few metres away. They were interspersed by an occasional truck or trade ute wanting to encourage a swifter journey.

A German couple caught her attention. They were in their 20s, weeks overdue for a haircut, wearing khaki singlets and baggy draw-string trousers that conservative Cantabrians would describe as *hippyish*. They were debating the merits of a whale watching tour. The giant mammals and dolphins were Kaikōura's biggest attraction. The tickets were steep for budget travellers.

Nearby an Italian family was comparing New Zealand ice cream to their beloved gelato in Firenze. Saffron didn't need to hear the next tourists approaching her café table to identify their nationality. The giveaway was the embroidered red cap: Make America Great Again.

Across the square, a couple in their 40s examined leaflets. Saffron wondered if they were reading about tourism highlights, or the mythology of the volatile New Zealand landscape. She loved the legend of Rūaumoko who causes the earth to move, rumble and shake whenever he stretches.

Tourists always struggled with the pronunciation. Saffron empathised; she still grappled with the Māori language. It was another reason for her extended stay in the South Island – there was so much to learn.

Saffron had been surprised by the evidence of Rūaumoko's most recent flexing. Roads were torn apart, homes destroyed, paddocks scarred, the coast uplifted by up to two metres. Most shocking were photos of mountains cascading into the sea: the main rail line and State Highway 1 buried beneath. It took a year to get the trains moving; the road repairs had segued to engineering projects to minimise similar damage when Rūaumoko next rolled in his earth womb. That was inevitable.

Saffron felt connected to Rūaumoko, sensing minor shifts minutes before the earth moved. Occasionally she was able to warn close friends to prepare for a shake. Not many could be trusted to understand her *gift*: a sensitivity to natural phenomena. Saffron had learned not to share these feelings widely; centuries ago, she would have burned at the stake.

Saffron finished the tea and checked her watch. It was time to shop at the supermarket on the highway. That was a 15-minute walk. Her rented studio apartment was back towards the pub, 10 minutes in the opposite direction. New Zealand was providing more exercise than she anticipated. At least she was dressed for the excursion: a blue, casual, floral print top and white calf length dress. Both were cotton, suitable for the warm afternoon.

The couple had completed their reading lesson. They greeted Saffron with a hesitant hello as she passed. *Spanish.*

'Hola. Cómo estás?'

Tourist eyes lit up with the fluent query about their well-being.

'We are *very* good,' the man said. 'Thank you. We love New Zealand and love to learn more. Our English not so good. But we get better.'

Saffron returned to her native tongue. 'You are doing very well. New Zealanders will appreciate you are making the effort.'

The man cocked his head. 'I think you are not local inhabitant?'

'No, an eager traveller, like yourselves. I am from England, the mother country for many white New Zealanders. However, I'm here to learn more about the Māori – the first arrivals who probably regret signing a treaty with the British.'

Her political opinion confused the man. His wife smiled politely, probably equally unaware of British colonialism. She moved to safer territory.

'Have you been on a whale tour yet.'

The man replied again. 'Tomorrow. Or the next day. We have just arrived from Christchurch in a motorhome. We find campsite, make plans. Do you recommend the whale trip?'

'Oh yes. However, I would not delay your booking. There is a cyclone on the way and sea creatures are sensitive to the conditions. They might move away to less turbulent waters ahead of the storm.'

'A cyclone?' The wife joined the conversation. 'We did not hear about this. When will it arrive? Do we need shelter?'

Saffron smiled to ease their fears. She knew the cyclone was coming but had no evidence of its power or track.

'The cyclone is a few days away. District officials and weather forecasters will send warnings when appropriate. Are you going north to Nelson? Abel Tasman?'

'Yes,' the husband replied. 'All these places. We also go Golden Bay and Takaka. The pictures look very pretty.' A frown creased both Spanish foreheads. 'Is safe to travel?'

Saffron winced; she had opened a can of worms.

'The cyclone last week caused flooding and damage on the West Coast and in Nelson. Listen to the radio for advice and warnings. You have time to plan a safe itinerary.'

Saffron felt conflicted. She had done the right thing; the Spanish tourists could have driven into the middle of the storm zone. However, she was annoyed about slipping into tourist-talk: speaking louder and using shorter sentences. It was the colonial habit of making foreigners understand English. *Shame on you, Saffy. Should have gone back to Spanish!*

A breeze blew along the street, ruffling her cotton dress. It wasn't a cold zephyr. But it reached her core, causing a shiver. The cyclone was gathering power. She waved goodbye to the Spanish tourists and hurried towards the shop.

An index finger tapped a message:

T1 met new T at pub What next?

Seconds later the phone was back on the rickety pine table, its owner reaching for a lager. Few people were outside to enjoy the gloaming: rich reds and deep blues contrasted the glowering ranges. There was a layer of white at the peaks, ice the summer couldn't melt. Tourists had departed for holiday homes, motels and campsites; most locals were indoors where the bar was closer.

The mid-30s texter sat beneath the main bar windows, where drinkers and diners were treated to a coastal panorama in all seasons. But the views didn't interest Heath Michel, although he frequently swivelled his head, as if admiring the dusk show.

Traffic to the New Wharf beyond the pub had been adjusting to free-range drinkers for more than a century. Heath was watching two middle aged men in the beer garden across the narrow bitumen. The meeting was important to Heath, another piece in the puzzle, but the conversation was impossible to hear. The man he'd designate as T2 was a local fisherman, judging by the uniform: All Blacks beanie, plaid shirt, dirty trousers, red band gumboots, dead fish cologne. Or was the smell coming from the beach? The man methodically rolled cigarettes as he listened. A new rollie was lit within seconds of a butt being flicked towards the sea.

T1 was an Australian, a toff by comparison: Boston baseball cap, dark hair, olive complexion, light blue polo shirt, clean denims, boat shoes. Heath was surprised T1 could tolerate the fishy stench. It was another validation for suspicions that a rendezvous was being arranged.

He wanted instructions for after the meeting: who to follow? The temptation was to track the new contact: the fisherman. The man and his vessel needed to be identified. But had T1 completed his business? This could merely be a social call. Or worse, a red herring to protect the real contact.

Heath didn't believe he'd been spotted. This was the first time he had been within 20 metres of T1. The surveillance job had been passed to him when the Australian had gone straight from Auckland's international airport to the domestic terminal. Heath had been mustered, sent a photo, given a battered Toyota Hilux with the grunt of a V8 and told not to lose T1. The plan was working, so far.

He'd dispatched a discreet image of the fisherman but didn't expect instant identification. It was a record: to be kept, investigated, or discarded. His role was to watch and follow the chosen.

Heath sipped beer and glanced at his mobile. They were invaluable tools; there was nothing suspicious about a man drinking alone and toying with his phone. He could be looking for messages, sports scores, playing games or chasing a Tinder hook-up.

He hoped a decision about the targets arrived before the pair separated. Their pints were close to empty. His task was to follow the Australian. A smart man would follow the order. An ambitious observer might try to progress matters by going after the new target. Heath weighed the options while he waited.

There was movement from the targets a minute later; the Australian had both empty glasses in hand. The fisherman didn't budge. Crisis averted; they were after refills. His own pint was three-quarters empty; he would have to nurse that through their next pint. A second beer wasn't possible. He could always try a coke. The targets might think it was filled with rum if they were even curious. It was all about hiding in plain sight.

Shadows spread across the foreshore as the sun dipped behind the mountains. The targets were settled, his mind was free to wander. It was his first time back in two years. He hadn't been avoiding Kaikōura, despite the potential demons; duty had taken him elsewhere. How did he feel? Was the angst still there?

The introspection was interrupted by a window opening above his head. The bar banter washed over him.

'Constable Naismith!' The room above was silenced. 'We presume you're off duty. But can you spare us any insights into the approaching cyclone? Or do you need to consult your oracle – The Witch?'

If there was a reply, it was drowned by raucous laughter.

A cyclone? That was news to Heath, if indeed there was an approaching storm. The merriment suggested a local cop was being ridiculed. Still, a wise man would investigate. The only supplementary information Heath had been provided, before scrambling to catch T1 at the airport, was that a *result* was expected in the next fortnight. They didn't need nature interfering with this operation. He picked up the phone and thumbed through to the MetService page.

A new message diverted him to the chat thread.

stick with T1

That sorted his dilemma. And the timing was perfect. The Australian had returned from the bar with one pint. They would be parting soon. Heath quaffed his beer and walked to the Hilux. It was more sensible to watch T1's rental than leave the pub behind him. The fisherman might have been a plant to flush out a tail. Heath was still in the hunt.

BASS STRAIT

Rafael Serrano's back was to the lights of Burnie as he lit a cigarette against a deck railing of the Cypriot registered *Hoplite*. It was the sixth time the 2nd mate's vessel had exchanged containers at the busy Tasmanian port. Yet, for a few minutes, he had to pretend he was interested in the coastal views. The 30-year-old turned towards the city and let the wind take the exhale.

'*Ola* Rafa.' The greeting was from a deckhand, a small Filipino man in blue overalls and a fluorescent orange vest.

'Fuck off Datu.' The response was dinky-di Aussie. Rafael's heritage was Spanish, via immigrant parents, but there wasn't much use for the mother tongue in the Melbourne suburb of Williamstown.

'Too late to fuck off, Rafa.' Datu Aquino pointed to Bass Strait. 'I not swim too good.'

They sniggered. Datu always tried to wind up the 2nd mate about his limited language skills. The deckhand had three decades at sea; that experience gave him the words to order food, alcohol and companionship – for a short or long time – in a dozen countries.

The deckhand joined Rafa at the rail and accepted the lit cigarette he was offered.

'All okay with the shipment?' asked Rafael.

'*Si, si*. I best hider on the oceans. No custom man or dog ever find what Datu not want found.'

'Good.' Rafael took one final puff of his own smoke and flicked his butt into the darkness. 'I'll send a message we're on target for the 13th.' Rafa turned and folded his arms. 'I hope the backup plan is in place by then.'

Datu sucked deeply on the nicotine. 'You get confirm?'

'Yeah. The Sydney boys said they will have a guy in Kaikōura.'

'Then no need worry for us.' The embers of Datu's cigarette flickered as he flung it towards the water. 'You get *Hoplite* to drop, I do my job. We get pay – end of story. Until next time.'

Datu slapped the 2nd mate's shoulder as he departed for official duties. No one could see the etiquette breach. Rafael knew the deckhand was right; their job was to get the vessel to the agreed location, drop the consignment without being seen and sail on. What happened after that was the gang's problem.

It was the change of routine that made Rafael cautious. The sea drop had only been done once before. It was successful, but there was a risk of millions of dollars going to the seabed if the next link didn't do their job properly. The organiser of the illicit shipment was a Lebanese gang in Sydney. They were not renowned for tolerating fuckups.

Rafael and Datu had combined for a dozen successful deliveries for the gang. Most had been in Sydney. The change was caused by the *Hoplite* picking up a contract for New Zealand. From Perth they would normally follow the southern coastal ports, turn north for Sydney, Brisbane and then do a run around several Pacific islands depending on what cargo was on board.

This trip required them to cross the Tasman for deliveries in Dunedin, Christchurch, Napier and Tauranga. Sydney was not on the itinerary, hence the change to a sea drop, and a pick up boat. Rafael was a professional smuggler – how reliable was the Kiwi crew?

That was the crux of Rafael's niggle. He could guarantee the goods would be dropped in the right place, but what would happen if the boat didn't find them? They might tell the gang there was nothing to collect, then sell the stuff privately. Things could get messy if the Lebanese came looking for their goods – or revenge.

FIJI

Gita was morphing from a playful infant into a mischievous toddler. Unsteady, energetic, uncertain of direction. Fuelled by the warm seas, it was growing by the hour as it wobbled towards the gap between Wallis and Futuna and northern Fiji. Her lungs were expanding, the exhalations peaking at 90 km/h, but not yet at a constant bellow that would cause serious damage. Nor was she powerful enough to concern the leaders in either nation.

The meteorological people took a different view. Semesa Bari was on the evening shift. He sipped instant coffee as he tracked every nautical mile and logged all the appropriate data: wind speed, sea temperatures and more. Gita was showing the signs of growing into a wild child. Science would determine the warning levels issued, Semesa knew instincts were just as valuable.

FEBRUARY 8

KAIKŌURA

Grumbling from behind a mountain of paper made Lachlan hesitate. Few cops enjoyed the bureaucracy of crime fighting; McCullers hated it. That's why the station boss allowed it to build to Mt Cook proportions. His offsider normally ensured the paperwork never clouded the senior sergeant's day. Dozens of signatures were all that McCullers usually had to worry about, until the underling went on holiday. A minor quake could bury McCullers under an A4 pile.

Lachlan couldn't help. He was filling in for a few weeks; if there were any mistakes it would be the regular crew who copped a blast from headquarters. Better computer skills kept Lachlan on top of his desk work. It also allowed time to follow hunches. He pivoted towards his boss.

'Baz?'

'What?'

The tone should have discouraged Lachlan, but the matter had to be raised. A cyclone with enough rain to worry Noah was forming near Fiji.

'Remember the professor's warning?'

Eyes surfaced over the paper pinnacle. 'Yeah. And?'

'There's one brewing. Samoa's about to get drowned – they probably should have been building an ark. They reckon it will be a monster by the morning.'

'Samoa? Is that north of Blenheim?'

'Yeah. About thirty-four hundred kilometres closer to the equator.'

'Then why the fuck should I be worried?' His head disappeared, the grumbling grew louder.

Lachlan persisted. 'Saffron is on target with her initial prediction. Could she be right about it reaching New Zealand?'

'Christ, Lachie.' McCullers stood, waved his arms. 'A cyclone pops up in the Pacific every other week in February. It doesn't make her a prophet of doom to guess that.'

'The climate's changing Baz. We're getting bigger storms down our way. Even Dunedin was flooded last week by the dregs of Cyclone Fehi.' Lachlan picked up the patrol car keys. 'I'm just raising a flag – we'd hate to get caught out.'

McCullers swung an arm in exasperation and infringement forms cascaded from his desk.

'Fuck!' McCullers glared. 'They were ready for the district court tomorrow.'

'Sorry Baz.' Lachlan grabbed his cap and hastened from the office. Chasing speeding drivers for a few hours was safer than the Kaikōura police station.

MELBOURNE

Jo moved a coke can and orange juice bottle to the café floor and spread a map of New Zealand on the table. The lunch plates were handed to a waiter; it was time for a swift planning session. 'What are you doing?'

'Texting Dugal. I need someone to look after Sexy Rexy.' Kim briefly lifted her eyes. 'He's not being banished like his crazy owner.'

Jo gritted her teeth. 'Spare me the anguish. I'd rather you stayed home with your bloody greyhound.'

'Fine.' The phone slammed onto the table. 'I'll do that.'

The silence lasted long enough for them to have remembered every major town on the map. Jo's patience snapped first.

'Look. It's too late to cancel the motorhome and I can't drive it by myself. If you don't come, Mac will get you locked up in a loony bin.'

Kim sighed. 'Alright. I've been told I don't have a choice. Do you have a plan?'

Jo tapped Auckland on the map with her left index finger. 'We land there on Saturday.' The opposite digit found Queenstown. 'We handover the motorhome here in two weeks.' She held her fingers up for an estimation of direction and distance. 'Easy peasy.'

Kim snorted. 'Hopefully there's a GPS on board. If you're going to be cuddling a wine bottle all day, I'll need a proper navigator.'

'I hope that's not all I get to snuggle up to.'

Kim's eyebrows shot up. 'Have you already arranged your Tinder itinerary? I'm not going to sleep under the awning the whole trip.'

Jo didn't reply. The penny dropped for Kim. Her hand reached for the scar.

'Oh! Have you spoken to Julian? I thought that flamed out?'

'It did. But we've exchanged the occasional email.'

'Why don't you get him to drive?'

'He's… busy.'

Kim pursed her lips. Julian Oliver was the instigator of the drama that almost cost their lives. He was an activist who cultivated a fling with Jo to frame a greyhound trainer for animal cruelty. It backfired. When *Spotlight* investigated the property, they found the trainer dead and Julian was the main suspect. It would be prudent if the reporter and the Kiwi never met.

'What date do we need to be in Kaikōura?'

'February 19.'

'You've never said anything about Byron. Were you close?'

Jo retrieved mints from her handbag. 'I was at Melbourne Uni and flatting when Dad remarried. Byron was doing the same. We only meet once or twice a year – Christmas, maybe a birthday.' Jo shrugged. 'Byron was… a nice guy.' She looked out the café window.

'Will flowers, prayer and a photo of the beach be enough to show your Dad and stepmum that you paid suitable homage?'

'Yep.' Jo dumped the bag on the floor. 'It was two years ago. Time to move on.'

Kim choked a response. How long would her friend and colleagues have mourned her death if the gunman had been more accurate?

'You've gone pale. Are you okay?'

'I'm fine. About to go on holiday.' Kim waved both hands. 'I'm a box of fluffies.'

'Bullshit.'

Kim reached for the scar again.

'You're having nightmares, or flashbacks, Aren't you?'

A slow nod. 'How did you know?'

'The personality change, the work anxiety, dumping Nathan – thumping two cops. There are a few major signs there. How long have they been happening?'

'I had a couple back in June. The doctors said that was natural. I spoke to a psychologist – but he was a pompous old git. Implied I was stupid for almost getting the three of us killed.'

Jo winced. 'Did the memories subside?'

'Yeah. I had the second surgery in July, then the extended rehab. That kept me focused for a few months. I was so happy when I returned to work – but those feelings evaporated.'

'You saw Stephanie had made herself an integral part of the team?'

A guilty smile. 'She was getting all the lead stories that should have landed on my desk.'

'To be fair, Stephanie found most of those through her own sources. She's a quality journo. Plus, Mac and Curly didn't want to destroy your health. You lost so much weight. No wonder you were permanently tired and grumpy. God knows why you volunteered to work for News over Christmas.'

'I was worried I was losing my touch. I wanted to tackle a variety of stories – to get the buzz back. It was also insurance – in case *Spotlight* dumped me. I might be able to find a desk down the corridor.'

'Is that when the dreams returned?'

Kim nodded.

'How often?'

'About twice a week. Sometimes three.'

'Jeezus Kim. Did Nathan know?'

'He guessed. Wanted to help – but I wouldn't let him. It's my problem – I caused it by going after a killer. I wanted to sort myself out.'

'It hasn't worked. You're lashing out at shadows. Pushing away those who care about you.'

Kim shrugged, fingers unconsciously fingering the scar.

'But you don't want to see a psychologist?'

'He didn't help. The dreams are more terrifying. The bastard stands over me and keeps shooting. I feel the bullets hit me – one after the other. I'm crawling away but he follows and laughs.'

'Does that wake you?'

'No – Rexy's usually my saviour. He must hear me screaming and licks my face.'

'Do we need to take Rexy as your emotional support? I don't want you scaring away my tinder dates.'

That prompted the first belly laugh of their planning lunch.

KAIKŌURA

Heath Michel yawned as he waited to turn off State Highway 1 at the racecourse. A police car approached from the north; blazing lights the deterrent for a snap turn. There were no obvious speeders.

The venue was more like a holiday park; tourists mingled between motorhomes, caravans and campers. Many lounged in folding chairs, cold beers and wine in hand. That made Heath lick his lips. Later. Maybe.

Heath's destination was South Bay, the whale watch and charter fishing sea base. It was the most likely location to find T2, the fisherman from the pub. The original mission to follow the Australian had concluded when he boarded a plane that morning.

The target had departed well rested; his nights spent in motels in Kaikōura and Christchurch. The latter was close to the airport. Heath knew the man enjoyed pizza; he could smell the pepperoni from the Hilux when they were delivered to both locations.

The stakeouts were the reason for his tiredness; Heath could only doze in case the Australian slipped away for a late night or early morning rendezvous. A home-cooked meal and 12 hours of sleep beckoned when T1 disappeared inside the international terminal. The men who paid his wages had other ideas. A new text command arrived before he could exit the airport car park.

find fisherman

Until then Heath assumed that duty had fallen on other shoulders. He'd sent the photo two days ago. Why the delay? He could only shrug and start the 180-kilometre journey back to Kaikōura. The winding coastal leg from Goose Bay to Peketa, south of the town, was the hardest. Road workers were still repairing damage from the quake and several stretches were single lane. A checkpoint guardian laughed at Heath when he nodded off during one delay. A smack on the bonnet got traffic moving again.

He parked the Hilux on the foreshore a few hundred metres from the marina. The vehicle was nondescript but training taught Heath to limit exposure. The same went for his clothes; experienced watchers changed their appearance subtly. He reached into a daypack and retrieved a khaki tee shirt and battered cap. The tan shorts and runners suited the tourist image he wanted to project.

It was Heath's first visit to South Bay since the quake. Without tourism and the bounty from the sea, there would be no Kaikōura. Tour operators and fishing charter operators were devastated when the seabed was uplifted. Access to the marina was restricted to a couple of hours around high tide. There would be no whale, dolphin, seal, or seabird tours if the boats couldn't launch. Dinner plates would be denied crayfish and paua. Everyone faced financial ruin. The rebuild was estimated to take 15 months: the job was finished in nine.

Heath loitered near the coastguard office and the hardstand where boats awaited their next charter. Four boats sat on trailers, two had crew working on deck. There was no sign of T2. He snapped a couple of photos, like a tourist.

Heath moved to the empty jetty. Whale Watch was Kaikōura's star performer: the biggest tourist drawcard and an important employer. There were six anxious days post-quake when no sperm whales were seen. Cries of joy echoed around the town when the first leviathan was discovered. Tours resumed 49 days after the quake. A repaired marina ensured the company and town had a future – if another natural disaster could be avoided.

Heath read every charter fishing and sea tour poster around the waterfront. In between, he kept an eye on the hardstand in case T2 appeared. The fisherman could be below deck, at sea or at home. If South Bay didn't produce a result, sleep would have to be delayed again. The pub and all the bars would be next on the search agenda.

A second day at South Bay could be a problem. He looked like a tourist, but a visitor who didn't join a tour would be too obvious around the marina. He had could fake one afternoon of being *undecided* where to spend his money.

Heath finished all the signs and safety warnings and slowly returned to the hardstand. Several boats had advertisements for charter options: two, three, four hour or full day trips, catch filleted and bagged. He could afford to inquire about prices. He chose the newest boat which was about 12 metres long. A deckhand in his 40s was coiling rope.

'Hi. What's the price for the two-hour charter?'

'$110, mate.' The deckhand rested a white gum boot on the rail as he gave a prospective client his full attention. 'We're doing a trip tomorrow morning if you want to book.'

'What am I likely to catch?'

'Shorter trips generally get sea perch or blue cod. Good eating that. Further out its grouper and mako.'

Heath nodded. He was happy to wriggle on the line to check out the other boats and their crews.

'What about crayfish? Any chance of coming home with one of those to please the missus?'

The deckhand's smile widened. 'Mate – this is *Kaikōura!* We check the pots every trip and rebait them. We usually find a tasty crustacean for the punters. Your lady will purr when you get home.'

'Sounds like a winner.' Heath was trying to think of another question when a rusty Land Rover pulled in nearby. 'Is that the skipper? Coming to check you're still working?'

'Nah.' The deckhand's tone flattened. He folded his arms and flicked his head towards the coastguard office. 'That's his heap of shit over there.'

A ripple in a mill pond could have sent that vessel to the bottom. Heath couldn't imagine any tourists who would risk a fishing expedition.

A car door slammed. *Bingo!* It was T2 – still in the same clothing and All Blacks beanie he wore during the pub rendezvous. The fisherman ignored Heath, scowled at the deckhand and carried a shoebox toward the battered boat.

'Friendly chap,' Heath said.

'Biggest arsehole this side of Cook Strait, to be honest.'

Heath saw the name on the stern: WOFTAM. That was a good start; the owner's name would make it a perfect day. Subtlety was required. 'Is that a charter boat, like yours?'

'Not anymore, thank goodness.' The agitated deckhand picked up another rope and coiled it. 'Tourism is an important business. We can't afford to have dangerous bastards like Gordie Tulloch taking tourists to sea. He's not long back from prison. Not for anything related to the sea but he's bad news in every way.'

Heath had what he needed – the boat name and its skipper. Further inquiries could be made by the power brokers. His fishing expedition to Kaikōura had produced quick results. The mission was accomplished, but Heath felt he could probe for more information without making the deckhand suspicious.

'What did he do?'

'He was reckless. Used to go out in gale force winds with minimal safety equipment. It's a wonder we didn't lose a few tourists overboard. They were chunder trips – spew from one end of the boat to the other.' The deckhand finished the rope. 'I worked with him that season.' The deckhand looked at his former boss. 'He's never forgiven me for jumping ship.'

There was no need for Heath to ask how the disgraced seaman made a living. There was one final question for the deckhand.

'WOFTAM – what does that mean?'

'Waste of fucking time and money.' The deckhand smirked. 'Gordie saw it on a photo of a double decker tourist bus years ago. It suits that rust bucket – and him.'

Heath had more than he needed; time to exit before the deckhand wanted to earn a commission for a trip booking.

'Thanks for your help. I might be able to get out tomorrow if I can promise the wife a crayfish. Cheers.'

Heath returned to the Hilux. There was enough light left to make the return journey to Christchurch. Or, he could find a motel, enjoy a pub meal on expenses and drive back after a good sleep. That option appealed. He engaged first gear and accelerated towards SH1.

Gordie Tulloch held the shoebox on the deck of WOFTAM as the Hilux departed. The guy looked like a tourist; nothing to worry about. He turned to glare at his former employee; the anger was wasted as the deckhand had his back turned. Gordie formed a pistol with his right hand and mimed shooting the traitor. A double tap, just like the special forces. Don't trust one shot to kill your opponent, finish the job.

Gordie had yearned to fix the bastard and the other smarmy wankers around the marina. He had the means if he wanted payback. They could wait. Tulloch stepped down into the congested cabin and shoved tatty lifejackets from the table. He lifted the shoebox lid and smiled.

Inside was a Sig Sauer P226. There were enough boxes of 9mm ammunition to fill the two 10-round magazines many times. They came from a former soldier in Christchurch, another contact of the go-between, Mutton Kineen.

It was supposed to be an easy job: cruise out, find the marker, haul in the package, ferry it ashore and pass onto the next contact. He wasn't told what was in the shipment, but guessed it was drugs. It had to be cocaine, heroin or meth to earn the cash that Gordie was going to be paid. It was a huge risk; the judge would throw away the key next time if he was caught with a gun and a boat full of drugs. Gordie's money problems meant he couldn't say no.

But why was the Sig Sauer necessary? The Aussie contact had been cautious; Gordie only knew him by a codename. The next link in the chain wouldn't be revealed until Gordie confirmed he had the shipment. Strange procedure, but it fitted the Aussie's pub boast about the group's security being tighter than a rat's arse. He advised Gordie to have a weapon handy if he wanted to play in the big league. The gun was part of WOFTAM's armoury; time to learn how to use it.

YouTube would be his instructor. Then Gordie would motor past the returning whale watchers. Only pesky dolphins would see and hear him test the weapon. A few would be good target practice – if they got too close. Gordie snorted. Nobody would find a bullet riddled carcass in the Kaikōura Canyon a few hundred metres offshore. It reached depths of 1200 metres and ran for 60 km.

Lachlan found there were advantages and disadvantages to staying in the pub. The pros were the coastal views, hearty meals, beer and companionship whenever he wanted a yarn. The cons were controlling the weight and getting too friendly with locals he might have to book for indiscretions.

The aromas from the kitchen made his stomach grumble. He'd ordered calamari, spicy potato wedges and salad. His stool by the window provided a commanding view of the bar, dining room and beer garden across the road. There was nothing to worry the constable; there were more diners than hard-core boozers.

Lachlan switched off his phone and examined the décor; it would never win any design awards. Fishing nets filled the spaces between crayfish pots, whaling photos and other seafaring memorabilia. He presumed not much had changed in the century since the pub was moved a few hundred metres from the Old Wharf to the New Wharf.

A customer being seated at a corner table in the main dining room caught Lachlan's attention. He was a similar age, although leaner, and there was something familiar about him, although he wasn't a local. His instincts were twitching. *Is he a cop? Okay, take mental notes.*

The guy was early 30s and dressed casually: jeans, polo shirt, runners. The dark, wavy hair was longer than his own. There was an *awareness* about him that pinged Lachlan's cop radar. He was studying the menu but also checking the room. Just like he was. Observing, without people knowing they were being watched. *Is he on a job?*

The guy could be undercover. The Kaikōura station would never be informed about sensitive operations. And it would be career suicide to mess one up. There was no need to offer a knowing nod if he attracted the guy's attention.

Lachlan then considered the other possibility, that he was totally off the mark. He might have booked the guy in the patrol car. Or encountered him in one of the few dozen New Zealand towns he had worked. Perhaps it wasn't surprising that he couldn't place the guy across the restaurant.

A door behind Lachlan opened. 'Ah! Constable Naismith – waiting for the TV weather update. Is the cyclone about to descend?'

Shit!

Lachlan swivelled to face the loudmouth. Brock Owen was a retired mechanic from Invercargill who moved north for more sun and fishing.

'Evening Brock. I think you'll find it's going be a threat.'

'Oh, really?' Owen's rheumy 75-year-old eyes made a quick scan of the bar. Lachlan assumed he was checking that Saffron Fernsby wasn't enjoying a sherry.

'The Witch was right? But correct me if I'm wrong, Constable. Isn't that cyclone going to hit Samoa?'

'I believe so.'

'And isn't Samoa a few thousand kilometres north of here?'

'Yes.'

'That's good. Because I don't think I'll need to batten down the hatches on the boat just yet. Or any time before winter.'

Two of the nearest tables joined in Brock Owen's laughter which, mercifully, drew him into their orbits.

Smart arse!

Lachlan dreamed of the night he could breath test the southlander. *Please, just one whiff over the limit!*

Lachlan had been tracking the cyclone's daily movements on the Fiji and New Zealand weather sites. Yes, the Professor was correct in predicting the cyclone. She just got its direction wrong. It was heading east, not south.

The aroma of calamari heralded the arrival of his dinner. He reached for the cutlery and condiments from habit, his eyes switching to the dining room. That was interesting: the stranger was gone and the waitress was removing his half full pint of beer.

FIJI

A tepid green tea had been pushed aside. Semesa Bari's fingers rippled over the keyboard: the data confirmed his instincts about Gita were correct. The *enfant terrible* gathered strength and ferocity with every nautical mile on her easterly track. Gita was loaded with water and the winds were escalating. Fiji's northern islands would escape the severest cloudbursts. Samoa would not be so lucky.

Apia was going to be hit hardest with up to 14 inches of rain overnight. Semesa knew the rivers there couldn't cope with that volume: villages would be flooded, homes destroyed. Landslides would be triggered, isolating communities at their neediest time.

Semesa was a professional meteorologist, he dealt with the vagaries of nature every day. Yet, he still felt frustration that his powers didn't extend beyond issuing warnings. Accurate forecasts helped villagers prepare and often saved lives. But they could not halt a raging tropical cyclone.

FEBRUARY 9

KAIKŌURA

Gordie turned the helm to port after leaving the South Bay marina. The whale fleet had gone south to hunt marine life. He wanted plenty of distance between himself and tourists armed with cameras. He didn't want his target practice to go viral on social media. The first shots with the Sig the evening before were exhilarating – but challenging. The results were best described as lacklustre; the buoy survived without a nick.

Who would have guessed it was impossible to shoot a chunk of plastic bobbing in the sea from a rolling boat? Gordie fired 30 rounds without endangering anything. The dolphins were smart enough to keep their distance.

The guy on YouTube made it look easy. Two hands, bam, bam; straight through the paper target. Reality was fun – the power in his hands was incredible as he sprayed the Pacific. The only problem was shooting straight. Still, it had been an invaluable experience. Gordie would have to be within five metres to hit anything. More practice might improve his skills. It couldn't hurt, and there were plenty of bullets in the shoebox. The supplier said ammunition was easiest to buy.

The former charter skipper didn't have any enemies in mind. He was following advice from an established crim: the new career path might be dangerous; the cargo was valuable. Gordie couldn't run to the cops if another *entrepreneur* wanted to take it away. They wouldn't say, 'hand it over, please.' It would be a sawn-off shotgun in his face. Fight fire with fire was Gordie's new motto. The pirates wouldn't know Gordie couldn't hit the broadside of a barn. Waving the 9mm might, at least, be a deterrent.

Gordie decided to bait a few hooks before he started shooting practice again. Just in case he encountered a fisheries patrol. Now was not the time to arouse suspicion. The contact told him to keep a low profile because the rendezvous was soon. He was a fisherman, a crap one, but he had to keep up appearances.

Gordie looked at the peninsula. The ants on the cliff were tourists searching for seals on the rocks below. Many had state-of-the-art cameras, which meant the skipper would need to go another dozen kilometres north-east. The sea was relatively calm; no white caps to jiggle his shots. In 20 minutes the buoy would be back in the water. 'This time you're going down.'

Saffron Fernsby inhaled the seafood aromas at Jimmy Armers Beach. It was another mild day with a layer of cloud; perfect for a cliff walk to South Bay. That contrasted with the morning radio reports about Cyclone Gita's drenching in Samoa. No lives were lost. But Saffron felt that Gita was only starting her rampage.

Her instincts were in tune with nature's whims; this was a bad storm and Gita would take a swipe at New Zealand. There was no scientific data to support her belief. That would come in the following days. Few Kaikōura residents had shown concern; Cyclone Gita wasn't on their doorstep.

The queue at the seafood caravan was 10 deep, the picnic tables were full. An occasional chowder was as much as her retirement budget would allow. Saffron's expertise was in ancient worlds, not modern finance. Global stock market crises in 1987 and 2008 had damaged two nest eggs. Thriftiness was a necessary skill to supplement her remaining savings.

Saffron saw helicopter pilot Mason Barnard talking on his mobile at the back of the line. He was dressed in a company shirt and chinos. They had chatted a few times in the pub. He finished the call and pocketed the phone.

'Hey Saffron. Are you joining the queue?'

'Sadly, my pension doesn't stretch to lobster these days, Mason.'

Saffron surveyed the crowd. 'Are you here with clients, or grabbing a meal between scenic flights?'

The pilot nodded towards the largest table; a group of four middle-aged men in LA baseball caps chatted amicably with other tourists.

'They're film executives, scouting coastal locations for a shipwreck movie. Money's no object – it's crayfish dinners all round, including the hired help.'

'How long are they here for?'

'Another three days. Have you got a movie plot to pitch?'

Saffron laughed. 'Hardly. No, I was thinking they might get a better idea of the wild coast in a few days.'

Barnard nodded. 'I heard that you predicted a cyclone. I've seen the alerts about Gita. But it's on an easterly course. Long way from Kaikōura, Professor.'

'Their paths have been known to twist and turn, Mason. I think you'll find that Gita is a strong-willed young lady. And dangerous. How much debris was shaken from the mountains during the earthquake?'

'About a million cubic metres of rubble from 85 landslides. I got sick of hauling buckets of seawater to the cliffs. The company loved the money – but it was hard work.'

'I fear Gita could provide a similar challenge, Mason. She's laden with water. And those mountains are full of sediment from the quake.'

'Jeez, that's a scary thought.' Barnard had progressed to the front of the queue – five crayfish meals at $54 a head took priority.

'Enjoy the meal, Mason.' Saffron didn't expect the pilot would have time – or any clients to buy crayfish meals for – after Gita's arrival.

FIJI

Semesa Bari nervously tugged at his beard as he watched a news report of floods and landslips in Samoa and American Samoa. Gita was a monster. Warnings had been issued, but they could not prevent torrents sweeping away homes and livelihoods. At least villagers had been able to evacuate to higher ground as no fatalities had been reported. She was at Category 1 and rapidly climbing the tropical cyclone intensity scale.

He checked Gita's track on a computer. If the cyclone stayed on its easterly course, there wouldn't be any large inhabited islands in her path until French Polynesia. Pape'ete was more than 2200 km away. Would Gita run out of puff before then? If not, would a change of direction see the fury vented in an isolated area of the Pacific?

That was Semesa's hope. Although there were other weather factors involved. His computer provided a better understanding of their region. There was an equatorial ridge to the northeast. Would that come into play? Could it shunt Gita in unwanted directions?

FEBRUARY 10

Bullets plipped in the mud. Kim was running, as hard as she could, but every step took an eternity in the sludge. The killer was closer, the gunshots louder. More bullets plunked close by. A dozen shots – when would he find the range? Kim struggled – but made little headway. Soon he would be right behind her – pouring bullet after bullet into her back.

She knew the pain was coming. Escape from the maniac was never possible. Yet, survival instincts would not allow her to flop and surrender, to accept the inevitable thud of a 9mm round.

Where the mud came from Kim had no idea. There was no rain before or after she and Jo set out on their body hunt. Yet, with her life in peril, the ground had turned to mush. It wasn't fair. She screamed in frustration – as she did each night – until a furry rescuer licked her back to safety. Sexy Rexy's tongue slobbered over her face, ending another rerun of the bush nightmare.

Kim rolled away from the adoring pet. Her breathing was ragged, the sheets saturated with sweat. The mud was a new dimension. Was it her subconscious telling her she could never shed those demons?

The greyhound bounded onto the bed and snuggled beside his mistress.

'Thank you, Rexy. I didn't get shot that time.'

A tongue flick found her cheek. Rexy was better than a psychologist; he understood everything.

'What am I going to do about these dreams?'

Rexy might understand, but there was no canine therapy beyond cuddles. Kim rolled to the alarm clock: 7.03am. There was no time for a Yarra River run if she was going to pack, drop Rexy at Dugal's and make her flight.

'Should I go for a jog in Auckland tonight?'

The pet psychologist nuzzled her.

'No, my darling. I won't hit any New Zealand policemen.'

CHRISTCHURCH

Long beach walks had been Heath's refuge from work and stress. He loved New Brighton when the tide was out and he could dawdle through the shallows. Heath wasn't a loner, but he had learned to become comfortable with his own company. The isolation was caused by career choices and their repercussions; work topics could never be shared with friends or family.

A vibration disrupted the solitude. It was the work phone.

'There's a been a change.'

Heath choked a bitter laugh. 'Okay. What's happening?'

'We need you in Kaikōura tomorrow.'

The original plan, barely two hours old, had him going north on Friday. He wanted to question the ad hoc decision making, but considered it wiser to listen. He had been praised for his professionalism on both hurried trips to Kaikōura; there was no need to earn a reputation as a stroppy field operative. Do the job, stay silent.

'If you're happy with the costs, I'll go back to the same motel on The Esplanade. It's discreet and convenient.'

'That's fine.'

'What about the rest of the plan?'

'The rendezvous might be earlier. The other parties will be in place for the takedown.'

'Okay. Anything else I need to know?'

'No.'

The call was cut. It was typical of most communications with his northern bosses. Minimal chat, usually terse, mostly oblique. Heath was used to that. Operational security had been drummed into him at police college at Porirua. That was a year before his first undercover operation. Heath loved the adrenalin charged atmosphere which made even mundane jobs exciting. There was no hidden aspiration to be an actor; the motivation had been to never get caught. Failed operations could end with a brutal beating or death.

Heath pocketed the phone and turned back for the carpark. An extended gig by the beach during the hottest month of the year would be welcome. The motel had sea and mountain views and he would have at least a week on expenses. No demons had surfaced during his two recent returns to Kaikōura. The cop getting a wind up in the pub had been a surprise. Heath decided to avoid that end of town, if possible.

AUCKLAND

Kim and Jo's cultural greeting to Auckland was via a Māori audio loop in the airport. The corridors were plastered with images of mountains and seascapes. Kim hoped the reality matched the advance publicity; her previous visit didn't extend beyond the southern ski fields.

Air New Zealand's business class service had lifted Kim's spirits. She hadn't thought about the latest nightmare or the breakup with Nathan all flight. But she knew her moods had been erratic for months. *I don't know why Nathan tolerated me.*

Their careers didn't help the relationship; murders and current affairs stories regularly clashed with dinner dates. Nathan had been supportive during her surgery and rehabilitation. It was her mental recovery that was beyond his skills. Not that Kim allowed Nathan, or anyone, to see the psychological impact of the trauma she was suffering. That would have been showing too much weakness. The solution of therapy by holiday would have to work, otherwise it was back to the shrink's couch. As Mac had reminded her before departure.

The cabin bags were towed another metre closer to the bio security officials. The queue snaked for 50 metres behind them. Many travellers were sneakily using their mobile phones.

Kim had instinctively checked news sites in the plane upon landing. There might have been a *coup d'état* in Wellington during the four hours in limbo. That ridiculous thought made Kim grin.

Jo's radar pinged. 'What are you thinking about? You want an international scoop to land in your lap?'

'Could be more interesting than being a motorhome chauffeur. A military takeover of the government. Jets strafing the parliament. Kim Prescott in safari suit reporting from the front line.'

The bags were bunted forward again. 'You lost me at the fighter planes. I don't think the Kiwis have any. Australia could probably invade the country with a squadron of F/A-18s. A fly past the prime minister's office and up would go the white flags.'

Kim kept the ball rolling. 'We could make them hand over the Bledisloe Cup as war loot.'

'What's that?'

'A rugby trophy that Australia wins once a century.'

They chuckled. The tall Māori official was still a few metres away.

'What's the plan after we get to the hotel?'

'We'll go to the Viaduct for dinner. There are supposed to be some cool bars there as well.' The bags were now one nudge from the desk. 'Do we need to call the motorhome guy to confirm the pick up tomorrow.'

'I texted him before we left. You just need to be sober enough to learn how it works and drive away.'

There was no time for Kim to be offended; they were ushered forward to complete the entry procedures. In a few minutes they would be out the door and starting their journey. She greeted the official with a smile.

KAIKŌURA

The television news report couldn't be heard over the chatter of pub patrons. It was peak hour; beers were poured and drained like the days of the six o'clock swill. Gordie's back rested against a timber wall as he rolled a second smoke. One rollie was never enough, although that pleasure would have to be taken outside.

Gordie glanced at the large TV behind the bar which showed the cyclone impact on Samoa. An elderly villager was being carried through floodwaters by a tourist. It didn't concern him; shit happened. It was a forgettable item on the telly, as long as the storm stayed in the tropics.

Cyclone Fehi hitting the upper South Island the previous week was an exception. It held Gordie's attention, briefly. His interest waned when the foul weather dumped on Nelson, the West Coast and even Dunedin. If that was a bad storm, there wasn't anything for him to worry about. Cyclone Gita was going east. His shooting had improved, he'd even clipped a shark's dorsal fin. A stationary man-size target would be easier. Gordie felt nothing was going to threaten his rendezvous and windfall.

The finished rollie was tucked behind his right ear with the first. He pushed off the wall and fished a lighter from his pocket. Gordie knew better than to light up inside; complaints from the old farts and reformed smokers were tedious. But the lighter would spark once the pub door opened, enough smoke would waft inside to tease and torment.

AUCKLAND

The Victorians weren't prepared for Auckland's mugginess. It wrapped them in a warm, damp blanket until they reached an air-conditioned taxi. The Mumbai-born driver doubled as a tour guide on the rapid journey; every green mound seemed to be a volcano. He pointed to the largest crater with an obelisk.

'That's the One Tree Hill made famous by U2.' The driver turned from the traffic to complete his spiel. 'They made the song for their Kiwi roadie who was killed in an accident. Very sad.'

'I suggest you keep your eyes on the road, thanks Ishant.' Jo habitually noted driver's identification. 'We don't want Bono singing about us.'

Ishant's tourist patter continued all the way to their hotel beside a racecourse.

'They will run the Derby and Auckland Cup there in a few weeks. You will stay for the big races?'

'Sorry Ishant,' Jo hauled her cabin bag from the Prius boot. 'Racing's dangerous for my health.' She grimaced as Kim blanched. *That was silly. You're supposed to be distracting Kim from her demons.*

The taxi driver thrust a business card at her. 'If you need safe travels during your lovely stay in Auckland, you call Ishant, please.'

Within an hour they had showered and been collected by an Uber driver for the journey to the waterfront. Another volcano loomed over the motorway soon after they departed the hotel. A Google search confirmed it as Mt Eden. Another 50 cones waited to be identified; if they felt inclined. The next startling feature was a giant syringe towering over the central business district.

'Is that a junkie's wet dream?' Jo asked.

'Gambler's heaven. That's Sky Tower – it's part of the casino and hotel.'

'You'd never get lost with that on the horizon.'

Minutes later the driver delivered them to the Viaduct, the waterfront entertainment hub where the restaurants and bars were overflowing.

'I guess we should have booked,' Jo said.

'Shall we go for a wander, see what else is available?'

It was the lure of multi-million dollar yachts and gin palaces bobbing at their berths that prompted Jo to agree. The stern names indicated the largest were registered in the Caribbean. Sleek designs and opulence attracted dozens of admirers.

They had to wait at the Te Wero bascule bridge for a late arriving yacht, and then crossed to Wynyard Quarter when the drawbridge descended. Restaurants on the west side had spare tables and the menus were cheaper. The water view encompassed the Tank Farm: massive bulk liquid storage containers destined for removal as part of urban beautification.

They tossed a coin between Thai and Mexican cuisine; tacos won. They sat at an outside table where Kim sipped a chilled Corona to take the edge off her spicy meal. Jo checked her phone between mouthfuls of guacamole and white wine. She texted her father, while hoping Julian Oliver's plans might have changed.

'Do I need to ask who you're texting?'

'No.'

'Are we going to see Julian before – or after – your stepbrother's anniversary?'

'Before.' Jo faced the tanks, the least appealing view. She looked over her shoulder to the CBD.

'You've never talked about his accident. It was obviously traumatic for your step ... for Melissa and your father. How emotional will a visit to the site be for you?'

Jo didn't turn her gaze from the city. 'That's a cheery holiday topic to explore on our first night.'

'Sorry. A reporter's curiosity can't be tucked away forever.'

They drank and people watched for a few minutes. Kim's hand drifted to the scar above her right ear. Jo spotted the nervous movement. A sacrifice was required.

'Byron met a Cook Islands girl,' Jo said. 'Jasmine was born there, but her family moved to Auckland before she started school.'

'Did he meet her while travelling here?'

'No – in Geelong. She was on a scholarship to study communications at Deakin University. It was a bit Romeo and Juliet – destined to be unrequited. The cultural ties won – Jasmine was always going to come home after her course.'

'Byron followed?'

'Yep. He talked her into a campervan tour. He wanted to explore the country, find out if he could live here. Convincing her family to accept him was going to be another matter.'

Jo poured more wine. The final part of Byron's story was always a struggle to share.

'What happened?'

'They were freedom camping. Just a few vans parked on the beach, a seal colony nearby. It was before the earthquake; everything was going well.

'On their last night in town, Jasmine had a headache. Byron wanted to watch cricket on TV, so he walked to the pub about a kilometre away.'

Jo's eyes dropped.

'He wasn't drunk. The barman remembered he had two beers and bantered with the locals. He left about 10 o'clock.'

Jo's wine glass trembled.

'Byron was hit by a car as he walked back to the camper. Jasmine didn't hear anything – she'd taken a sleeping tablet. He was dead when they found him the next morning.'

'Could he have been saved if it was reported immediately?'

'The doctors said it was possible. That's what set Melissa against New Zealand forever. If the bastard had stopped and checked – there might have been a chance for Byron.'

'What happened to the driver? He was found, wasn't he?'

'Yeah. Turned himself in the following afternoon in Christchurch.'

'Was he drunk?'

'No proof he was over the limit. But whether the delay allowed it to dissolve – or whatever the fuck it does…' She gave a frustrated wave.

'Did he offer any explanation for not stopping to check Byron?'

'That's one of the most upsetting parts.' Jo sipped. 'He never explained. Only Dad and Jasmine were in court. Melissa couldn't face him. The driver wasn't there either.'

'Why not?'

'He was on a video link from prison. He wore a hoodie and tried to hide his face. Dad used his mobile to get a photo from the monitor. He pleaded guilty and that was it.'

'I'm sorry Jo. I didn't realise it was such a traumatic experience. I hope they threw the book at the driver.'

'He got four years. He should still be some hairy ape's love interest.'

'Where's Jasmine now?'

'She's got a new bloke. They're getting married in Rarotonga next year.' Jo drained her glass. That was more than enough painful family history to share. 'Okay – it's time to test Auckland's night life.' She noticed a runner in shorts and sweaty singlet weaving through the post-dinner crowd. 'Let's find a bar–'

That face!

Jo bumped the table as she rose, her glass smashed on the ground.

'Jo!' Kim steadied her empty bottle. 'What's the rush?'

Everyone stared at her. She didn't care. Phone, purse and Kim were left behind as Jo ran for the first time in almost a year.

FIJI

Semesa Bari nervously tapped a pencil against his desk as he watched Gita skip up the intensity scales to Category 3. The data was scary: sustained wind speeds between 118 – 157 km/h, gusts up to 225 km/h. Samoa copped a deluge, but these winds would tear villages apart.

Where are you going Gita?

He was troubled that Gita had turned in a southerly arc that put Niue in danger. Warnings had been sent across the region and islanders were doing their best to shelter. That was all humans could do – nothing could stop or deflect nature at full roar. Semesa knew the next few days were going to be wild in the South Pacific.

AUCKLAND

Kim had no idea what made Jo bolt, or how far she could even run. Any thoughts of following were blocked by the restaurant staff who arrived swiftly to clean up the mess. It took five minutes, and a generous cash tip, before Kim could join the pursuit. And that's what it had to be; Jo would never run anywhere without her mobile or money to buy the next drink.

Kim's only option was to walk towards the CBD. She found her disgruntled friend still puffing against a rail at the bascule bridge, its span pointing at the stars.

'Did whoever you were chasing cross before you could?''
Jo grunted.
'Who was it?'
'The bastard who killed Byron.'
'What? It couldn't be. He's only halfway through his sentence. Surely a hit-and-run driver wouldn't get an early release.'
Jo pushed herself upright and looked at the descending bridge. 'Do you have my phone?'
A few seconds later a photograph was presented for Kim's assessment. 'That's who I was chasing. He's supposed to be rotting in a Christchurch cell.' Jo watched the span slot into place. 'He ran across there a few minutes ago. I wasn't fast enough to catch him.'
The gates opened; they joined the pedestrian flow.
Kim had learned that the Trescowthick family refused to use the killer's name. 'Was it the jogger you were chasing?'
Jo nodded.
'You only had a few seconds to see his face.' Kim waved at the lights. 'Can you be sure?'
Jo stopped and turned. 'I'll never forget the face of the man who killed Byron.'
They walked to the main street in silence. Dancing and drinking held little appeal for Kim; she suspected it was the same for her travelling companion. 'It's been a long day. Shall we catch a taxi to the hotel and find out why Byron's killer is already a free man?'
Jo silently followed.

FEBRUARY 11

KAIKŌURA

Gordie's Mazda Bounty rolled heavily to the right as he turned off State Highway 1 onto the marina road on Sunday morning. The neglected vehicle was renowned for its woeful steering; it hadn't magically improved during Gordie's prison stint.

'Shit!'

Gordie was used to wrestling the grey ute onto the correct side of the road after the junction. Rarely was there other traffic to avoid. However, his latest sweeping turn had been witnessed. Two hundred metres along the road was a red police car. It was the new constable and he was shaking his head.

There were many reasons to find fault with the corroding vehicle that recently clocked 366,000 km. The Warrant of Fitness was two weeks overdue, the diesel road user charges had expired, the tyres had little tread. Every bump left a layer of rust on the bitumen. Individually the fines would hurt, collectively they could see the ute forced off the road. Gordie couldn't let it happen. The rendezvous had been brought forward.

'Fucking Baz!'

The permanent cop in town could be relied on to give a nod at the pub when a road-check was planned for South Bay. Baz always allowed leeway for the unfortunate few who didn't pop in for a drink the night before. He set his roadblocks closer to the marina. Gordie would have time to spot the danger and park on the foreshore across from the racetrack. The Bounty's big sway could made it look like a natural manoeuvre. He could sit and roll some smokes until Baz resumed his highway patrol. The system worked well; but no one had told the new bloke.

The Bounty was well past its use-by-date. No arguments from Gordie about that. It should be on its way to the scrapyard within a fortnight, along with the decrepit Land Rover, if everything went to plan. The second-hand F150 Raptor on his TradeMe watchlist would be the envy of the town by autumn. As the Bounty coasted to the copper, there was a strong chance Gordie could be back in prison before then.

Nestled, uncomfortably, against his butt was the Sig Sauer. Gordie wanted to be like the studs he saw on television. Cops, gangbangers and spies slipped canons into the back of their trousers. They drove, walked, chased, fought and probably fucked with their gun snuggled close. It was always within easy reach, a split second away from being drawn for wasting good guys or bad guys. Gordie found that almost a kilogram of metal stuck in his arse was not as cool as he expected. Much of the time he was terrified a wrong move would flick the safety and blow him a new arsehole.

There was nowhere for Gordie to run. There was only one road into the marina. If bravado tempted him to drive through the roadblock, the Bounty's cumbersome turning would allow the copper time to make a cup of tea and then block the road. The only good news was that he hadn't been drunk on Saturday night and he'd left his weed at home. Maybe the cop wouldn't make him get out of the vehicle?

Lachlan tapped the bonnet as Gordie stopped. He looked at the front wheel arch as if he expected it to collapse in a mountain of rust.

'Good morning sir. Your tyres aren't in the best shape.'

Gordie's default setting was surly, even with Baz McCullers. It took a monumental effort to be polite to the new cop.

'Yeah, I been meaning to get them sorted. I normally use the Land Rover, but it's out of petrol.'

Lachlan checked the label on the windscreen.

'Your warrant of fitness is overdue.' He peered closer. 'A fortnight.'

'The tyres have been the problem, boss. They're hard to get in the South Island. I've been waiting weeks.'

Lachlan stepped back to assess the rare rubber. 'They look fairly standard.' He walked to the other side of the vehicle to check the registration and road user charges label.

'What's your mileage?'

Gordie looked at the dashboard. '366,137.'

'You're overdue by more than 10,000 ks.'

'Nah. I paid, boss. I just forgot to put the label in. It's mixed up with some paperwork. I'll dig it out it when I get home tonight.'

That might buy Gordie a couple of days. He used a sleeve to wipe sweat from his brow as the cop returned to the patrol car. He pulled out a pad and a roadside breathalyser.

'I need to do a breath test sir. Please state your name and address.'

Gordie complied and watched anxiously until Lachlan confirmed it was a pass.

'Do you smoke cannabis Mr Tulloch?'

'Very rarely boss. It's been months since I had a puff. Too bloody expensive.'

Lachlan nodded then looked to his left; a white Corolla stopped behind the Bounty. It was a rental.

'I'll take your word on that. I'm going to have to ticket you for the WOF and bald tyres. You'll need to present your road user charges label or receipt at the Kaikōura police station within the next 48 hours, otherwise that will be another fine.'

Lachlan stepped back and started writing. 'This ute has really reached the end of its days, Mr Tulloch.'

'I know boss. I'm getting back into the charter business soon and I'll be trading this up to an F150.'

Not having to leave the vehicle made Gordie garrulous.

'That Ford's an expensive beast,' Lachlan said. 'I thought fishing was tough around Kaikōura because of the post-quake restrictions.'

'Oh, yeah, yeah. It's a struggle for those who don't know what they're doing. No problem for the experts, like me. I know how to catch the big fish beyond the restricted zone.'

Sweat trickled around the Sig Sauer in Gordie's bum. There were some regions deodorants never touched. He hoped the pong couldn't reach the copper.

Heath saw the cop writing and switched off the engine. He wasn't in a rush. The rental was a step down from the V8 powered Hilux, but low-key was the order from up north. He was meant to be a tourist.

A police road check was no drama, he had two beers with dinner on Saturday night and the car's paperwork was in order. The guy ahead appeared to pass the breathalyser test – he was still in the ute – but the cop found plenty of faults with the rust bucket.

The detour via the marina on the way to the motel was a spur-of-the-moment decision as he approached Kaikōura from Peketa. He wanted to make sure Gordie Tulloch's boat was still on the hardstand. No firm date had been established for the rendezvous. It could be any time in the next week according to fresh information from his sources. The shipment was at sea, that was all Heath knew. His job was to keep an eye on Gordie Tulloch – the transport from ship to shore.

Following a target would be a challenge in a small coastal town. The peninsula provided a few main streets, the highway, shops and the marina. Most people had to use them every day. The same vehicles could be seen trundling to and from work or shopping.

A new car parked in the fisherman's street would be too obvious. It would be safer to anticipate Gordie's movements. Rather than follow him from home, Heath could find a discreet park near the marina. The boat was the key; the time for action was when WOFTAM left the hardstand.

Kaikōura provided some advantages for the watcher. The locals treated visitors as cash cows, lining up every day with credit cards to be milked. How many registered the faces? Or remembered them? Pay for this sea trip, eat your crayfish here, buy that woollen jersey or scarf, wave goodbye, next bus please. Good trade craft would keep him anonymous for the duration.

Experience would also guide him through the next phase. It wasn't Heath's duty to intercept the shipment; that was a job for the Bruisers. All he knew was that they would arrive soon and stay in a different motel. Heath would not have contact with the guys with guns. His only communications would be with Auckland. They would relay the information and decide the time to strike. That might be in the marina, at Gordie's home or somewhere away from the public. It wasn't Heath's concern; he should be out of Kaikōura by then.

The plan was straightforward, but operations can go awry. Heath preferred to have a mobile number for the team leader. There would be nothing more frustrating than watching Gordie Tulloch disappear with the shipment because the communication links broke down. Heath was a foot soldier; it was not his place to question the decisions.

The cop, who was familiar from the pub last Thursday, handed several tickets to the Mazda driver. There'd been no reason for Heath to slip away the smartarse drinker had poked fun at the local plod but it was an undercover cop's instinct to steer clear of police while operational. A surprise look or comment could be fatal if witnessed by the targets.

Smoke billowed from the diesel ute as it drove away from the checkpoint. The driver even offered a wave with the paperwork as he departed. The Corolla eased forward; Heath lowered the window for his breath check.

'Good morning sir. I'm doing random checks and require–'

The cop paused when he saw Heath's face.

'Um, I need your name and address, thank you.'

Heath was spooked. He had been recognised – but from where?

'Your name sir,' the constable prodded. 'Or, perhaps your rugby team. Just a brief sample and you can be on your way.'

He knows me!

The cop could ask for identification, but Heath didn't expect to be unmasked before showing a licence. He chose the national sport option.

'I'm a Crusaders supporter. The Super Rugby title is ours this year.'

'You'll have to take it off the Hurricanes.' The officer barely glanced at his instrument. 'That's all good, sir. You have a nice day.'

They separated with smiles; Heath's effort required every scrap of his professionalism. He looked in the rear mirror and saw the cop watching.

How does he know me – and what does he know about me?

AUCKLAND

Kim and Jo were unusually subdued tourists on the taxi ride to collect their motorhome. The journey didn't prompt comments about yachts on the Waitemata Harbour or volcanic Rangitoto Island. An internet search for Byron's killer had yielded few hits beyond the first reports of a pedestrian death two years ago. They couldn't find anything about the guilty plea, sentence or an early release. The journalist understood the rapid disappearance from the news cycle. The victim was Australian; there were no relatives or friends to provide emotion for local cameras and reporters.

Kim knew not to push Jo about a wrong identification, even though it was possible. It had only been a glimpse in the Wynyard Quarter. At night. Kim had barely registered the runner in the crowd. Yet, Jo was certain it was the man who left her stepbrother to die on the beach. Kim dared not suggest it might have been a kneejerk reaction to her emotional revelation about Byron's death only moments before.

The trip was meant to be an escape for Kim, a chance to shed her demons from the shooting. Perhaps Byron's killer had done the same after his prison release. Did he move north to Auckland to start a new life? If that was the case, he had inadvertently added to Jo's pain.

Neither had slept well. Jo wanted to tell her father. Melissa would find out and that would engulf the family in a new wave of distress. The two hour time difference with Australia allowed Jo to delay that family shock until Sunday morning.

The restless night might have saved Kim from a new nightmare. She yawned, then her eyes widened when the taxi parked opposite a white motorhome.

'How long is it, Jo?'

'Seven metres.'

'It's massive!' Kim didn't know if she was nervous or excited. 'I hope the roads are wide enough.'

Jo's mood brightened. 'That's a palace on wheels.'

A lean man in his 50s approached from a townhouse with a broad smile.

'Hello. I'm Declan. Are you ready to meet Kwozzimoto?'

Over the next 20 minutes, the proud owner explained the intricacies of the motorhome. The beige leather driver and co-pilot seats swivelled to include the table. The kitchen was in the middle with a gas hob, oven, sink and a 145-litre fridge. Two single beds were at the rear and a bathroom and toilet made it fully self-contained.

Jo grinned when a double bed lowered over the dining area at the press of a button.

'The penthouse suite's mine.'

Kim shrugged and made notes as Declan explained the power/gas/water operation. A solar panel on the roof meant they could freedom camp.

'Are you going to Napier?' Declan asked.

'A wine stop – or two – is on the itinerary,' Jo said. 'My chauffeur will have to stay dry.'

Declan laughed as Kim winced. 'There's a freedom spot on the foreshore in the city. Get a park there and book a winery tour. They'll drive you to all the best vineyards in Hawke's Bay.'

That made the designated driver smile. Kim pointed at the large storage section at the back of the motorhome.

'What's in there?'

Declan opened what he called 'the garage'. It was huge, running under the single beds from one side of the van to the other.

'It's big enough to take four bikes – but we're paddlers.' He pointed to two grey cases. 'Those are inflatable kayaks. Brilliant on rivers and lakes, okay on calm seas.' The paddles were suspended on cables.

'There's also a barbecue, tables, chairs, boogie board, snorkel, flippers, spare water container, clothes rack, cleaning stuff – everything you need for life on the road.'

'Goodness Declan,' Jo said. 'There's still enough room to fit a clothes dryer in here.'

'Don't suggest that to my wife – please!'

Kim did a circuit of the motorhome exterior, checking various hatches. She half raised a hand to caress the hidden scar, then let it drop.

Jo stood beside Declan. 'Where did the nickname come from?'

'My wife's a Kiwi, I'm an Aussie – Kwozzimoto was a no-brainer with that hump over the living area. He's one of the family.'

Kim found the bonnet release and checked the engine: spotless, like the rest of the motorhome. 'How easy is it to drive?'

'Like a car. The gear box can be automatic or manual. You sit higher on the road and it gives you a better field of vision. Just remember you've got seven metres behind when turning corners.'

Kim lowered the bonnet. 'I guess it's time for Kwozzimoto to show us Aotearoa.'

SOUTH ISLAND

Banks Peninsula was a dark outline in the distance when Rafael Serrano heard a fearful rattle: a metallic scraping along the hull. Rafael had experienced it before – and dreaded a repeat. It was most likely a lost container, doomed to bob like an iceberg until it sank – or smashed into vessels like the *Hoplite*.

Rafael was on the bridge, which had views to the stern. There was one final clunk, which made the boat shudder.

'Fuck! That's probably the propeller.'

A few seconds later Rafael saw a rectangular shadow rolling in the wake. There was a degree of comfort in that his speculation was confirmed. It would have been worse if the collision had been with a yacht running without lights.

The crew's training kicked in. The speed was reduced, the captain summoned, everyone waited for a damage report from the engineer. There was no panic. Their ship wasn't the *Titanic* in the icy Atlantic.

Nobody was going to drown, but Rafael could be in trouble. Not because they bunted a 40-foot container in the gloom. His problem was the deadline for his drop off at Kaikōura. That was scheduled for the 13th. Any serious damage could delay the *Hoplite*. That would make Rafael's special clients extremely grumpy.

Fifteen minutes later Rafael's fears were confirmed; the chief engineer reported a vibration in the tail shaft. They were diverting to Lyttelton to check the damage. It wasn't far – but there was a cyclone lurking in the Pacific and Rafael had no idea when the ship would leave.

FIJI

Semesa Bari was worried. He wanted to walk, to release the pent-up energy in muscles cramped by hours in front of the computer screen. His snack of almonds and dates lay untouched on the desk. The tea was cold, the cup almost full. The data had been too absorbing, the danger to island nations too immediate to waste time.

Tropical Cyclone Gita had done the unwanted, but not unexpected or impossible. Her southerly arc turned into a westerly trajectory. Instead of meandering wildly out to sea, Gita turned back towards inhabited islands.

She was intensifying every hour, a pattern likely to continue for at least the next day and a half. She was at Category 4 – sustained winds of more than 160 km/h with gusts up to 200. Niue had been lucky; there had been no significant damage from the winds or flooding.

Not so Tonga. The change in direction put her firmly in Gita's sights. The cyclone would be close to maximum power by then. That would mean winds of more than 200 km/h, drenching rain and waves up to 10 metres. Dozens of villages could be swamped by the storm surge.

Gita was not going to simply brush by either. The capital, Nuku'alofa, would bear the brunt. The most populated centre would experience the worst cyclone in more than half a century. A state of emergency had been declared. Public shelters were opened. There was nothing more that Semesa Bari could do except pray.

FEBRUARY 12

ROTORUA

The screech of a campervan sliding door less than a metre from Jo's head woke her – again.

'Jeezus!'

She rolled onto her side in the dropdown bed and pulled the pillow tighter around her ears, waiting for the next step. Bam! The closing. It was the eighth time she had counted the sliding cadence since 7.13am. That was half an hour ago. Declan O'Connell never warned them that sleep-ins were impossible at freedom camping sites.

Kim was also awake in a rear single bed. 'Now I know why that English motorhome couple moaned about *sliders* last night.'

Rotorua's chorus of native birds was regularly disrupted by the occupants of converted mini vans. Many were held together with duct tape; most were more than 20 years old. All proudly displayed the blue badge of a self-contained vehicle: cooking, sleeping, bathroom. The portable toilet in 99% of the vans had never been unpacked. Hence, the early morning quest for a public loo.

'I guess we can't complain,' Kim said. 'Ingrid and Emilia were sweet last night.'

Jo groaned beneath the pillow. 'Yeah, we'd still be hunting for a park without them. Wish I had taken a video – you reversing a seven-metre motorhome into a space I wouldn't park a shopping trolley.'

It must have been the holiday spirit, or a second night without a nightmare, that made Kim chuckle.

'What's for breakfast?' Jo asked. She sat up and retrieved her mobile phone from a shelf. 'I fancy scrambled eggs.'

'Sounds good. I'll catch the chooks; you look after the toast.' Kim slithered out of bed and tucked in the sheets and a light blanket. 'Now, which button gives us hot water?'

The idiosyncrasies for the shower and kitchen were worked out over breakfast. Many laughs were shared as they juggled the space. The Germans next door joined in the banter from their slider.

'This is closer than camping,' Jo said through the open doors.

'Ja, but without the snoring.' Ingrid replied. 'We were happy to see two women arrive rather than an old man.'

'Or worse,' said Emilia. 'Two old men!'

The travellers shared eggs, toast and travel tips over breakfast at Kwozzi's dining table.

'What are you going to see today?'

'We're going to start with a swim at the Polynesian spa.' Jo pointed to the hot pools complex 60 metres from the park. 'We did the mud pools and Māori village at Whakarewarewa when we arrived.'

Her butchered pronunciation made everyone laugh.

'After that, we're tossing up between zip-lining through the trees or white-water rafting.'

Emilia finished her coffee, stood and placed the mug in the kitchen, one step away. 'I think you must do the forest walk or canopy tour. We did our rafting in Turangi. Tongariro River Rafting was excellent and exciting.'

Jo's good mood changed in a heartbeat. She stepped out of the motorhome to check the text from her father.

> I haven't told Melissa. Will make calls today
> for verification. Update you later.

Jo sighed. She was certain it was Byron's killer running free on Saturday night. But it was probably wiser not to upset her stepmother until it could be confirmed. It was likely to be a long battle with the Department of Corrections and police. The bureaucrats hadn't been helpful two years ago. She didn't expect them to change.

'Was that your father?' Kim checked the engine oil. The Germans packed their camper.

'Yeah. He's going to make more calls today. See if anyone will talk.' Jo sent a thumbs up reply and tucked the phone into her shorts.

'How did Melissa take the news?'

'He hasn't told her.'

Kim dropped the bonnet. 'That might save some anxiety – or delay it.' The breakfast vibe was dissipating.

'Come on. We're on holidays in the land of endless grapevines. There are wineries waiting for my seal of approval. Let's hit the road Fangio.'

KAIKŌURA

Heath found the South Bay Reserve was a perfect observation post. The loop road with a grass centre was filled with cars and campers. The peninsula walkway started – or ended – there, loitering tourists were not out of place. Neither was a little white Corolla.

The reserve was about 400 hundred metres from the marina where *WOFTAM* sat on its trailer. The beach, Kaka, Moa and Tui roads gave Heath several approaches to check his target. Daylight observation could be looser; the rendezvous was expected to be early morning or evening. A night run out to sea in the decrepit 12-metre boat would be too suspicious. Heath believed his expectation for a twilight or dawn rendezvous would be a safe bet.

A daypack, water bottle, sandwiches and mystery novel reinforced the tourist disguise. Walkers never lingered before a hike across the cliffs. They wanted to search for whales, seals, dolphins. The quest would be capped with a few cliff-edge selfies in the camera; tick it off the bucket list and move to the next attraction.

As he drove past the marina, Heath had been surprised to find Gordie collecting a box from the tray of the rusty ute the cop had pulled over ahead of him. He hadn't realised his prey had been the driver who'd been given a fistful of fines. Heath turned the rental around near the Coast Guard office, drove back along Moa Road and into Kaka Road. It took him to the reserve. From the safety of the shoreline, and his novel under the sun, Heath was able to watch Gordie potter around his boat for an hour before driving away.

The second vehicle was a wake-up call; Heath should have checked last week when he located Gordie's home near the Catholic church. It was at the end of a cul-de-sac, with paddocks either side. Heath couldn't tell whether that was a blessing for the other residents. They weren't close to their neighbour, but they could not avoid the eyesore.

Gordie's home was in worse condition than the vehicles or boat, with paint peeling from the weatherboards and window frames. Heath couldn't guess the original colour – or when it would have been applied. Even real estate agents would suggest a bulldozer renovation. The Land Rover had been parked on the front weed patch. The ute must have been around the back.

It wasn't Heath's responsibility to investigate the hovel as a potential takedown location for the Bruisers. His motivation was simply the professionalism and team ethic instilled at police college. He hadn't heard any dogs on his first visit but that didn't mean a pit bull – or three – were not lurking in the backyard. Shooting angry dogs was not the best way to launch a takedown. Another late night inspection would be required.

Heath also wanted to check the boat on the hardstand. Did Gordie Tulloch know the value of the shipment? If so, would he have a gun? Heath reasoned there was no need for the fisherman to carry a weapon around town. The danger would come when the goods reached shore. Did he have protection until they were handed to the next link?

He hadn't been tasked with finding that information. The Bruisers were experienced; they had enough firepower and the skills to take down a fledgling drug runner. But any shooting would attract public attention and media scrutiny.

STATE HIGHWAY 5, NORTH ISLAND

Jo slipped into the navigator seat without spilling a drop of wine. Kwozzimoto provided cup holders, but not big enough to hold a bottle. The frequent trips to the fridge and kitchen for refills were easy. She had mastered the skill of pouring on the move as they motored from Rotorua to Taupo. Her limited navigation skills were redundant with an onboard GPS.

'This wine is good.' Jo sipped. 'You'll enjoy it when we get to the campsite.'

'Will there be any left?'

'We can always buy more in town.'

Kim grunted and wriggled her left shoulder. Vibrations from the rough roads reminded her of the two surgeries. She stabbed at the dashboard screen, switching from Jo's Spotify favourites to a news channel.

'Oh, come on Kim! We're on holiday – you don't have to listen to every bulletin. Chill out.'

Jo rested bare toes on the dash. They were grimy from their walk through the redwood forest in sandals. It won selection over zip-lining through the treetops – they wanted to save their courage for a bungy jump and jet boat ride in Queenstown.

Kim shrugged. 'I guess you're right. Why do I want to be dragged away from this luxury for a story?' She reached for the music button. The announcer stalled her.

'In the headlines: Tropical Cyclone Gita heads for Tonga with 200 kilometre-per-hour winds. New Zealand could be next.'

Jo's feet dropped to the floor. 'Um – perhaps we should listen to that.'

KAIKŌURA

Saffron Fernsby's evening dry sherry sat untouched on the table of her studio rental. It was better quality than anything served in the pub. Her appetite had soured when she turned on the six o'clock radio news. Cyclone Gita was growing more powerful.

A lesser person might have danced around the room, shouting 'I told you so'. But confirmation that the cyclone Saffron predicted was likely to reach New Zealand was not a cause for celebration.

Winds above 200 km/h could sweep aside traditional timber structures in a heartbeat. Even modern builds were likely to lose roofs and windows. Villages would be inundated by coastal surges, fishing boats smashed by massive waves. Lives would be lost, homes torn apart, crops destroyed, livelihoods ruined. Saffron understood that it was a time to offer a private prayer.

The broadcaster said Tonga would not be the end of the cyclone's serpentine trail. Computer models forecast that Gita was likely to run wild through the Pacific and Tasman before a final twist towards New Zealand. That could be by the weekend.

The projected track was between the lower North Island and the upper South Island. That was a wide range, many towns and cities would be at her mercy. Gita would lose some of her sting in the Tasman's cooler waters, yet she would still be dangerous. Saffron knew her temporary home would experience that energy.

The sherry was carefully returned to the bottle. It was too precious to waste; her brand had to be sent from Christchurch. The regular tipple might have to be rationed in the coming weeks. The news broadcast continued as Saffron prepared dinner. She rinse the red lentils, and chopped pumpkin, spinach leaves, coriander, onion and a green chilli. The coconut dhal could be the staple for a few weeks if Kaikōura was isolated again.

TAUPO

The peak of Mt Ruapehu loomed over the south end of Lake Taupo. That fact was established after clearing a smear of hummus from the map spread across the picnic table. A wine bottle and two glasses held the map in place against a zephyr, and Jo held the fourth corner while Kim hunched over her shoulder.

'There's no avoiding it – we have to pass through the cyclone impact zone to get south,' Jo said.

Kim swiped at her mobile phone, shuffling through news sites for an update.

'It's not expected to arrive until the weekend – at the earliest. Predictwind says it will pass Norfolk Island Saturday morning. That's still miles away and we'll be in the South Island before then. I don't think Cook Strait will be too rough for our Friday ferry crossing.'

'I hope not.' Jo managed a gulp from the closest wine glass without the map flying away. 'I saw a news video about a stormy crossing there with 10-metre waves! It was terrifying!'

'The ferry arrives in Picton and – judging by the map – Abel Tasman Park and Golden Bay aren't far down the road. We can decide on Saturday whether to book a kayak trip – or to hurry south to avoid the cyclone.'

'Excuse us, ladies.'

The interruption was from the English tourists who had squeezed their slider into the narrow gap beside Kwozzimoto. They were less than a metre away, which did not impress Jo. She had given the travellers short shrift when they tried to start a conversation over dinner preparations.

The Five Mile Bay freedom site was massive compared to Rotorua – but also full. More than a hundred motorhomes, campers, caravans and SUVs were crammed higgledy-piggledy by the lake. There were no parking bays and much of the site was undulating. Kim and Jo were grateful for their onboard bathroom as the only facility was a long drop.

'Did we hear that you're heading for the top of the South Island?' The new gambit was made by the male Jo had dubbed Oxford. His mate was Cambridge; they sounded like they were on a post-graduate adventure, but Jo never warmed to space invaders. She didn't raise her eyes from the map, which left Kim to be the diplomat.

'Abel Tasman hopefully, we'll see about going over the hill to Golden Bay.'

The pair were eating noodles which Kim had established was a staple meal for tourists in sliders; they were cheap and easy to make. Both men were in shorts and singlets, also uniform attire from what Kim had seen.

'We were in Nelson for the first cyclone: Fehi,' Oxford said.

That attracted Jo's attention. 'We didn't know there'd already been a cyclone. How bad was it?'

'A lot of wind and rain.' Cambridge placed his empty bowl on the ground. 'The worst part was the king tide and ocean surge. A few suburbs were swamped. Residents had to be rescued from flooded homes. Roads were washed away. It was a mess.'

A few seconds later Jo had a news report on her mobile. She read it and showed Kim.

'It's not the place to be for a second cyclone then?' Jo said.

The Brits shook their heads. They were left to clean dishes as the Australians considered their options.

'We could do the rafting trip in Turangi tomorrow morning, then drive to Wellington,' Kim said. 'That gives us a day in Wellington and maybe a ferry on Thursday.'

'That would mean missing the wineries around Napier!'

'There are more vineyards in Blenheim. That's almost out of the danger zone.'

Kim's suggestion was ignored as Jo flicked through the ferry booking service.

'Can't do it.' Jo displayed the website. 'The ferries are booked solid. We either take the crossing on Friday – or go back to Auckland.'

Kim's hand reached for the scar behind her right ear. Annoyed, she dropped it immediately. 'I guess we stick to the schedule.'

'Yep.' Jo pointed at the map. 'We raft the Tongariro in the morning, then drive to Hawke's Bay. We'll book a winery tour for the next day. You'll love it Kim – great food and wine and you won't have to drive.'

Kim shrugged and stepped inside the motorhome to finish dinner preparations. Jo's phone rang. She took it down to the lake edge.

'Hey Dad. What did you find out? Is he out of gaol?'

'I don't know.' Sterling Trescowthick sounded exhausted. 'The bureaucrats haven't been helpful. They said there are *privacy issues* to deal with.'

'Privacy!' Jo picked up a pebble. 'A killer's fucking privacy is more important than our right to know! We should have been told if he was free.' She chucked the pebble into the lake.

'They didn't confirm that. They rarely say anything unless the offender wants to return to the same location as a victim's family. We're in Australia – not even on their radar for warnings.'

'Shit.' Jo eyed a rock to boot. She scuffed the ground; a broken toe would not help them outrun a cyclone. 'I'm sure it was him running around Auckland. Can you make any more calls?'

'Yeah. I'll try the ex-cop tomorrow. He should be able to find out.'

Jo turned back to the motorhome. Kim stood in the doorway waving a pot.

'I hope so. I wish there was more I could do. Anyway, it's dinner time here.'

'Where are you?'

'Lake Taupo.'

'Leave that man to me. You and Kim enjoy yourselves.'

'Yeah. This trip keeps getting complicated. We have a cyclone to consider now.'

'That one in Tonga?'

'Yep. They say it could hit the top of the South Island by the weekend.'

'Are you going to cross Cook Strait early?'

'Every other camper and motorhome has the same idea. It's booked solid the rest of the week.'

'Well, head south when you reach Picton on Friday. You should be safe once you get past Kaikōura.'

Jo looked at the sky, not a storm cloud in site. 'We've got the weather apps, Dad. We'll be well out of range.' There was no need to worry him about kayak trips and wineries before the safety zone.

FIJI

Semesa Bari's stomach churned all afternoon. It was the most helpless feeling in the world – knowing a catastrophe was going to happen and not being able to stop it. He watched Cyclone Gita rapidly escalate to Category 4: torrential rain with wind gusts of more than 200 km/h. And she was right over Tonga.

Damage reports would not arrive until the morning because Tonga's power grid was switched off. Live lines draped over damaged houses and flooded roads post-storm could be just as lethal. The only solace Semesa could take was his advance warnings; it gave residents time to find stronger shelters.

Semesa checked the computer again; Gita was smothering the main island of Tongatapu. The capital in the middle of the destructive forces. That meant more people and homes in danger. Dawn could reveal grim scenes and statistics.

That would not be the end of Gita. Semesa was certain she would reach full power: Category 5 with wind gusts up to 280 km/h. She would be beyond Tonga by that stage, on course for Fiji again. This time it would be the Lau Islands to the south in trouble.

FEBRUARY 13

Weekend paperwork awaited Lachlan Naismith's return to the office on Tuesday morning after a day off. He noted the fisherman had not produced his road user charges tag or receipt. He turned to the senior sergeant who was at his locker putting on his stab-proof vest.

'Hey Baz. Did a Gordon Tulloch report to reception yesterday?'

McCullers paused. 'I didn't see Gordie. What's he done this time?'

'Road user charges are overdue. He claimed he'd paid but forgotten to display the label. I gave him until Wednesday to avoid the fine.'

McCullers snorted and went back to making the vest comfortable for several hours in the pratol car. 'Save yourself the paperwork, Lachie. He'll never come near our shop – too scared we'll bust him for something else. Where did you catch him?'

'The marina road on Sunday morning.'

McCullers grunted as he eased the utility belt a notch. 'He'll be pissed off with me.'

'Why?'

'Small town policing 101, mate. I used to give him a nod at the pub the night before we did a block at South Bay. That meant if he had to go to his boat, he would use the most roadworthy of his vehicles. Or walk.'

'Doesn't tipping him off defeat the purpose of the checks?'

'Yeah.' McCullers scooped up his road snacks, water bottle and police gear from the desk. 'But that rogue will never be fully compliant.' McCullers waved a pad. 'I could fill this with infringements from Gordie alone – but he wouldn't pay. Then there's the hassle of a court summons, which he'll ignore, or *forget*. The fines would add up, that leads to more paperwork for me. Finally, we get him before a judge who listens to Gordie's latest sob story with a tear in his eye. He'd waive most of the fines – and then we start the circus act again. Not worth my time. Gordie's been careful since getting out of prison. He only ever drives the few kms from home to the marina. He can't cause too many problems.'

'We won't have to worry about him for much longer.'

McCullers lifted the car keys. 'Why not? Gordie's never going to leave Kaikōura – no other town would take him.'

'Says he's about to buy a Ford 150.'

'He's dreaming. Gordie could never afford anything roadworthy without winning Lotto.'

He spun his keys on a finger. 'Process whatever else you got him for on Sunday and forget about the road tax. I'll give him a rev up at the pub when I see him next. At least I'll enjoy that!'

The door slammed before Lachlan could mention his other concern: Tropical Cyclone Gita. Breakfast radio reports said it was almost certain to hit New Zealand. Tonga copped a hammering overnight with hundreds of homes destroyed. Shouldn't Baz be making plans with the district council, civil defence and police headquarters?

Lachlan returned to the keyboard, tapped a few letters, then stopped. Gordie Tulloch was back from prison? He'd almost missed that nugget during his lecture on the practicalities of policing Kaikōura. Was he put away for unpaid fines, or something more serious? It was worth investigating the database.

The fisherman didn't appear to be prone to violence. He was tall and sinewy, strong enough to handle ropes, boats, life at sea. Maybe it was a different story after a few drinks? Or was that the cause of Gordie's incarceration – was he caught driving under the influence? If so, it must have been a bad case to involve prison time.

Lachlan was about to solve that mystery when a crime call took him away from the office. Two teenagers were nabbed shoplifting at the supermarket. It was the third time in two months for the offenders, the manager wanted to prosecute. High crime in Kaikōura.

MELBOURNE

The *Spotlight* office was quieter than normal. The dungeon numbers were down by only one; Mac had snaffled a PA from Channel 5's newsroom to cover for Jo. Carla Olson was a recent communications graduate, eager to fit in anywhere. She was on the bottom rung of the news hierarchy down the corridor; two thirds of the way through a six-month internship with no promise of a job at the end. A chance to impress the current affairs gurus – Mac and Curly – was another lifeline for the 22-year-old.

Mac knew that Carla was highly organised, pleasant and no danger to his ankles. Carla walked rather than hunted flesh like Jo in her death chariot. Yet, the office lacked a spark that Jo and Kim generated by default. Curly confirmed that change in ambience over the latest espresso prepared by Carla.

'She'd make a good barista if News don't offer her a job.' Curly sniffed the aroma. 'And she smiles before her first caffeine infusion in the morning.'

Mac chuckled, then drained his cup. He was sitting at Kim's empty desk; Carla was quietly tidying the kitchen. Jo always made sure everyone in the dungeon knew when she was doing the domestics.

'I bet Carla never expected her media future depended on six months grovelling in a newsroom after three years at Uni.' The cup was shunted to the desk edge for Carla to collect. 'Imagine if I was straight out of school and trying to get a journalism job?'

'Can you work the coffee machine?'

'No.'

'You'd be stuffed, mate.'

Their laughter was interrupted by Pete Benson, the only reporter left in the office. He was on Facebook.

'Hey guys – have you seen Kim and Jo's photos from New Zealand?' He turned the screen. 'Looks like they're having a great time.'

Mac and Curly didn't need to lean far to view the pictures, there were only half a dozen reporter desks in the office.

'That's a great looking motorhome,' Curly said.

There were 10 photos in chronological order. The first was Kim and Jo with big smiles in front of their transport in Auckland. There were two of Kim at the wheel, the mud pools and hot springs in Rotorua, drinking with young travellers, a forest walk. The most recent was the *Spotlight* tourists rafting.

'I think the plan is working.' Curly locked his fingers behind his head and tilted the chair. 'We haven't seen a proper Kim smile for months.'

Mac stood, scratched his ginger beard. 'I'm not just a pretty face mate.' He returned to the command post as Carla reclaimed the empty coffee cup.

Benson closed Facebook and found an update on the cyclone that had devastated Tonga. The parliament building had been flattened. Without an Australian connection, the story might rate a 20-second reader voice-over on the news – if the pictures were dramatic.

'Have you seen this story on the cyclone, Curly?'

'Just the headlines. It sounded like a wild night for Tonga.'

'Did you read they expect the cyclone to swoop on New Zealand?'

'No.' Curly unlaced his fingers. He skipped the opening paragraphs to find the Kiwi connection. 'Shit. They think it's going to hit both islands.'

Benson's seat swivelled. 'Do we know Kim and Jo's itinerary?'

Curly scratched his head. 'Vaguely. I think they had a ferry crossing from Wellington on Friday. They should be able to outrun the storm.'

'Do you want them to?'

More than 30 years as a journalist had given Mac the ability to tune into peripheral conversations. He held up a hand to stop Carla mid-sentence and turned to his reporter.

'What are you suggesting Benny? That Kim could report on the cyclone when it hits New Zealand?'

'Why not? I would.' Benson shrugged. 'Imagine a live cross to Kim and Jo in their motorhome. Torrential rain and wild winds. They could use their mobile phones. Once the program is over, they could record a few videos and shelter from the worst of the storm. We could package it the next day and do another live cross. It gives us a dramatic story over a couple of nights.'

Mac and Curly exchanged glances. It made sense, a *Spotlight* reporter in the middle of a cyclone.

'How dangerous would it be for Kim and Jo? Curly asked.

'From what I've read, most cyclones get downgraded by the time they reach New Zealand.' Benson pointed at his screen. 'They had one a couple of weeks ago that caused flooding in Nelson and the West Coast – but no one was in real danger. Check this out.'

Benson played footage of a tidal surge swamping half a dozen residents. They were wet and embarrassed, but not hurt. The *Spotlight* crew laughed; it was perfect TV fodder.

Curly sat up. 'The story could be great. But wasn't the idea to get Kim away from the stress for a couple of weeks?'

Mac gestured for Benson to replay the footage. 'Yeah. And it seems to be working – judging by those Facebook photos.' The clip finished – the Kiwis were still wet. 'What day are they predicting it will hit New Zealand?'

'Late Monday, or Tuesday,' said Benson.'

'That means Kim would have been chilling for 10 days.' Mac worked one hand into the beard. 'She would be hungry for a story by then. Knowing our Kim – she's probably thinking the same as us. I'll give her a call – sound her out.'

Mac returned to the command post and retrieved his mobile phone. Curly silently focused on his script.

'Are you annoyed that I suggested the story?'

'No mate. It's instinctive – we all would have suggested a story once we read where the cyclone's going. I'm sure Kim's mentally fit to cope again.'

'Okay – so what's making you worried?'

Curly's fingers paused over the keyboard. 'It's the knack those two have for getting into trouble.'

KAIKŌURA

Heath yawned for the sixth time in an hour. The words on the Kindle in his lap were blurred. It was not the writer's fault. It was being behind the wheel of a rental car in the afternoon sun. Another walk past the hardstand would serve two purposes: clear his head and ensure Gordie Tulloch had not gone to sea.

Much of Monday and most of Tuesday had been spent in the South Bay Reserve. He arrived before dawn and would not leave until after sunset; unless he could establish that Gordie had settled into the pub for a few pints.

WOFTAM wasn't going anywhere near water. The fisherman had pottered around the boat for 90 minutes the day before, but was a no-show today. The tip from the bosses about an earlier rendezvous must have been off the mark.

He stifled another yawn. The tiredness wasn't entirely due to the summer heat. Heath had sneaked into the boatyard at 3am to search *WOFTAM*. There was nothing out of the ordinary. A night vision monocular confirmed the boat was in a poor state: dirty, outdated equipment, ready for the scrap heap. Most importantly, there was no sign of weapons.

The marina was an unlikely location for the Bruisers to confront Gordie. They would choose a discreet location, away from the public. But, in case the Bruisers went in for a quick snatch, Heath didn't want unexpected firepower complicating matters.

Sleep would also be limited again tonight. Heath wanted to search Gordie's home to check for killer dogs in the backyard and to find out if the house had spotlights or cameras. A look inside would be difficult as burglary skills were not taught at police college. The Bruisers were likely to use 'shock and awe' tactics anyway; the target would never get to use a gun if he had one nearby.

Heath stepped from the rental and stretched his arms, back and legs. Hourly walks to the marina and hardstand weren't enough to prevent muscle tightening.

'Hello. You seem to like this reserve.'

A small, elderly woman with wispy hair had glided to the car in hiking boots without him being aware. That spooked Heath, a surveillance man prided himself on never being caught out. The constant flow of tourists through the parking bay to the walking track and beach had lulled him. She was more observant than most walkers.

'Oh, yes, it's, um, it's a peaceful spot.'

The woman smiled as she looked at the rocky foreshore. 'I guess it is. Not as inspiring as the views from town, or the other side of the marina. I guess you like your solitude?'

'Yes. It's good to get away from the crowds.' Heath recovered. She sounded English, perhaps a curious old lady. He turned the conversation.

'That coastal path has lovely views. Do you walk it every day?' It sounded innocuous, but Heath needed information. Was she likely to be walking again tomorrow? A tourist found in the most unglamorous reserve in Kaikōura three days in a row would be suspicious.

'Not every day, normally. But there's a cyclone on the way. I think the coast is going to suffer badly from slips and erosion. I'm trying to get more walks in before it arrives.'

'Oh? I didn't realise the forecast was that bad.'

The woman eased a daypack on her shoulders and switched a stout walking stick to the opposite hand.

'The meteorological service is still gathering data – but I'm sure it's going to be a rough time around Kaikōura. How long are you staying?'

'A few more days.'

'You'll be safe enough then.' She wriggled the pack to a more comfortable ride. 'My name is Saffron. Perhaps I'll see you again on one of my walks?'

'You never know.' Heath waved Saffron away without offering a name. He had half a dozen aliases at the tip of his tongue. But, for some reason, he felt that Saffron would know they were lies. There was an intellectual sharpness about her that made him shiver. It would be better to avoid her, which meant finding another location to watch Gordie Tulloch's boat.

The weather was another complication. Would it speed up, or delay, the rendezvous with the shipment? What about the delivery vessel? Was it large or small, able to ride out stormy seas? If not, would it shelter in port, or in a bay? These were issues for the bosses to ponder. Were they already working on Plans B, C and D? Or, as they were in Auckland and far from the cyclone impact zone, were they unaware of the local weather threat?

Heath pondered the possible scenarios as he strolled towards the marina one final time. He could not use the reserve tomorrow. It might be possible Thursday or Friday. Unless the rendezvous had happened. His preference was to be in Christchurch by the weekend for the start of the Super Rugby season. It was a split round; the Crusaders were not playing until the following week. But it was the return of quality rugby and he had been waiting for that since November.

NAPIER

Jo kicked a stone as she wandered the waterfront car park at Ahuriri in Napier. That required skill in thongs; the toes had to be curled to ensure rubber and not skin made contact. Behind her was a grassy reserve, walking tracks, motels, Hospital Hill. The Pacific Ocean views from the heights were even better than from where the grumpy tourist lined up another stone. It was sent over the path, across the dry grass and onto the grey beach.

Jo looked at the motorhome 50 metres away. Kwozzimoto faced the sea, his white hump shone brightly in the late afternoon sun. Kim, wine glass in hand, sat on a folding chair chatting to tourists from France, Spain, the Netherlands.

They had been lucky, once again. The larger freedom camping park on Marine Parade was full. They were told about a handful of spaces at Perfume Point, near the port, and arrived in time to claim the last berth. Restaurants and bars were a few hundred metres away; there was no need to make a mess in the kitchen.

The free waterfront abode should have been an idyllic end to another day of adventures: the drive from the central plateau to Napier, exploring the art deco city. The mellow mood was spoiled when Julian Oliver cancelled their Thursday meeting. He had been sent to Tonga by the Red Cross to help with the Cyclone Gita clean-up.

Jo kicked another stone. It bounced into the kerb a metre away. Wine sloshed from her glass as she dodged the ricochet. *Shit!* She was equally annoyed by the form of the message: a text. *Couldn't he spare a few minutes to call?*

She was about to pocket the phone when it rang. Hope flickered briefly until she saw the caller ID. She finished the wine.

'Hey Dad. Did you make any progress?'

'No. And I'm not likely to for a few days. Our contact is on holiday until the end of the week. We'll be in limbo until then. I wanted to update you – and find out how things are going. I don't want it to overshadow your trip.'

Jo gritted her teeth. She didn't want her father to suspect her anger about Byron's killer running free around New Zealand.

'We're in Hawke's Bay. Napier's lovely and the weather's fine. We've got a wine tour booked for tomorrow, so we'll be here a couple of nights.'

'How's the motorhome?'

'We're converts. You'll never find me in a damp tent again.'

'How are the Kiwis treating you?'

'They're good – especially when we give them money.' Jo looked at the empty glass. She held it high, but Kim didn't see the hint to bring the wine bottle. 'We can't wait to get to the South Island – everyone says it's like Switzerland in the south seas.'

'I hope you get to see it properly. Sounds like that cyclone is nasty.'

'People are telling us it won't be a problem Dad. They lose their energy before they reach New Zealand. The alps should block much of the storm.'

Jo walked towards the motorhome, eager for a refill and to end paternal concerns. Most of what she said was true. She just neglected to tell her father they would be doing reports for *Spotlight* during the cyclone.

Kim had been enthusiastic when Mac broached the subject. A few days travelling had recharged the reporter's batteries; Kim was keen to be a foreign correspondent. They would produce a video report on Monday about Kaikōura's preparations, followed by a live cross. A pub was confirmed as the logical location.

The worst of the weather was expected Tuesday evening. Mac and Kim agreed that report should be flexible, depending on the severity of the cyclone. The easiest broadcast option was Skyping on the iPad, or a mobile phone report. It made sense to try the pub again if it was open. Or still standing.

Jo snorted at the gallows humour; she spent too much time with journalists. Her normal role as chief fixer would expand to camera operator during the live shots; basically, keeping the mobile phone steady. Kim would manage interviewees and story production. Jo didn't mind Mac's imposition on their holiday; it could be a welcome distraction in Kaikōura. Every kilometre was taking them closer to the accident scene and emotions Jo had been suppressing for a long time.

KAIKŌURA

Gordie watched a dozen seagulls scrap over the remains of a pub dinner in the beer garden, mashing the chips as they were claimed and stolen several times. The screeching distracted him from his cigarette rolling.

'Fuck off, ya noisy bastards!'

It had no effect. The battle waged until the plates were rescued by kitchen staff. The victors scoffed their rewards on the rocks, then flew back with the first-round losers to await the next course.

One rollie dangled from Gordie's lips, another three waited on the pine table for ignition. His agitation would probably extend the production line until the pub shut. The source of his ire was a phone call he'd got at the marina. The boat making the drop had been diverted to Lyttelton with a steering problem. His payday would have to wait.

Gordie needed the money. His credit card was maxed out by the pistol and *WOFTAM*'s fuel bill. There were also the fines collected on Sunday. They were on the floor of the Bounty, along with a dozen similar infringements. Baz McCullers never chased paperwork, but the temporary cop would be a pain in the arse. Gordie might have to pay the road tax arrears if Lachlan stayed a few more weeks. That was a thousand bucks Gordie would not have until the deal was completed.

'Fuck!'

'I see you're as cheerful as ever.'

Gordie turned to find two deckhands from the marina with full pints. Spike Moloney and Wiremu Henare were occasional drinking companions. They still wore their charter uniforms of dark trousers, shirts with company logo and gum boots. The lads were in their mid-20s, hard workers and ambitious. They wanted to run their own charter business and didn't have many scruples about how their plans were funded.

The pair bracketed him at the table. Spike, leaner, with the gelled hair that earned him the moniker, sat to Gordie's left. He was usually the talker. Wiremu's bulk made him a first-choice prop in every rugby scrum since primary school. Gentle giant was never a term used by his on-field opponents. His size was a valuable strength on a fishing boat too. Perched so close at the picnic table, Wiremu looked intimidating.

'We haven't seen you for a while Gordie.' Spike sipped his lager. 'Not since you chatted to that convict.'

Gordie used the cigarette production to mask his surprise. The dead butt was flicked towards the beach, a reserve from the table was lit. He thought the meeting with the Sydney man went unnoticed. The contact bought the beers while Gordie sat outside in the gloom. Somehow Spike and his mate heard about it. They were fishing for an easy score, not the types to welcome being told to *fuck off*.

'When was that? I talk to lots of people.'

'Bullshit, Gordie. You'd rather hold up the pub wall and smoke your rollies than communicate.' Spike sniffed, hinting the All Blacks beanie, plaid shirt and grungy trousers were overdue for a wash. 'You talking to anyone was bound to be noticed. The same with his accent. That wasn't smart; everyone knows you wouldn't piss on an Aussie if they were on fire.'

Gordie spat a strand of stray tobacco across the table, away from Wiremu, as he pondered that assessment. It was true enough; he hated Australians normally, unless they offered a shit-load of money. But the pub deal highlighted the trouble with Kaikōura: no privacy.

Were Spike and Wiremu nibbling, or threatening? Probably a bit of both, Gordie reasoned. If he didn't include them in the action, would they try to bash him and take the booty? The lads might have been a threat a few days ago. Not anymore. The Sig Sauer and a box full of bullets bolstered Gordie's confidence. It was tucked under the seat of the ute. He didn't need it now, there wouldn't be any confrontation until the shipment arrived.

'I remember that guy now. Tourist from Sydney. Wanker thought the Waratahs might be a threat in the Super Rugby this season. I told him he was a dreamer.'

Wiremu shifted on the bench seat. Just a few millimetres, enough to issue the message: don't talk crap. Gordie found himself in similar squeeze plays during his stint in Rolleston Prison, south of Christchurch. The Department of Corrections classified it as low-security. Prisoners were housed by their crimes, not size. There were inmates bigger than Wiremu inside Rolleston who required careful handling. Gordie survived his stay unscathed, these two were not going to make a scene at the pub. He called their bluff.

'What makes you so curious about my drinking habits and conversations?'

'You've been rather busy since that chat,' Spike said. 'You've made a couple of runs to sea by yourself. No fish came back with you. Ernie Drake tells us you've topped up the fuel tanks for the first time in living memory.'

Wiremu suddenly found his voice. 'That suggests you might be prepping *WOFTAM* for a special *contract* – soon.'

Shit!

Small marina, small town. Someone was always watching. Anything out of the ordinary becomes gossip. Gordie hoped the locals might attribute his burst of activity to getting over the prison blues. They weren't stupid. He was banned from charter work and commercial fishing was strangled by the restrictions imposed after the quake. There were few options for *WOFTAM*. The budding entrepreneurs made the correct assumption: Gordie had been hired for an illegal pick up.

The delivery vessel breakdown gave Gordie breathing space. It could take days, or even a week, to fix. Spike and Wiremu couldn't watch him around the clock because of their charter commitments. It was peak season; they were at sea with the punters every day. He would have to make the pick up and handover as swift as possible. There would be nothing to steal if Spike and Wiremu came knocking after their day duties.

'Nah. You boys have got the wrong end of the stick. I'm selling the boat – I'm just making sure it's running well.'

Wiremu spluttered in his beer.

'You've got to be joking!' Spike said. 'Who would ever give you money for that piece of shit?'

'A dumb Aucklander. I listed with an agent in Picton.' Gordie licked and sealed another rollie. 'He's found a guy doing a house renovation in the Sounds. *WOFTAM*'s the perfect size to run builders and supplies back and forth.'

Gordie liked the sound of that story. There was plenty of repair activity since the quake. Builders were stretched; it sounded plausible that a gullible homeowner, with deep pockets, could be conned into buying a 12-metre boat. His peripheral vision caught Spike and Wiremu exchange a glance as they drank.

Yes! Everyone believes Aucklanders are stupid.

Gordie embellished his story.

'I learned some carpentry skills in Rolleston. They're crying out for chippies all over the country. I'm thinking of moving to Christchurch.'

That suggestion made Wiremu blink. The Tullochs had been working the sea around Kaikōura since the first whaling stations in the 1840s.

'You've done a deal for *WOFTAM*?' Spike asked.

'Almost. The agent reckons it'll be signed off within a fortnight. He said to keep the engines running sweet for the handover.' Gordie stopped his rollie preps to gauge Spike's reaction. 'I'll have to make another run, or two, out to sea.'

It was plausible. Gordie couldn't make a living from the boat. It made sense to get rid of *WOFTAM* to a latte drinker from the North Island. Aucklanders had more money than sense.

Spike grunted, emptied his pint. Wiremu's was already drained. The bench seat lifted under Gordie as they stood.

'I can't imagine you as a chippy,' Spike said. 'Bloody roof would leak in the first rainfall.' The deckhands walked across the road and entered the bar. Gordie did not expect them to return with a refill for him.

An unexpected threat had been averted. When the lads realised *WOFTAM* was not moving to the Marlborough Sounds it would be too late. The shipment would be gone. Gordie also had cover for his next trip to sea; he was testing the engines for the run up to Picton.

His own pint was empty, but Gordie didn't want to risk another chat at the bar. The collective incredulity from the boozers might scupper his story if Spike mentioned the sale. A smartarse would want to know about the cheeky agent. Someone else would know them. It was wiser to go home. He could clean and play with the Sig Sauer again.

FIJI

Semesa Bari and his supervisor Isa Lelea tapped their mugs in the late evening in Suva. One held green tea, the other coffee. It was not a celebratory toast, more a case of a salute to survival in the South Pacific. Tropical Cyclone Gita was still capable of causing carnage. Indeed, she was escalating, expected to top the scale at Category 5 by midnight. But her fury would be vented at sea, beyond the inhabited Lau Islands.

Bad Girl Gita passed Oni-i-Lau during the day. She was preceded by a tidal surge which flooded villages. Communications had been lost early with the island and nearby Vatoa. Semesa and his boss were hopeful the southerly course might have spared Fijians the worst effects of the storm. Homes were bound to be destroyed and crops devastated. But Gita's strongest breaths were 60 km from the nearest land; that would spare some properties, maybe save some lives. They would know more the next day – if contact could be re-established with the islands.

Isa stood and stretched his arms and back. 'Cyclones are strange beasts.' He collected both mugs. 'Gita looped around us to the north and south, yet she played havoc with Samoa and Tonga. Two nations suffer, one is more fortunate.'

Semesa stopped typing. He was working on the next forecast. 'We can see the meteorological influences that drive cyclones. That's the science. But I agree with you Isa, there is something eerie about them. Gita is not a good girl – she wants to cause trouble.'

Isa nodded as he walked to the kitchen. Semesa went back to his next warning. Gita would be over open water for a few days. Their data showed her tracking south of Noumea. Would she use that time to re-energise? The computer models indicated she would track past Norfolk Island and swing left. That track on the computer looked serpentine and weird. It was almost as if Gita was eager to reach New Zealand.

FEBRUARY 14

Heath's cross trainers made little noise as he walked on the verge beside the church. The rental car was parked around the corner in front of the bowling club. A handful of houses shared the lane with Gordie Tulloch, although there was no indication the residents were early risers. The only light came from a solitary streetlamp on the opposite side. That was helpful; the grass strip was narrow and sloped steeply into a large drain.

No dogs betrayed his nocturnal scouting mission before he reached Gordie's drive. The home, a century-old villa hemmed in by massive macrocarpa trees, looked even gloomier at 2.47am. Heath waited beside the rusting iron fence. There was a slight southerly breeze over his shoulder. If there were any dogs, they should pick up his scent soon enough. The house was dark, the Mazda ute parked in front. The Land Rover was down the driveway. No barks, yips or howls emerged to wake the occupant. *Surely nobody else could live there!*

Heath stepped through the gateway, confident there were enough weeds over the stones to mask his approach. The property had been a classic Kiwi quarter acre paradise at some stage. The history about who built it, or left it to rot, didn't matter to Heath. He wanted information about potential four-legged residents who could tear apart the Bruisers.

The house was set 20 metres inside the boundary. The original garden had been buried under old tyres, scrap metal, the ute and other detritus. There was a bay window to the right of the front door, a veranda to the left. The guttering clung precariously to the roof, unlikely to survive the next downpour. A shabby couch beneath a bedroom window showed no signs of canine occupation.

There were no lights or sounds from inside. The weeds and stones had been compacted to a noiseless avenue suitable for an intruder. Heath hoped the villa followed the traditional layout; the bay window usually indicated a formal lounge. The bedrooms and bathroom would be adjacent to the driveway. There was little moonlight, but Heath could not avoid offering a silhouette through threadbare curtains as he passed. The kitchen would be on the other side of the house.

Each window was negotiated in the blink of an eye, with no reaction from inside. Even better, there was no growling. Normally Heath would hug the side of the building to reduce his profile. But he spotted loose stones close to the weatherboards. He reached the rear of the house and observed the backyard from behind the Land Rover. It was even messier than the front. Rusting junk, assorted motor spares, a dozen crayfish pots and plastic fenders were scattered throughout the untamed grass.

Heath held his breath when he saw two large cages beneath the trees on the rear boundary; there were kennels inside. He exhaled slowly when no rottweilers emerged to tear him apart. The decay indicated the inhabitants had run away; or died of neglect.

It was mission accomplished for Heath. The takedown team would not have to worry about vicious dogs when tackling the target. If they chose his home. Heath had never been in the frontline, but it made sense to catch Gordie here. The neighbours were not close, and, judging by Gordie's surly nature, he doubted if anyone would rush to help. There was nothing appealing about Gordie's personality.

'Who the fuck are you?'

Heath had made a costly error – losing focus on the job.

Gordie Tulloch stood on a battered porch four metres away. His upper body and arms were covered with tattoos; his hand was pointing a gun. Heath wasted no time – he sprinted back down the drive.

'Oi! Stop, you sneaky arsehole!'

Gordie watched the man disappear. Should he have shot first, rather than challenge? Too late now. He ran to the corner of the villa. The man was fast, almost at the front gate. He jinked left and right; the runaway had no idea that the gunman was the world's worst shooter.

'I'll fucking find you.'

The adrenalin was pumping but Gordie hesitated. He didn't care about waking the neighbours, but the cops would be another matter.

It was okay to defend his property from a burglar, but how would he explain the gun? There was no receipt for the purchase. Or licence. Everyone in Kaikōura knew he was an ex-con; he could never pass the requirement to be a fit and proper person to handle a firearm.

Then there was the Australians; they would be pissed off if Gordie was locked up. The shipment might sink to the bottom of the sea if they couldn't find a replacement skipper. Gordie's life would really be in danger then.

The intruder was a nimble weaving shadow at the end of the road. A few seconds later he turned towards the main highway.

Who was that fucker?

Gordie had been going to the loo when he saw a silhouette through the lounge curtains. He thought it was Spike, and raced to the bedroom for the gun. It was loaded, but he only intended to use it to scare the crap out of Spike. And Wiremu. The big bastard would have been sneaking around the other side of the house. He wanted to teach them that Gordie Tulloch would not be an easy mark.

To find a stranger in the driveway instead had shocked Gordie. The guy didn't have a bag – he wasn't even looking at the house when challenged. Perhaps he was scoping the place? Gordie looked around the waste-ground. There was fuck-all worth stealing. He had tried to sell the wrecks for scrap metal but he dealer suggested Gordie pay to haul the junk away. *Bloody cheek.*

Gordie ran a hand through bristles on his chin, cheeks and scalp. It felt strange not to be wearing the beanie. It had covered thinning locks for almost 20 years. The mystery intruder raised a question. Should he tell the Australian, or would that jeopardise his payday?

The guy had been alone, which meant he was unlikely to be a cop. Unless he was undercover? *Nah.* Gordie had given the police no reason to be curious since getting out of Rolleston. Maybe he was a junkie, roaming the coast, stealing from isolated properties. There was enough separation between Gordie and the neighbours to make him semi-rural. The silly fucker had no idea Gordie had nothing of value. There was nothing smart about his television apart from the on/off switch. He had an iPad, but the screen was fractured. You couldn't give it away.

It would be different in a couple of weeks. The F150 would be his first buy. The Australian indicated there could be regular shipments if everything went well. Gordie would get a 4K telly next. Then a Sky Sport subscription, so he could watch the Super Rugby and the All Blacks. That would be sweet for the winter. He could sit at home, drink, smoke and not run the cop gauntlet on Saturday nights.

Given what he might lose by telling the Australian about his intruder, Gordie decided it was wiser to remain shtum. He would be more wary now, plus he had the Sig Sauer. That cheered Gordie as he peed onto weeds at the back of the hovel. Anyone comes after him or the drugs, they'll get a double tap; two 9mms between the eyes. *Maybe the torso would be an easier target, unless they get close.*

Heath panted as he sheltered under a conifer across the road from the bowling club. There were no sounds of pursuit, which was a good sign. Gordie Tulloch's nightwear – boxer shorts – wasn't suitable to chase trespassers. How long would it take Gordie to start one of the rust buckets? A sanctuary, rather than the rental car, was Heath's immediate goal after turning the corner. He didn't want a farcical chase across town if Gordie's vehicles were more reliable than expected. But the empty street indicated the pursuit died in the driveway.

Running was a safe bet. The house protected him inside a split second, if Gordie was going to use his weapon, which Heath doubted. Most people would assume the gun would be enough to make an intruder quake. Experience taught Heath to react. He would have been 10 – 15 metres down the driveway by the time Gordie rounded the corner. A handgun over that distance, with a weaving runner, was never guaranteed to be accurate.

Another 10 minutes in hiding should be sufficient. Waiting was no hardship for a watcher, patience had been his most important job skill for the past decade. As he crouched, thoughts returned to the pistol – and almost getting caught. Heath's report would have implications for the takedown crew and could cost him his job. Who wants a secret spotter who can't stay hidden?

Darkness hid the embarrassment. What Heath saw as professionalism could now be interpreted as foolishness. The target had been alerted. Heath hoped Gordie Tulloch assumed the stranger was a burglar. Further reflection ruled that out. Few thieves in the South Island would bother investigating the property.

Heath's pulse returned to normal, yet he waited. The house behind him was dark. He was unlikely to have woken anyone. These were the skills he had honed through dozens of jobs. Not all went according to plan. Heath was aware of the problems – and penalties – when a mission unravelled.

How much should he tell the bosses? Was it a full bladder or a sixth sense for trouble that woke Gordie Tulloch? That didn't matter. What *did* matter was the gun; how could he convey that message to the Bruisers without getting himself into trouble? Should he tell his bosses everything – or anything?

It was the middle of the night; he could decide over breakfast. Possibly even lunch. The target was not leaving Kaikōura, the product still had to be collected. Gordie Tulloch might be more aware than Heath would have preferred, but he could deal with that. He could be a chameleon when required.

Heath silently emerged from his conifer shelter and crossed the road. The Corolla was already unlocked, the interior light switched off. There were no beeps or indicator flashes to disturb restless sleepers. The 1.3 litre engine had no delusions of V8 grandeur when ignited. Heath pulled out and headed towards State Highway 1.

NAPIER

Kim smoothed her blue cotton dress as she settled into a leather seat in the Mercedes transporter at midday. They decided wine tastings required more decorum than t-shirts, shorts and jandals. They were picking up the local lingo. The other eight tourists sharing the journey also opted for smart casual. They were a cross section of the travellers they had encountered in New Zealand: four Germans, two Brits, one American and another Australian. The ages ranged from early 20s to the retired gent from Canberra. They had seen thousands of Asians enjoying Aotearoa's summer, but most used their own guides and buses.

Jo was the last to claim a seat. Her white dress was a risky choice for vineyards, in Kim's opinion, but it was not her only surprise for the day. 'I can't believe you agreed to my suggestions.'

Kim expected a battle at breakfast after another nightmare-free sleep. Drinks and French language lessons at the motorhome had progressed to dinner and more wines on West Quay. It was a 10-minute walk to the bars, a long stumble home around midnight. The hangovers were quelled with mashed avocados and vegemite on toast.

Perhaps it was the lingering mental fog that saw Jo calmly agree to the plan: find a powered campsite, visit the National Aquarium, wine tour in the afternoon. Kim expected Jo to fight hard to spend their morning and afternoon in the wineries.

'Don't flatter yourself.' Jo flicked through her Twitter account. 'I checked the extras you get on full-day trips and the prices. It amounts to one extra winery and a lunch we had to pay for. An afternoon binge will suit me nicely.' Jo dropped the phone into her bag.

Kim looked out the window. 'And there was I thinking you were giving your liver a rest.'

'Plenty of time for that in heaven – or hell. I'm sure the Devil serves wicked cocktails.'

Kim smirked. 'That was neat watching the reef fish feeding.'

'Yeah. The sharks at two o'clock would have been cool.'

'You were never going to choose that over a winery tour.'

'Nah. If I really want to see a shark feeding frenzy, I'll throw burley in the sea at Torquay when Kenny goes diving.'

'I'll book the camera with Dugal Cameron.'

'Oooh! Would Stephanie Grant come along as well?'

'Bitch.'

The banter had been brutal from day one of the adventure, but Kim's stress levels had dipped with every kilometre in Kwozzimoto. No barb from Jo could wound and it had been a day since she'd noticed Kim unconcously tracing the scar.

Jo sighed. 'I wonder if we'll get to see the other national treasure – a Kiwi?'

Kim watched the tour guide slip into the driver seat. 'It would be awesome to see a Kiwi in the wild.'

Daniel turned to his guests. 'You want to see a Kiwi in the bush? That's probably easier than finding an Aussie with the Bledisloe Cup.'

The only laugh came from the pensioner; clearly they cared about rugby in Canberra.

KAIKŌURA

'Fucking typical!' Baz slammed the phone back into its cradle.

Lachlan's chair swivelled towards the source of the outburst. 'What's the problem?'

'Headquarters. They said we're on our own when the cyclone arrives. They can't spare any staff.' The senior sergeant slumped in his seat. 'They reckon if this Gita is anything like Fehi, they're going to get another hammering.'

Lachlan shrugged. 'Nelson was a mess. Parts of it still are. I can understand their thinking.'

The *faux pas* was immediately obvious as McCullers took his coffee mug for a refill without offering any to Lachlan. The temporary copper had shown his true allegiance: Nelson. Lachlan should have turned back to his paperwork but he was indignant. McCullers had laughed off the first warnings about a new cyclone, so Lachlan jabbed again.

'Cyclone Fehi didn't cause the same problems, or damage, on this side of the coast. Those mountains were a reasonable shield.'

McCullers emerged slowly, stirring his drink. 'Have you seen the rainfall projections – or can't The Witch tap into that cosmic forecast?'

'I've no idea. But you have to admit she was right.'

McCullers sat, sipped, grimaced. Lachlan couldn't tell if it was caused by boiling water or the crap coffee.

'I've been told the weather gurus are predicting more than 200mm of rain over the ranges,' McCullers said.

'Shit! That's almost eight inches.'

'Yep. And there's tonnes of debris up there from the quake.'

Lachlan finally understood the concern. That shingle could wash down the creeks and ravines over the recently restored rail line. The state highway was still single lane in many places. Kaikōura might be isolated again.

'How bad could it be – as bad as the quake?'

McCullers sipped again. 'Worse.'

FIJI

The cyclone watch in the Fiji Meteorological Service never wavered through Wednesday night. The problem child had moved beyond their homeland. No lives, homes or businesses were threatened. Semesa Bari and his colleagues breathed easier.

Their Pacific neighbours had copped a battering though. The damage was severe in Tonga's case compared to Samoa. Gita was the fiercest cyclone to sweep through the Kingdom in more than half a century. But the forecasters knew it could have been a greater catastrophe if villagers ignored the warnings to shelter.

Gita was now tracking towards New Caledonia, with a southerly curve. Semesa knew the tropical cyclone would continue that drift, away from land, into the cooler waters of the Tasman Sea. That would defuse some of the danger as Gita slipped back down the category warning levels. But she was not a spent force.

The Fiji office would continue to monitor and issue advisories and bulletins, in between looking for new tropical disturbances. When Gita passed through the 25th parallel south in the next few days, that responsibility would shift to New Zealand's MetService. All the data confirmed that Gita would take a left turn in the Tasman and plunge through the middle of the Land of the Long White Cloud.

FEBRUARY 15

Saffron Fernsby stood at the top of the stairs at the community hub on Thursday morning. She had spent the previous hour reading historic documents at the museum, which shared the building with the district council, library and environment agency.

A few clouds clung to the Kaikōura ranges to the north; the temperature was in the low 20s. The car park beside the information office was packed with campers, motorhomes and cars. A change in seasons was not likely to slow the tourism business; the star attraction – whales – featured all year round.

Helicopter pilot Mason Barnard chatted to the senior sergeant at the bottom of the steps. Saffron knew Baz McCullers referred to her as The Witch. She spoke to him politely – when he could not be avoided. Even morons had to be treated with good manners.

The mayor, a district councillor and the civil defence co-ordinator joined their conversation. Saffron assumed a planning meeting for Cyclone Gita was about to start. Four of the men nodded politely as they passed her. Mason stopped.

'Morning Saffron. Another lovely day – who would ever guess we're about to experience a cyclone?'

'Good morrow to you Mason.' Saffron glanced at the decision makers. McCullers had entered the building first. 'The approaching tempest your topic *du jour?*'

'*Oui*, Madame.' Mason grinned sheepishly. 'But that's the extent of my French. Yeah, just an update from civil defence and Baz about procedures. The company choppers will be in demand if the storm causes problems. They want to know if we have enough fuel and crew to cope with emergencies.'

That confused Saffron. 'Surely you can fly over any problems?'

'We can. But dashing back and forth to Blenheim to refuel costs time and money. I have to reassure the wise men we're prepared.' Mason took a step towards the entrance. 'I heard the cyclone has dropped back to a Category 4. What's your take on it? Your instincts have been ahead of the weather gurus.'

Saffron clutched her shoulder bag tighter. Secretly she was chuffed that Mason and the young policeman gave credence to her gift. There would be no gloating; nature had blessed her for a purpose – to save lives.

'I fear it is going to be much worse than anyone expects. I don't have any science to support my opinion – it's just a feeling that water will be the key element, not so much the wind.'

Mason looked towards the northern ranges. 'There's still a lot of crap up there from the quake. I dread to think what the coast road will look like if it washes down.' He turned towards the foyer where Baz McCullers beckoned. 'I'll do what I can to prepare them, Saffron. I can't guarantee they'll listen. Cheers.'

Saffron waved him away. She descended the stairs in search of a cup of tea and muffin. A convoy of 10 Britz and Maui motorhomes dawdled past, each searching for a gap to park. Saffron knew she wouldn't have to rush for a café table; the quest for a park might take half a day.

Early arrivals filled tourist shops, boutiques and cafes. The bars weren't far away from opening, most wouldn't close until the next day. These were important weeks for traders; peak summer had to sustain them through winter. Whales couldn't attract the same international tourism numbers during the northern hemisphere summer.

Saffron quietly hummed Blondie's *Heart of Glass* as she walked. Her Kaikōura interlude had been enjoyable, but her relentless quest for knowledge would soon take her to warmer Pacific islands. That would be June or July, after the cyclone season, and only if she managed her pension carefully.

Saffron's walking daydreams of a possible future were hijacked by the odd behaviour of a pedestrian ahead of her. The man had darted into the lane beside the real estate agency in a manner that suggested a serious avoidance tactic. *Exit, stage left!*

The man was gone in the blink of an eye, as if trying to avoid someone. She looked at the approaching pedestrians: a nuclear family of tourists, a window washer, a scruffy local in an All Blacks beanie.

Curiosity made Saffron stop at the lane, which continued behind the shops along the base of a limestone cliff. There was no sign of the man. She turned back to the footpath, just in time to step aside to avoid being run into by Gordie Tulloch, the vile beanie-wearing fisherman from the pub. He was totally focused on rolling a cigarette, as he walked. *Typical.*

Saffron wouldn't blame anyone for wanting to avoid the obnoxious man, even so there was something familiar about the other man that piqued her curiosity. It would niggle at her for the rest of the day; unless she waited for the man to return to the main street. She wasn't in a hurry, apart from a desire for herbal tea. Saffron drifted back to the real estate agency to pretend to look at the houses for sale. That would be entertaining. *Who on earth could afford these prices on New Zealand wages?*

Heath wondered if it had been wise, or silly, to avoid Gordie Tulloch as he returned to the main street five minutes later. He was fortunate there was a kink in the lane, which allowed him to hide behind the real estate agency. Heath pretended to browse his phone in case a delivery driver arrived. It wasn't necessary.

Gordie's head had been down as he walked; and he probably hadn't got a good look at him the night before anyway. But instinct had taken control and flight seemed the best course. True, Heath's sudden movement might have drawn Gordie's attention but as no one followed him down the otherwise empty lane he was hopeful he hadn't been recognised. Heath still had the issue of the bastard's gun: how to tell the bosses their target was armed.

Heath reached the main street. He stayed to the left of the lane, reasoning that Gordie had continued on beyond the real estate agency. He used his phone as cover again, casually checking it while also scoping the street. There was no sign of Gordie, who was probably halfway to the pub, as he had shown no indication of going to sea. Heath headed to the ATM to make a withdrawal. He always operated with cash – fewer traces.

Saffron was more than ready for a cup of tea by the time the man returned to Kaikōura's main thoroughfare. He held his mobile, as if checking for a number or browsing, but it was obvious he was surreptitiously checking the street. *I really should have been a spy!*

A colleague at Oxford had been recruited by the security services during their student days. Saffron was miffed that she didn't get the same shoulder tap. She presumed an ancient history scholar had been no use during the Cold War.

The man walked away from where she was window shopping, so Saffron followed him, her curiosity still not satisfied. It was the same man she'd seen at the reserve near the marina, which had struck her then as an unusual place to linger. Darting into lanes in a tourist town added to the odd behaviour. Saffron enjoyed a tingle of excitement as she followed her *target*.

The buzz and pursuit lasted barely 100 metres. The man stopped at the ATM and inserted his card. Saffron had no choice but to keep walking. She fought the urge to turn for 30 metres and then disguised a sneaky look by stropping to ferret through the shoulder bag.

The man was pocketing cash. He returned the same way, which was disappointing. Was he up to nefarious purposes? Or was her imagination too active? Saffron pondered those options while humming another Blondie tune as she resumed her walk to the café.

HAWKE'S BAY

Jo squirmed in the navigator's seat on State Highway 2 as Kwozzimoto trundled towards Wellington. Summer had baked the paddocks golden; good for the vines, harsh for sheep and cattle.

'I thought this was supposed to be a green wonderland. It looks like Australia.'

'Yeah.' Kim checked both wing mirrors again. No traffic behind. 'This could be anywhere between Ballarat and Horsham.'

'And boring.' Jo unclipped her seatbelt and slipped between the seats. 'The GPS is programmed for Te Papa. You can't get lost. I'm going for a nap.'

Kim didn't mind driving solo. She was in sync with Kwozzimoto. The power steering made him easy to control and the gears were automatic; Kwozzi shifted up and down as he pleased on the few hills they encountered. The view from high in the driver's seat was brilliant; she felt like a queen of the road. If *Spotlight* dumped her, she could always get a job driving mine trucks. And she'd always wanted to cross the Nullabor Plain, and go all the way to Darwin along the Western Australian coast.

Traffic was light going south. Dozens of motorhomes and campers passed in the other direction. The Australians had found the regular motorhome salutes entertaining. There was an etiquette that took a day to learn. Members of the New Zealand Motor Caravan Association sported red logos – shaped like wings – on the front and rear. They would greet club members with a variety of gestures, ranging from a casual raised index finger to wild waving from driver and passengers. But only if you had wings, which Kim and Jo did, courtesy of Declan's membership. No wings, no salute. Jo went rogue on the trip from Turangi to Napier – she waved at the sliders and caravans. That caused a few stunned looks.

Kim felt bright-eyed. It had been almost a week without a nightmare. Granted, most sleeps followed hectic tourism activities: driving, eating, drinking, having fun. She had crawled into bed about 11 o'clock the previous evening and heard nothing until the door of a nearby slider slammed at breakfast. No guns or madmen returned to torment her. Mac and Curly were right, a few days away from the media world pressures had been refreshing.

She checked the wing mirrors again. It was second nature to do that every few minutes. Local motorists hated being delayed behind campervans. Kim had learned to let them overtake when possible – or risk being run off the road.

Kim also checked the interior rear-view mirror. Jo still slumbered. Probably snoring, although that couldn't be heard from seven metres over the road rumble. The entrance to Dannevirke provided Kim with what she had been seeking; a long, wide parking bay. She needed a pit stop. No smelly public facilities were required with an onboard loo.

'I thought the capital city might be a bit more impressive.' Jo rubbed sleepy eyes.

'We're not quite there. I needed a pee. Shall we make a coffee and press on?'

Jo nodded and slumped into a seat at the table.

'Right. Guess I'll make it,' Kim said. It took only a few minutes to boil the water and make enough coffee to fill their cups and a thermos. The instant jolt encouraged Jo to buckle herself back into the front seat as Kim returned to the highway.

'Where are we?'

'Dannevirke.'

Jo fumbled with her mobile. 'It's still another two and half hours to Wellington.'

'You're on holiday. Enjoy the cultural experience.'

They went through the town without a photo stop.

'I'm glad I can tick that off my bucket list.' Jo yawned. 'Maybe we should come back for the Agricultural & Pastoral Show?'

The GPS guided them through Palmerston North without problems. Kwozzi was soon up to 100 km/h, occasionally overtaking slower SUVs hauling caravans.

'We've got the Wētā Workshop tour booked for tomorrow morning before the ferry.' Kim said. 'Are you going to look around Te Papa this afternoon, or shop?'

'I'll join you for a cultural fix. We should pay homage to Phar Lap's skeleton.'

'That's weird.' Kim waved to a winged traveller heading north. 'His skin is in the Melbourne museum, the heart's in Canberra and the bones are in Wellington.'

'Should we kidnap him? We could hide him in Kwozzi's garage, let the scientists at home reassemble him. Imagine how pissed-off the Kiwis would be?'

'Shall we souvenir their original pavlova recipe as well?'

The giggles lasted until the next radio bulletin.

'Leading the News. The MetService warns people to spend the weekend preparing for Cyclone Gita.'

'Shit! I thought that storm was fading away.'

The bulletin continued.

'Cyclone Gita weakened to Category 4 today as it tracks towards Noumea. However, meteorologists say she still has the potential to pack a powerful punch when she arrives in

New Zealand. Computer models project that will be between the lower North Island and upper South Island. Her arrival is expected to be Tuesday, with the effects starting Monday.'

'Monday? That's the 19th,' Kim said.

'Yeah. Byron's anniversary.'

FIJI

The map on Semesa Bari's computer marked the 12 days of Gita's existence. She was like a giant serpent, slithering her way through the South Pacific. It was data on a screen, not a true reflection of her real power. Not a record of the fear, damage and heartbreak she had caused.

Semesa's uncle on Oni-i-Lau described Gita as the worst storm in his lifetime. The root crops were devastated. All four villages on the island needed help to rebuild. Food and water supplies would take weeks to return to normal. The islanders would survive, as they always did, but it would be a struggle. Relief supplies from Suva and aid agencies would be required.

Semesa looked around the office. Everyone was focused on their duties and computers. He hurriedly opened a sport website. The Super Rugby season would start on the weekend with two matches in South Africa. The time difference meant kick off was on Sunday morning in Fiji; Semesa would be tied up with church and family duties. But there were likely to be replays on the television schedule.

Semesa found what he wanted and returned to weather-related information with just a tinge of guilt. The current cyclone danger for his part of the world was over. Gita should be in a watery grave beyond New Zealand by the time his favourite team – the Crusaders – played their first match. That was something to look forward to after a stressful fortnight.

FEBRUARY 16

BLENHEIM

The drive to the rental company in Blenheim had taken Heath an hour and 40 minutes, not a bad run considering the road works. The temperature, to Heath, always seemed to be about five degrees warmer in the region. It was open country; the soil and dry summer heat ideal for New Zealand's premier winemaking centre. Not that Heath had ever stopped for a tour or tasting.

There would be no time again to sample the grapes. He was at the depot to swap the *broken* Corolla. There was nothing wrong with the vehicle, but a change was necessary because of the elderly English woman. Heath had noticed her watching him the previous day at the bank. She had spoken to him at South Bay Reserve on Tuesday. Her curiosity at the ATM made no sense. Was she just a nosey tourist, or something else?

Heath did not want another encounter with the busybody. He needed to make changes, starting with the car. The woman had seen it near the marina, and it had been parked near Gordie Tulloch's house during the aborted inspection. He doubted the dodgy fisherman would alert police or a neighbourhood watch group about his *prowler,* but Heath knew it was wiser to ditch the white car.

Erik, the rental clerk, picked up a clipboard. 'We're terribly sorry you've been inconvenienced, Mr Mitchell.'

He'd used a false identity for the hire, which was standard practice. Heath preferred the *Mitchell* alias after an awkward experience at Auckland airport. Another cop was behind him when he was issued a car under a different surname. Fortunately, the only query from the senior officer was a raised eyebrow. A convenient compromise was Mitchell; it could always be interpreted as a mispronunciation.

Erik pointed to the front door. 'I'll need to do a visual inspection of the car first, then we can get you underway again.'

He led the way to the yard.

'It's unusual for this model to have mechanical problems. You say it keeps cutting out?'

'Yeah. At traffic lights and stop signs. Might be something electrical – a loose wire?'

The workshop could spend a week investigating but would never find a mechanical problem. Erik swiftly moved around the car with his check sheet; there were no scratches or dents to worry about.

'It looks in good nick, apart from the stalling.' He passed the clipboard to Heath to verify his assessment. 'We've got another Corolla that's running perfectly. We can knock $5 a day off the price for your troubles.' Erik smiled proudly for his largesse.

'Actually, that Highlander caught my eye.' Heath pointed at a blue Toyota in the front row. 'Is it available?'

'Yeah. But it will cost more.'

'That's no problem. My boss is paying.'

Erik smiled and pointed the way back to his desk for the new paperwork. Heath followed, content with his selection. The SUV had tinted windows.

Heath was back on the road to South Bay within 15 minutes. By lunchtime he would be anonymously parked at South Bay Reserve. The nosey parker could stroll past the vehicle a dozen times without a clue about who was inside.

It was a risk leaving the target for half a day. Gordie Tulloch had spent three hours at the pub Thursday evening, mostly by himself, drinking six pints. Heath calculated no late-night or early morning pick up was scheduled. To be sure, he drove by the marina before the dash to Blenheim: *WOFTAM* was idle on its trailer.

The issue of Gordie's pistol was also dealt with. He'd sent a text the previous evening. His oblique description, to avoid using the word 'gun' in the message, had resulted in several exchanges before the bosses understood. It was up to them to pass that along to the Bruisers. He did not mention the embarrassment of being seen at Gordie's home. He claimed he had seen the target handling a *defensive device* on the boat.

Heath reached for the radio tuner, but a news headline stalled his search for music.

'New Zealanders warned to spend the weekend preparing for Cyclone Gita.'

MARLBOROUGH SOUNDS

The Bluebridge ferry glided majestically through the Marlborough Sounds. The bush-clad hills dipped steeply into green, watery depths. The sun had returned, which tempted Kim and Jo onto the viewing deck in front of the lounge. It was breezy, despite the gentle pace.

'Spread your arms Kim.'

She turned to find Jo framing her with the camera.

'Do the Rose move from the *Titanic* movie. Imagine Leonardo Di Caprio wrapping his arms around you.'

'We're not on the bow, Jo. Besides take a look at the total absence of any inspirational blokes among this lot.' She waved at the middle aged European, American, Asian and Australian tourists sharing the views. 'Plus, I don't want to look like a dork.'

Jo snapped a picture regardless. 'You're no romantic.' Seconds later it was texted to Mac and Curly with a reassuring message.

She's no Kate Winslet

Jo turned to get photos of a timber house in an idyllic setting on the shore. It was double storey with floor to ceiling windows. Sea kayaks waited on the narrow lawn and a gleaming cabin cruiser was tied to the private dock. There were no power lines or neighbours; splendid isolation in the sounds.

'This is beautiful,' Jo said. 'I could imagine myself spending a summer here. Relaxing, fishing, swimming, paddling, eating mussels.'

'I can't.'

'Why not?'

'You'd run out of wine every two days.'

Jo pointed at the gin palace. 'That's what the boat is for. I could send the servants to do the shopping.'

'Servants now? How can you afford them?'

'I'll have to be rich to afford a holiday at that home.'

'Who are you going to kill to get the inheritance?' Kim rested her elbows on the railing again. 'It's cooler than I expected, even in the sun.' A couple on an outboard boat waved as they zipped past. 'I'm glad we left the clouds behind in Wellington.'

'Yeah. I was worried the cyclone was closer than we thought.'

'I think I've managed a compromise for the weekend – which includes the vineyards – and keeps us on schedule for the Queenstown handover.'

Jo lowered her camera. 'You really thought the wineries were *negotiable?*

Kim ignored the zinger. 'I suggest we do a kayak and walking trip in Abel Tasman tomorrow. Sunday morning, we drive to Blenheim. Do a winery tour in the afternoon. Stay the night. Another early start for Kaikōura on Monday where we can lay some flowers for Byron.' She paused. 'Are you religious?'

Jo shook her head and raised the camera.

Kim noticed her friend's eyes were watery. Was it the sea breeze, or the reference to Byron? 'Okay. We have two options for Monday night – a small park beside the pub or the racecourse on the coast. Either would work for a live cross – there would be people or motorhomes in the background.'

Jo nodded; her eyes glued to the camera.

'Both locations are close to the marina. If they're still operating, we can book an early tour for Tuesday. They last about three hours, which gives us time to prepare for the second *Spotlight* live cross. How does that sound?'

'Only a half day winery tour?'

'My body can't survive a full day. I want to reach 30.'

Jo snapped pictures of a cluster of homes above a headland. 'No visit to Golden Bay?'

'No.'

'What about the seals?'

'I'll need some shots for the *Spotlight* story on Monday.'

'What's the latest projection for the cyclone hitting New Zealand?'

'Tuesday.'

'But we still don't know where?'

'Correct.'

The tranquil waters stretched ahead to Picton. They had already agreed to be adventurous and take the scenic route to Nelson via Queen Charlotte Drive.

'I can live with that itinerary,' Jo conceded. 'As long as the winery tour includes my two favourite vineyards: Cloudy Bay and Spy Valley.'

KAIKŌURA

The beer bottle shattered as it struck metal hidden in the weeds. It wasn't dark enough to be pissing in the backyard, but there were no neighbours to complain. Not that Gordie cared. Gordie's home, Gordie's rules.

He returned to the house and retrieved another beer from the fridge. He was sick of waiting for his ship to arrive; and the frustration soured a temper that rarely improved beyond grumpy. Gordie slumped into a battered Chesterfield three-seater that extended along a kitchen wall. His grandfather had bought it back in the days when the home was treated with respect. The old boy was a devout Catholic, as evidenced by the classic portrait of a haloed Jesus on the wall, which the whole family would kneel before on Good Friday to recite the rosary. He had even seen his father, with head bowed in a silent prayer, standing in front of it before going to sea in rough weather.

The only time Gordie had asked for a miracle from the Lord it hadn't worked; he still went to prison.

Religion and domestic pride left the villa along with the male role models; the couch's torn leather reflected the decline in family values. Several of the feature buttons were gouged with a knife by the juvenile grandson, but Gordie never moved the picture of the Lord, and couldn't admit it was superstition that stopped him.

His father's antique radio only worked on two channels: Radio New Zealand and Trackside. It was merely background noise when Gordie was thinking. The sea pick up occupied one hemisphere of his brain, hunger the other. The latter could be fixed by the beef sausages and frozen wedges in the fridge. If he could be bothered putting the oven on. The alternative was a takeaway curry. That would mean driving down to the highway, a risky move after an afternoon with a carton of beer.

Gordie hauled himself to his feet. One oven tray would suffice for the snags and spuds. A bit of oil, heat and half an hour would sort one issue. The other – the delayed rendezvous – he had no bloody control over. The dial came off in Gordie's hand when he cranked the oven to 180 degrees.

A greasy tray sat on the electric elements. He sniffed – something spicy. From when? It was treated to a quick wipe with a grubby tea towel before a splash of oil. He scattered the wedges, added the sausages from the supermarket plastic and *voila!* dinner was underway.

He slumped back onto the couch as he listened to a cyclone update. 'You're a fucking bitch Gita!'

Nobody heard Gordie's tirade at the radio. But it didn't stop him.

'First the fucking boat breaks down. Now a storm wants to totally fuck my life. What if I can't find the drugs?'

That possibility ended the rant. That was his biggest fear; that the consignment could not be retrieved in big swells. His employers would not be happy. There was no need to voice the obvious ramifications. *They'll cut off my balls!*

Gordie shivered at the repercussions if he failed to deliver. These guys were part of an Australian crime gang. Heavy hitters in Sydney. Do the job right by them and everything was sweet. Fuck up – kiss your pride and joy goodbye.

Gordie smashed a fist onto the rolled arm of the chesterfield. What did those bastards know about the problems Gordie faced? They were more than 2,000 kms away. Safely out of the path of a raging storm. He wallowed in self-pity for a few minutes as a radio presenter and a meteorologist pontificated about Gita.

'Do your computer models indicate which parts of New Zealand are likely to be the hardest hit?' asked the interviewer.

'Every hour Gita tracks across the South Pacific gives us more information, but we can't say whether it will be more of a North Island event, or an upper South Island event. The only certainty we have is that Gita will hook left in the Tasman Sea and impact New Zealand.'

'We have listeners from all over the country. What districts should be on greater alert?'

'Residents in Taranaki and the Kapiti Coast are likely to experience strong winds and heavy rain. That could extend east to southern Hawke's Bay and Wairarapa.

'The Nelson-Tasman region is being proactive after the previous cyclone. Their emergency management group is on standby and urging residents to be prepared.'

'*We're seeing Gita slide down the scale of severity since pummelling Tonga,' the interviewer said. 'They had winds above 200 km per hour. That's what caused the most damage. Are we expecting winds of that magnitude to strike New Zealand?'*

'*Gita might lessen in severity, but she will still have fierce winds, heavy rains and storm surges. We saw what happened along the coast of Nelson and Tasman with ex-tropical Cyclone Fehi. That could happen again with Gita. Residents should take precautions and fill their own sandbags to protect their property – or find a safer location. This is going to be a significant weather event for our country.'*

'Fuck!'

Gordie tuned out as the program moved onto other topics. There was a shit-storm coming his way. No avoiding it. But what would it do for his payday?

Another empty bottle and growling stomach urged Gordie to his feet again. Check the sausages, another beer, in that order. Mission accomplished, back on the sofa, Gordie's thoughts returned to the delayed sea journey. He was told to wait for a message that the repaired boat was leaving Lyttelton. There was nothing to be done until the vessel was fixed, apart from ensuring *WOFTAM* was ready. Which she was. Fuelled and with secret firepower – the Sig Sauer.

The temptation had been growing to text Sydney on the phone they provided. Or could he call? Would a cryptic phone chat attract attention from the cops in either country? Gordie had enough common sense to never mention the word drugs. Or shipment. Even packages. The most he would ask is when the boat was leaving. That wasn't too much. There was a fucking cyclone about to smash through his town, he had to be able to plan.

The aroma of roasted meat and spuds drifted across the kitchen. No additional vegetables or healthy salad were required, just tomato sauce, bread and butter. Fuck the arteries.

Before dishing up Gordie walked to the oak sideboard in the hallway where the burner mobile was on permanent charge, ready for the call or text. It was to be handed over with the consignment, and Gordie assumed it would be destroyed rather than re-used. But they obviously didn't trust him to get rid of it.

He picked up the cheap Nokia and fingered the keyboard. There was only one number in the contacts. What harm would there be in a simple question? He tapped out the inquiry.

any news?

That was innocent. It could apply to a thousand things. Who could make a connection between that Trans-Tasman query and a ship full of drugs? He could be an uncle asking about the birth of a baby. Or maybe a job. *Yeah, nothing wrong with that.*

Gordie thumbed the send icon and replaced the phone in the cradle. He tried to check the state of the sausages without opening the oven door, but the glass was too greasy.

The snap of a bottle top indicated a text alert. The Aussie response:

no

The terse message angered Gordie. 'Don't those dropkicks know how dangerous it is at sea in a fucking cyclone?'

Gordie tapped that question into the mobile; but restrained himself in time. He took several deep breaths, holding each to the count of four before exhaling. It was one of the rare anger-management exercises he remembered. It helped; he deleted most of the reply.

cyclone?

Gordie's prison counsellor would have been proud of that measured response. He dropped the phone on the kitchen table. The snags and wedges were ready. Melted butter and tomato sauce were dribbling over Gordie's fingers when the bottle top clanked again. There was no need to lift the mobile to read the response.

understood

The answer partly mollified Gordie. The Aussie paymasters knew about the storm. He presumed they knew the difficulties it posed for the operation. He could be trying to retrieve their drugs in mountainous seas. That was dangerous for Gordie and the Aussies. There were no guarantees the buoy would remain afloat, or in the drop zone.

'I hope you wankers understand if I come back empty.'

Gordie shoved more sausage in his mouth and felt better. It was followed by a swig of beer and two spicy wedges. His simple pleasures could make the payday last a long time. The Aussies hinted it could be the first of many. Any money was welcome to a permanently cash-strapped Gordie. He looked around the dingy kitchen. A regular income might provide enough for renovations. A paint job at least, although the F150 took priority.

The Chesterfield twanged as Gordie slumped into a corner. Maybe it should be replaced before doing any painting. He considered the drugs about to be dropped at sea. What were they? Heroin? Cocaine? Meth? Precursors? He knew nothing about the shipment. He would be sent co-ordinates for the buoy. Anything attached was to be ferried ashore for the handover. Gordie only assumed it would be drugs. What else would need a backdoor entrance to New Zealand?

There was no moral dilemma for Gordie in being a drug smuggler. He loved a toke when weed was affordable. Cocaine had been a once in a lifetime treat, supplied at a party. Gordie was so stoned he couldn't remember what buzz it gave him. Could have been white flour for all he knew. Aucklanders loved it. That's where the money was, in the cities.

He marked the end of dinner with a loud belch. It coincided with the birth of an idea; an extremely risky proposition that could provide a bigger payday.

MELBOURNE

Mac dropped his lager bottle into the bin beside the command post. The glass-on-glass contact was loud enough to distract camera operator Ken Withers as he regaled Pete Benson with a shooting story: guns and wild pigs, not videos. The click from Mac's shoulder stretch was also audible.

Friday night drinks in the *Spotlight* office lacked their usual ambience. Kim and Jo were in New Zealand, Curly had departed early for a child's birthday party, Stephanie Grant said she had a date and Mac had no idea where Dugal Cameron was. Withers had merely shrugged when Mac inquired about the unusual absence.

Half of Carla Olson emerged from the kitchen; she waved a chilled lager at Mac. He gave the temporary PA a thumbs up as he scrabbled under a pile of scripts for his mobile. Withers, Benson and the handful of other freeloaders extended Carla's time at the fridge. Mac scrolled through his contacts, then thumbed the phone icon.

Ten seconds later, Kim answered. 'Hey Mac. You know it's Friday – the cyclone is still a few days away.'

The cheery admonishment made Mac smile. It was the *old* Kim – before the shooting.

'Kimberley Prescott. Lovely to hear your voice from across the waves.'

'Now you're living dangerously Mac. Jo hasn't drawn blood in a week. I can send her back with a contract on your ankles. I presume her death chariot is still working. Or did you smash the casters and put it on blocks in Sunshine?'

Mac almost choked on the lager. Kim was in better spirits than he expected.

'Tell the tiny assassin we've gone to a chairless office. We're too busy to sit without you two. That'll make her sweat for a week.'

'She's a few motorhomes away getting some tips about kayaking.'

'That sounds like fun. Where are you staying?'

The clash of pots filtered across the Tasman. 'Sorry for the noise. I'm making a pasta dish for dinner. We're at a place called Brightwater, about 15 km from Nelson. It's an old military drill hall in the middle of nowhere.'

'Away from the city lights for a change?'

'Yeah. There was no room at the inn for us in the city. I've never seen so many campervans and motorhomes. It was like a beehive. There's another six vans around us, so we won't be lonely.'

'I'm glad you're having a good time, Kim.' Mac placed his bottle on the desk. 'But we might have some extra work for you.'

'I'm ready Mac. My head's in a good space. But there's no indication that a cyclone is bearing down on us.'

'No sandbag work-parties on the beaches?'

'Nope. It's been hot and sunny, hardly any clouds and barely a puff of wind. The beach was full of swimmers. There are plenty of warnings on the radio about Cyclone Gita, but nobody is paying much attention.'

Mac scratched his ginger beard. 'Oh well, that might save you a weekend intrusion from News. I told Ciaran O'Malley you would do a phoner if the cyclone arrived early.'

'I'm happy to do a cross, or whatever they need Mac. But there really isn't anything to show.'

'No worries Kim. News can dig in their own backyard this weekend. So, are you still on target for Kaikōura?'

Strange kitchen noises drowned Kim's reply. 'Sorry Mac. The pasta is ready – but the bolognese sauce needs remedial work. Let's see – the wineries in Blenheim are Sunday afternoon and then we drive to Kaikōura Monday morning. It's not far. We can pay a tribute to Jo's brother and gather shots for overlay on my story. There's a seal colony where I can grab vox pops – any fears about the weather etcetera. We'll have a better idea by Sunday how big and bad the storm is going to be – and where it's likely to hit.'

Mac laid the final empty bottle to rest. 'If it's going to be a dud, we'll pull the pin early Monday. But if this Gita decides to get nasty, make sure you and Jo are somewhere safe.'

'No problems Mac. We'll stay at a small campsite beside the hotel near the wharf. We can shelter inside if it gets too rough. The pub's been there a hundred years, we reckon it can survive another storm.'

Mac stood and stretched. The fridge was empty, Carla remained for the clean-up. He waved her away with a smile. 'It sounds like you two have been having a great adventure.'

'We're a trio Mac.'

'Oh.' Mac wondered whether it would be rude to inquire if any hitchhikers joined the party. Or was the extra passenger someone they knew? The Kiwi who almost cost his two colleagues their lives perhaps.

'I can read your silence Mac.' Kim laughed. 'There's no hitchhiker – and no Julian Oliver. He flew off to Tonga with the Red Cross to help with the clean-up. It's Jo, me and Kwozzimoto – the three musketeers.'

A background babble told Mac that Jo had returned, and with more dinner guests by the sounds of things.

Mac picked up his car keys. 'Curly and I will give you a call before the Monday conference.' The computer was switched off. 'Pass on my regards to young Josephine. Ciao.'

Mac disconnected before Jo could reply.

FIJI

Semesa Bari sipped tea as he checked the latest status on Gita. She was midway between Noumea and Norfolk Island, at Category 3 and about to lose her fearsome designation. The bulletins would refer to her as ex-Tropical Cyclone Gita from the morning.

That change could be misleading to the uninformed. Gita was being downgraded, but she was still dangerous. Often the weather associated with the system spreads out. Wind and rain can cause damage over a wider area. That made the modelling for a New Zealand landfall trickier to fix. The regions between New Plymouth and northern Canterbury were in the firing line. It was still too early to predict which centres would experience the fiercest elements.

Semesa could only hope that the wild child mellowed in her old age, that Aotearoa would be spared the damage that had been wrought on Tonga. He bowed his head at the terminal and prayed silently.

FEBRUARY 17

As Rafael Serrano approached London Street from the waterfront, it was the sound of buskers that announced the weekly Lyttelton Farmers Market was in full swing. The musical *artistes,* ranging from jazz players to violin prodigies, at least to their parents, usually earned a few coins of encouragement. The market attracted hundreds from all over Christchurch to sample stalls laden with fruit, vegetables, cheese, bread, herbs, and plants.

The aromas were a pleasant change from those aboard his damaged ship. But indulging in food would have to wait until he found an internet café. He had a new departure time for the *Hoplite.* That information must be passed up the chain. The captain would tell the vessel owners; Rafael had to worry about the Lebos. It was safe to use the ethnic slur – he was 2,000 km away from the Lebanese gang's base in Sydney.

His contact had been bombarding Rafael's mobile with the same message since the *Hoplite* limped into the port to inspect the damage from the submerged container.

> when?

The sim card was disposable. But two dozen one-word inquiries through the same cell site? That could be too suspicious in Rafael's understanding of clandestine work. He had switched the phone off and removed the battery the previous evening. Ironically, at breakfast, the marine engineers had finally given them an estimate for the repair completion. The gang would get their answer, but Rafael felt more information had to be conveyed. He didn't want an extended exchange on the phone, or via text, in case the morons were too indiscreet. Who knew what the Kiwi customs service or spooks were monitoring?

There was always a backup channel for communication: email. It had been used regularly enough that Rafael felt the Lebanese would check the site when the texts from Lyttelton stopped. It was a simple method; both parties had access to the same email address. Messages would be left in the draft folder and deleted after being read.

Rafael had no idea how secure the method was, but it had to be better than communicating with volatile clients on a phone. He also didn't want any record of the messages on his laptop. It had never been used to log into the message service. Hence the need for an internet café.

Rafael spotted an internet sign behind the stalls; it was a proper café with computers along a side wall and actual coffee and food which might be welcome if he had to wait for the Lebanese to respond. He was on a deadline: four hours until he was back on watch.

The most important information was the departure time. That would have to be conveyed to the go-between in Kaikōura. Rafael had the primary responsibility for navigation; he could ensure the drop would be in the right location, thanks to his conspirator on deck. In theory, the consignment was waterproof and should be safe until scooped out of the sea. It was not wise to leave it to the mercy of the waves for too long.

The local contact needed as much warning as possible. The complication that the gang might not be fully aware of was the approaching cyclone. The *Hoplite's* departure, which he had no control over, meant the Kaikōura drop-off would be Monday evening. About nine o'clock. Rafael could only give an estimate because speed was likely to be a matter for debate. Perhaps even conflict.

The captain would want to make up for the wasted days in port. Below decks, the chief engineer would want to stay beneath maximum speed for the first hours to ensure the damaged equipment worked properly. To Rafael, there seemed little wrong when the ship arrived in port. They were only doing a few knots because of the *awful* vibration. Nobody on the bridge could hear or feel it, just the chief engineer. Frustration above deck had grown in the following days as damage inspection and repairs had to be done while afloat; the *Hoplite*, at 140-metres, was too big for the only drydock.

She would be ready for sea again Monday afternoon. The captain was pleased because it gave him an opportunity to outrun Cyclone Gita. He wanted to be beyond the wind funnel through Cook Strait by midnight. The worst of the storm was not expected until Tuesday. However, experience taught the seafarers that all coastal waters would be churning ahead of the cyclone.

Rafael knew that his drop zone could be like a washing machine for the pick-up skipper. There was nothing that he could do to stop nature. And he could not delay, or hurry, the *Hoplite*. The consignment would go over the side on Monday night. It was up to the Lebanese, and the Kaikōura contact, to make sure it was collected before the cyclone swept it away. Could Rafael make the Lebanese understand that message? He didn't want them coming for his balls if the shipment never reached land.

KAIKŌURA

Baz McCullers loudly drummed the fingers of his left hand on a keyboard as he listened to the one o'clock radio news. It annoyed the hell out of Lachlan Naismith, but the latest cyclone information outweighed the irritation. He sat at his desk with arms folded, legs outstretched.

Cyclone Gita was down to Category 3 with wind speeds of almost 120 km/h. Further downgrades were expected in the next 36 hours. But, according to the radio reporter, that did not reduce the threat for their region.

> 'Weather models suggest Cyclone Gita will cross central New Zealand during Tuesday and Wednesday. Heavy rain is expected from Monday night, with the potential for rapidly rising rivers and floods in a broad area north of Canterbury. The MetService says people should be aware of coastal inundation, especially where high waves, low atmospheric pressure and strong onshore winds come together. Cyclone Gita will also bring severe gales. Residents in the projected path have been advised to spend the weekend securing their properties: roofs, trampolines and other items that could be at risk from high winds.'

Lachlan looked through the cottage window to his left; a few stray clouds and sunshine mocked the warning.

'It still looks like summer out there Baz. How many people are going to listen to that advice?'

The station commander finally ceased his drumbeat. 'Bugger all.

They won't react until the cyclone takes their neighbour's roof off.' McCullers stood, thrust hands into his pockets and circled the office.

'It's so hard to predict how bad the storm will be. We might get a bit of a buffer from the wind with the mountains.' McCullers jerked a thumb in their direction. Then he swung his hand towards the sea. 'And the quake has lifted most of the coast along here. That should nullify some of the surges, apart from high tide.' The prowl resumed.

'So, what's your main worry? The rain?'

'Yep. I was talking to Mason Barnard at the civil defence meeting.'

'A chopper pilot would have an interesting perspective.'

McCullers nodded. 'They washed away a lot of debris from the hills after the quake. Took them months. But Mason says there's still a lot of loose shit up there.'

'What? They reckon a heavy downpour could bring it all down?'

McCullers completed the worst-case scenario. 'Burying the rail tracks and coast road again.' Fingers kneaded tight muscles in his neck. He had been on early patrol. 'Christ – the trains have only been running again since Christmas.'

Lachlan picked up his coffee mug, pointed at his colleague's.

McCullers shook his head. 'I've already had a thermos full.'

Lachlan mixed coffee granules with milk and three sugars from McDonalds as the kettle boiled. He was surprised by the never-ending supply of sachets, considering the nearest golden arches were in Blenheim.

'So if the rain is heavy enough, we're looking at multiple land slips.'

McCullers slumped into his seat. 'Yep, all the way from the Hundalees to beyond the Clarence.'

'What about houses?' Lachlan opened three cupboards in a futile search for biscuits. 'How many are in danger?'

'A few dozen. There's a couple of families down at Goose Bay that I'll be telling to get out before the storm arrives. One place is right on a creek bank. They could get washed out to sea.'

'And there's nothing we can do to stop nature.'

'Exactly.'

'Have the Transport Infrastructure Recovery teams been briefed?'

'All the diggers and trucks are on standby. They'll need half of them for the overtime pay they'll collect.'

Lachlan paused before the first sip. 'You mean there's a New Zealand company that still pays overtime? Maybe I should do some moonlighting.'

ABEL TASMAN NATIONAL PARK

The seabed was three-metres beneath her kayak, yet Kim was certain she could count every shell. Abel Tasman was filled with native birds, chattering tourists, the splashing of water and the occasional clunk of paddles against plastic. Cyclone? What cyclone?

Kim dipped a blade on the left, then the right; the foot pedals helped maintain course for Split Apple Rock a few hundred metres away. It was a double kayak, but the passenger in the bow wasn't providing much momentum. Jo had been moody since a phone call with her father during the tour briefing.

'Do you think we've used more than our quota of luck on this trip Jo?'

'What do you mean? Julian raced off to Tonga. What was lucky about that?' Jo snapped a shot of the bush-clad coast above the sea caves.

'Okay, apart from *your* barren sex life, we've had a good run. We were lucky to get this motorhome to ourselves, lucky Mac sent me on holiday, lucky to get the last parking spot most nights.' Kim turned the rudder to the right to steer around a struggling member from another tour group. 'And we were bloody lucky to get the last double kayak from Kaiteriteri.'

Jo grunted and framed more of the national park in her camera. They'd faced disappointment when they arrived at the beach mid-morning as all the guided tours were booked. They assumed there would be ample kayaks available; it was peak season after all. The operators were apologetic; the best they could offer was to take a phone number in case of a cancellation.

Kim and Jo had retired to a nearby café to debate Plan B. A week of adventure had seen the diminutive PA walk further than she had in the previous six months. Lush bush tracks beckoned nearby. They were attractive to Kim, but not her co-traveller.

'Nope. I read the brochure – it's three hours to the next point where we can get a water taxi back here. I'm not walking that far.'

They finished their lattes and were about to resort to the back-up plan of lying around on the sand, when fortune smiled on them again with a cancellation. It was not Kim's preferred trip, and only a five-kilometre glide along the most sheltered part of the coast, but it would take in scenic nooks and crannies, sea caves, and the famous rock formation. It would also include a beach swim, lunch and more paddling on the homeward leg. So, plenty of photo opportunities, no walking, Kim providing the power at the rear – a perfect outing from Jo's perspective.

Kim manoeuvred their craft into the best location for photos of the granite showpiece. It was an impressive sight; a massive 120-million-year-old boulder cleaved neatly in half, earning it the dual moniker of Tokangawhā / Split Apple Rock.

The boulder and the story of the battle for its possession was a must-see for every visitor to Abel Tasman Park. The guide paddled ahead of their group of eight kayaks to deliver a spiel about its creation; and in this case mythology trumped geology, as legend said two feuding gods broke it apart.

There were dozens of kayaks floating around the rock and closer to shore. Further out, a handful of jet skis almost drowned out the guide. Kim, the once-stressed reporter, would have been annoyed at the wild posse a week ago. She might have even thrown her water bottle if the intruders blasted within range. But seven days in a motorhome touring Aotearoa had worked wonders for her mental health.

Kim was even secretly pleased about a text from her ex-boyfriend, Nathan Potter. It arrived during the kayak briefing on the beach. It was a friendly *hello* from the police detective, wishing her well on the New Zealand adventure. The guilt that might have overwhelmed her in Australia was suppressed by the surrounding beauty. Abel Tasman Park was not a place to get angry with someone who had your welfare close to his heart. She sent a quick response; grateful for his kind thoughts – and hoping to make him a little bit jealous about their pending kayak trip.

Maybe I'm still a bitch! That prompted a chuckle, which interrupted Jo's photo taking. 'What are you laughing about?'

'Nothing. Just enjoying the view. I'm glad we didn't miss out.'

Jo smirked and made a half-hearted effort to propel them forward with a few fake strokes. 'So, nothing to do with a text from Nathan then?'

'What? How did you know he messaged me?'

'Easy guess. You are literally glowing now. No one else can get you smiling like Nathan.' Jo pointed at the guide trying to usher their group towards shore for a swim. 'I mean that hairy pig hunter isn't your type, so it's obvious he's not the view you're admiring.'

Kim struggled with a response. Her vibrating mobile rescued her from the moment. She wrestled it from the waterproof pouch while praying it wasn't the former beau. A text she could cope with, not a chat. Especially with Jo half a metre away. It was an Australian number, but not from her contact list.

'Hello?'

Jo paused her camera work to find out who would dare to interrupt their holiday.

'Kim! It's Ciaran O'Malley. Have you got a moment?'

Kim left the call on speaker, but turned the volume down. Jo shook her head and waited to be paddled ashore. She dangled a hand in the water.

'Hey Ciaran. Mac gave me a heads up that you might call. What's he done to owe you guys a favour?'

'He stole my last Kit Kat – and that was after he tried to pinch the news diary.'

'That's the Mac we love – and know to hide valuable stuff from.' Kim watched the guide unhitch his spray skirt and assist other kayakers ashore. She waited at the back of the queue. 'He told you about Cyclone Gita hitting New Zealand?'

'Yeah. How dangerous is it? Are people boarding up their windows, filling sandbags and that sort of shit?'

Jo and Kim both laughed.

'You must be desperate for a story Ciaran,' Kim said.

'There's fuck all happening in Melbourne, Kim. The producer's threatening to cut me out of the pie and cake run if I can't find a lead story by lunchtime.'

Kim tapped the foot pedals to keep the five-metre kayak pointed towards shore. 'You're going to be hungry Ciaran. It's a beautiful day here. Not a sign anywhere that there's a big storm on the way. We're on the water, in fact, doing a kayaking tour.'

'Fuck!'

'Sorry. There's just nothing visual to record. The sea is a lovely green, mostly calm. Just a few clouds. I can't see anything changing in the next four hours to help you. If anyone is preparing for Cyclone Gita – we haven't seen them.'

'Shit. I'm looking at a website; it shows the cyclone lumbering towards you like a concussed Collingwood ruckman. But there's obviously no gale force winds or coastal surges for you?'

'Nope.'

Kim watched the seventh kayak in their group edge towards the sand. They were a large, middle-aged American couple. It might take them a minute to haul themselves from the plastic cockpits.

'What about tomorrow? The weather might deteriorate. Are you and Jo staying at the top of the South Island?'

'Not quite. We've got a wine tour booked near Blenheim. Do you want to ask Jo to cancel that?'

'Jeezus Kim. I'm not that brave – or stupid. I thought cyclones are supposed to be terrifying. I mean, look what Gita did to Tonga last week. Mac promised me it was going to happen to New Zealand.'

The guide waved to Kim; it was her turn to paddle through the gentle shore-break. She held up a finger.

'I have to go Ciaran. To be honest, we're driving away from where the cyclone will hit land. We have a commitment in Kaikōura on Monday that can't be changed. If it turns to custard tomorrow, I'll give you a call and we can sort something out then.'

Thirty seconds later Kim and Jo were hauling their kayak above the tide line. Thoughts of news stories were banished by the prospect of a swim in the crystal-clear water.

Jo looked at the hampers being unloaded from the guide's hull. 'Do you think wine comes with the lunch?'

KAIKŌURA

Saffron Fernsby felt conflicted as she walked through town. Weather forecasts were coming every hour, yet the tourists and townspeople continued as normal. There was little to indicate nature was ready to turn their world upside down.

Her own instincts were in tune with Cyclone Gita; she was still a powerful force despite the downgrading. Saffron had conveyed that message many times. Were people being blasé, or naïve? Perhaps the South Island had endured so many physical and economic disasters in recent years that another threat barely raised their adrenalin.

Saffron adjusted the strap of her shoulder bag and trudged on. Her destination was a stall near the supermarket. It might be her last chance to stock up on fresh produce before Gita arrived. There were ample tinned supplies of pulses and flour to bake bread. But nothing could beat fruit and vegetables.

Three people queued at the ATM outside the bank. It reminded Saffron of her amateur sleuthing. There had been no further sightings of the *suspicious* tourist. Most likely he was in Christchurch, Queenstown, or Fox Glacier. Some tourists travelled far and fast, making use of every daylight hour to explore Aotearoa. His actions were unusual: darting down a lane and lurking in a dull reserve. But who was Saffron to question his motives? *You're just a nosey old biddy!*

Saffron smiled at her folly, which prompted a well-muscled islander to respond in kind as he passed on the pavement. His taller, and equally fit companion presented a grimmer visage. They were both in their 30s and – to Saffron's over-active imagination – looked as if their physiques had been sharpened by military training. She slyly glanced as they walked towards The Esplanade. Both were over six foot, had broad shoulders and narrow waists. They walked with confidence, not a swagger. Few people would want to mess with them. Her heart might have fluttered 30 years ago. Now, it raised a curiosity akin to the other tourist. *Interesting.*

On the other side of the street, Heath watched the grey-haired woman appraise the Bruisers from the cover of a raised takeaway coffee cup. He had spotted the steroid pumpers as they left a cafe near the railway bridge. To his professional eye they had to be part of the takedown crew. The only thing missing to confirm the id were guns. But even these guys wouldn't be silly enough to parade around town with pistols strapped to their hips. Staying under the radar was their mantra as well.

There was no need to communicate with the Bruisers, but Heath *was* curious about where they were based; he didn't want to run into them at his own motel. A decade of undercover work instilled in him the need to know where the guys with guns were based.

His coffee cup was empty, not that any pedestrian would know that. Heath blended into the crowd, pretending to sip occasionally as he glanced in tourist shop windows. The Bruisers were easy to keep in sight, even from 80 metres.

The nosey pensioner doing a double take at his targets, however, meant Heath had to abandon his pursuit of them. She was walking towards him. He didn't want to draw attention with any sudden moves, so he very casually crossed the road, the coffee cup raised to his lips. Heath needed to stay out of sight of everyone; the Bruisers could wait. He binned the cup and stepped into a men's clothing shop, where he browsed the shirts near the window, waiting for the extremely curious woman to pass. *Does she have a bloody sixth sense or something? Or am I just paranoid?*

Gordie reversed the Land Rover into his preferred spot in the wedge-shaped park at the pub. That piece of good fortune did not improve his mood as he gathered tobacco, papers, wallet and mobile from the passenger seat. A pint, or half dozen, might help. He glared at the phone, the source of his grumpiness. The Sydney wanker had texted the drop would be Monday night.

'Fucking brilliant!'

A cyclone was swooping on the South Island – and the Australians want him to go to sea to snare their precious cargo! They had a fortnight to get their act together. Now, when the danger is escalating, they want him to risk his life and boat.

Gordie's sour face when he ordered his first pint did not prompt the barman to inquire about his day. There was no need to stay sober, the rendezvous was two days away. No other patrons offered a greeting either as Gordie slunk past the regular cliques for the beer garden. A crawling motorhome slammed on the brakes to avoid Gordie as he free-ranged across the bitumen. A toot on the horn from the frustrated elderly tourist earned a raised middle finger.

Gordie threw his tobacco pouch and papers onto the table, and the rollie production line resumed. The beer and repetitive actions calmed him. He was able to rationalise the Australians' thinking. Their ship had been delayed by a breakdown. It would leave port when fixed. It was Gordie's bad luck that would be Monday.

The television news indicated the cyclone was most likely to hit the upper South Island. *Great.* But the current modelling had the worst of the weather hitting Tuesday and Wednesday. There was some solace in that prediction, although Gordie knew the seas would get rougher as the cyclone approached.

He'd rolled three smokes by the time he flicked the first butt onto the rocks. Gordie's record was six in reserve before the second was lit. He inhaled deeply, enjoying the moment – until Spike Moloney and Wiremu Henare spoiled it.

'Evening Gordie,' Spike perched facing the sea. Wiremu took the pub view, which put him directly in Gordie's eyeline. He didn't offer a greeting.

Gordie nodded, continued to wrap tobacco in paper before sealing it with a lick.

'How much are you asking for *WOFTAM*?'

'What? You want to gazump the *JAFA*?'

'Shit no, Gordie. I wouldn't give you a hundred bucks for that rust bucket.'

The rollie production stopped. 'Then why the fuck do you want to know what I'm getting paid for it?'

Spike drank his pint, glanced around the garden. The other tables were full, but no one could hear their conversation.

'The grapevine says you're buying a fancy new F150. They're not cheap Gordie. Not even a JAFA is going to give you that much for *WOFTAM*.'

Shit!

The only person in Kaikōura who knew about the Ford was the copper. *Small town gossip!* Probably everyone from Clarence to the Hundalees knew about his 150 plan.

Spike and Wiremu hadn't fallen for his story about selling the boat. There were probably a few other people sceptical that he could find the money for a new vehicle. The pick up was 48 hours away, the handover soon after. He had to keep these pirates at bay.

'A new F150?' Gordie said. 'What gave you that idea?'

'Pub talk Gordie. Straight from Baz McCullers.' Spike took a long swallow as he held Gordie's eye.

The gabby sergeant would be Gordie's salvation. 'Ah! That explains it.' He made them wait as he finished and flicked another stub towards the beach.

'I got pinged by that new copper on the way to the marina. He gave me a fistful of fines and was going to order the Bounty off the road. I told him I was getting rid of it after the boat sale. I've always dreamed of a 150 with a confederate flag – I gave him a story that bought me some time.'

Gordie smiled as he lit another smoke. 'I wanted the cops off my back – I never thought Baz and the other wanker would take it seriously.' He blew smoke across the table; confident the bluff would work.

Wiremu stood with his empty pint. Spike gave him a chin up, confirmation he was ready for a refill. Gordie suppressed a sigh. The deckhand was yet to be convinced.

'It sounds believable Gordie – except I know what a bullshitter you are.'

Gordie shrugged, not taking his eyes of the rollies. Seven waited on the table and the pouch was almost empty. Wiremu's absence made him bolder.

'I don't give a fuck what you think Spike. My boat is my business – not yours. I didn't invite you to sit down for an interrogation. In fact, I'd prefer it if you fucked off – *right now!*'

Gordie was gambling a busy Saturday night at the bar would delay Wiremu long enough for Spike's bravado to fade. The pair stared at each for half a minute, until the younger seaman blinked. He stood.

'You're up to something Gordie. I can smell it – you're in for a payday and it's something to do with *WOFTAM*. You should be a smart man and include Wiremu and me. We'd have your back.'

Gordie looked over his shoulder. Still no sign of the muscle.

'Fuck off Spike. Your big Māori mate doesn't scare me. I learned a few things at Rolleston.'

Gordie turned back to the sea; the upstart dismissed. A few seconds later he was alone – and smiling. It felt good to head off a coup. How long Spike and Wiremu would be kept at bay was debatable. They were suspicious, but Gordie just had to avoid them.

His own pint glass was empty. There would be no slinking away tonight. He left the rollies on the table and crossed the road for a refill, certain Spike would not bother him again. Perhaps it was time to get used to carrying the Sig everywhere? That would keep both pushy bastards in their place. And that fucking intruder; if he ever came back.

FIJI

Normally Semesa Bari's interest in cyclones and abnormal weather patterns waned once they moved beyond his patch. There were always new threats to investigate and warnings to prepare for the island nations in his Pacific region.

Yet, Semesa could not bid adieu to Gita as it entered the Tasman Sea. He found himself drawn to every update for the projected path.

'You were never a good girl Gita.' Semesa stood and stretched back and arm muscles. 'What mischief do you have in store for New Zealand?'

FEBRUARY 18

BRIGHTWATER

Kim sat at the wheel of Kwozzimoto on Sunday morning and traced the scar above her ear – for the first time in days. She had enjoyed another deep sleep without nightmares, an indication of the holiday therapy. Maybe she was taking on some of Jo's new tension?

Kim wriggled her shoulders. The kayak tour hadn't been long, but it exercised muscles and bones that had gone through reconstruction surgeries. The aches were justified; Kim had paddled for two.

Their departure was delayed by another call from Australia. Jo said her father was worried about safety in a cyclone. Kim hoped Sterling Trescowthick put their welfare ahead of the luxury motorhome.

Kim watched her friend pace in ever-decreasing circles, a sign of waning patience; a concerned parent would not stand between Jo and a day among the grapes. She turned to scan the motorhome for loose items. Clothes, crockery and food spilling from unsecured cupboards in the first two days taught them the need for a daily check list. A wine bottle rolling from the fridge on a sharp bend had earned Kim a severe rebuke.

All latches and windows were fastened. And Jo was reaching for the handle. A toot from a departing slider prompted a farewell wave from Kim. There were four German girls in a van half the size of Kwozzimoto. Kim was impressed they had survived six months together on the road. The Europeans were heading north for fruit-picking work in Hawke's Bay to fund the rest of their gap year.

There were more clouds, but no sign of heavy rain or the destructive winds that were forecast every hour on the radio. The temperature was comfortably in the early 20s. A live cross to a dry Kim in shorts and t-shirt would not be a ratings winner for Mac. That was 36 hours away, perhaps the weather might turn more dramatic. Further musings about work were diverted by Jo's entrance and the tail end of the phone call with her father. Kim started the engine.

'Ignore those promos about Kim reporting live from the eye of the cyclone, Dad. Mac got a little too eager after watching footage from Tonga. It's down to a Category 3 now and dropping all the time. It's likely to be a non-event. If we weren't going to the wineries this afternoon we'd be on the beach. That's how safe Nelson is – and it's supposed to be in the firing line. I'll call again tomorrow.'

'It's a wonder your parents haven't ordered you a rescue helicopter,' Kim noted.

Jo shook her head. 'Honestly, Mac never lets the facts get in the way of a good promo.' She plugged the mobile into the charger and buckled her seat belt. 'Okay skipper. I can smell the wineries in that direction.'

A salute preceded the gear selection. Kwozzimoto wasn't in the groove; he stuttered two metres before Kim braked.

'Shit! What was that?' Jo said.

'I don't know.' Kim looked out the side window. 'We're on grass, but it's dry. I don't think it was wheel spin.'

'Try it again – maybe a bit slower this time.'

Kim accelerated. The shudder was less pronounced, within a few seconds they were moving smoothly.

'That was weird.'

Jo waved to another van load of travellers at the exit. 'Well, it's working now. Drive.'

There were no further problems as Kwozzimoto reached the first set of traffic lights in Richmond. Kim pressed the accelerator gently on the change to green – no shuddering.

'The gremlin has been vanquished,' Jo patted the dashboard. 'Behave yourself for another week, please.

KAIKŌURA

'Fuck!'

Four tabs of paracetamol couldn't ease the pain in Gordie's head. He rolled over in bed, aware that he was still dressed, although the beanie had slipped to the floor. The night at the pub lasted longer than Gordie anticipated. Fuelled by the adrenalin buzz of putting that little Spike turd in his place, five pints had been followed by four bourbons. He then stupidly drove home in the Land Rover, because he still hadn't paid the charges on the Bounty, and then had three large whiskies.

It was madness to drive. If he had been caught by Baz McCullers, or the temporary copper, he would be back behind bars again. He wouldn't even have to hit anything. The judge would look at Gordie's record and shake his head. He couldn't expect anything as reasonable as time in Rolleston again.

Gordie tried to lift his head from the pillow but it flopped back, striking something hard.

'Fuck me!'

He reached out for the offending item, then realised it was the Sig Sauer. He had been sleeping with a loaded gun. Gordie's stomach almost heaved when he saw the safety was *not* engaged.

'Fucking brilliant Gordie! You blow your brains out the day before your biggest payday!'

He set the safety and moved it to the bedside table. Fluids were the next priority; he needed to drain his bladder and refill with water and coffee. Daylight required some decorum with the ablutions; Gordie used the inside loo instead of peeing on the weeds.

Five minutes later, he'd consumed a pint of chilled water and carried a mug of milky instant coffee with three sugars out to the backyard to check his makeshift intruder alarm. He'd tied half a dozen empty beer cans with string and hidden them in the long grass between the corner of the house and the back door. They should be impossible to see in the dark unless any future intruder had night vision goggles. But hopefully the first guy had been scared off by the gun.

Gordie grunted and returned to the kitchen for toast. What was the bastard even after? Every small town in New Zealand had its share of petty thieves. But the Tulloch household had never been a target since Gordie inherited the property after his father's death. Everyone knew he had nothing of value.

That strengthened the niggle that the intruder knew something about the drugs pick up. Gordie slumped into the Chesterfield with thick slices of toast dripping cholesterol. He fancied baked beans but was too lazy to open a can.

The job had come through Mutton Kineen, a Rolleston connection. There was no hope of anyone like Gordie emerging from corrections department care with a revised social attitude. Prisons were a training ground; learn better skills to avoid getting caught next time. The encyclopedia of dumb mistakes would run to hundreds of pages. If you didn't take heed, you deserved to be locked up.

Thinking about Mutton made Gordie wonder about his share from the deal. Would it be enough to satisfy a career crim? Perhaps Mutton had been sneaking around Gordie's home to earn himself a bonus. The payment would be cash; too much to put straight into the bank without attracting attention.

Gordie tried to recall the physique of the intruder. Did it match Mutton? Possibly, he was always scrawny, although he'd never seen him run inside Rolleston. The guy on Tuesday night was fast. It was too dark to match hair colour. Maybe he had a beanie or a balaclava.

But, if this is the start of a regular service, why risk pissing off an Aussie gang by taking down their boatman? If Gordie dobbed in Mutton everything would be fucked. No, Gordie didn't think Mutton was that dumb, or sneaky. The intruder was someone else. Who – and were they still watching? He should pay more attention to unusual faces around the marina. That would give him an advantage, along with the Sig Sauer.

The pain in Gordie's head eased to a dull throb. Give it another hour and he would drive to *WOFTAM* and hang out there for a few hours. Keep his eyes open, see who showed interest in the boat.

MELBOURNE

It was the fifth day of Lent; Ciaran O'Malley believed the Lord was punishing him for failing to make a traditional sacrifice. A crumpled Kit Kat wrapper on the desk was the damning evidence of his guilt. Was it too late to start the period of self-denial? Would it even help his current plight, the need more stories to fill the Channel 5 News six o'clock bulletin? *Probably not.*

O'Malley swivelled his chair, hoping three of the four reporters still in the office might have tapped a source for a story. They were all on their mobiles; they could have been chatting to friends, partners, lovers or bookies. In the case of the cadet, Matthew Gunn, he was probably telling his parents about his wonderful job listening to police scanners.

'Oi! Matty!' The lad jumped like a startled rabbit. 'Any police activity? I'd rather a hostage scene two streets away, but I'll take anything – anywhere in Victoria.'

A mobile was tucked against a scrawny chest. 'I'm checking reports of shots fired in Mildura, Ciaran. The patrol car is about to report back.'

'Fuck! O'Malley scratched his head furiously. Great, there could be his magical shooting/hostage drama, but it also created a dilemma. Mildura was almost 500 km away. Scheduled commercial flights took 80 minutes to get there; it was more expensive in a private plane. There was a local television station, but its weekend staffing levels were probably more dire than O'Malley's.

He was about to punch in the speed dial for the airport when the cadet blotted his career prospects.

'Sorry Ciaran. It was kids with homemade fireworks.'

O'Malley let his finger hover. 'Did they start a fire?' That might save the day – the Mallee ablaze in a late summer firestorm.

'No bushfire, Ciaran. The cops are reading the riot act to two 10-year-olds by the Murray River.'

O'Malley threw away the phone. 'Maybe the cops should give those kids swimming lessons – with rocks in their pockets.'

The cadet smiled, obviously thinking his boss was joking.

'Matty! Get me a coffee – and a Kit Kat. Fuck Lenten sacrifice. God's doing nothing for me.'

The cadet scrambled from the room, not daring to ask O'Malley for cash.

A finger drum roll didn't improve the story inventory. His desk was covered with a pile of weekend media releases from the usual suspects: Greenpeace, Amnesty International, fringe political parties and the conspiracy theorists. No self-respecting chief of staff could stoop that low. They were television, not radio.

A ping from his mobile announced a text. O'Malley's heart rate lifted when he saw it was Kim Prescott. Had the cyclone arrived early? Were the cadaver crew about to serve him up another exclusive? The fleeting hopes were dashed within seconds.

No sign of cyclone. Can't help your bulletin

'Fucking brilliant.' The phone clattered against the timber console.

Matthew Gunn's return prompted a sigh from the veteran newsman.

'Young Matty,' he said, accepting the coffee and chocolate with a nod. 'Did you see the Samoa and Tonga footage on the cyclone?'

'Yes, Ciaran. It was dramatic.'

'Okay, that cyclone is about to slam into New Zealand in a matter of hours.'

'Really? I thought it was downgraded.'

'Oh no, young man. It's still lethal. Haven't you seen *Spotlight's* promos? They reckon it's going to be the worst storm to hit the Kiwis in years. The change in the cyclone means its fanning out – going to hit a wider area. More people in danger, more damage.'

'Wow. There could be some great pictures and stories in the next few days.'

'Yep. But I think we need to start the ball rolling.'

Gunn's eyebrows lifted. 'You want to use the file vision to indicate the disaster about to hit the New Zealanders?'

'You got it Matty. Hustle together some pictures and a script. I'll spice it up for the producer.'

It was a big opportunity for a cadet whose media life didn't extend beyond the lottery results and the police scanner. He ran to his desk.

'I just remembered that Kim Prescott is in New Zealand – should I ask her for a phone interview?'

'Ah, no Matty. We'll let Kim do her report on *Spotlight* tomorrow.'

O'Malley swivelled to his terminal to add the cyclone story to his thin rundown. It was a beat-up that no senior reporter in the room would touch. For Ciaran, it was another 60 seconds of news vision to fill the gaps between the commercials which paid his mortgage.

KAIKŌURA

Lachlan's patrol car stopped behind three camper vans and a motorhome at Jimmy Armers Beach. They were parked close enough to pass food, drinks, books without having to get out and touch the sand. It was too cosy for Lachlan's camping tastes; he hated listening to every burp or fart from the neighbours.

'He pulled on his cap and stepped out to perform his duty. The tourists weren't in trouble, Lachlan was there to warn them about the approaching storm. He found eight Europeans in their mid-20s: Germans, judging by the accents. Communication wouldn't be a problem; their English skills were usually better than his.

'Hello. I'm Constable Naismith. Can I talk to you for a moment?'

'Ja. You may constable,' said a blonde woman in dungarees and a khaki shirt. The rest of the group nodded, putting aside noodle bowls and water bottles. 'I hope there is no problem with us staying here. We only arrived this morning.'

'That's okay.' Lachlan held up a hand to reassure the tourists. Few locals treated him with such deference. 'I'm not here about the freedom camping. You're all fine.' He looked from the battered vans to the sea. 'You've got a great spot. But I need to warn you that it could be dangerous when the cyclone arrives.'

The tourists were surprised. 'We have not heard anything about it, constable. We have been in Otago.' Their relaxed mood swiftly evaporated. 'When is this storm coming? Do we need to evacuate?'

Lachlan wasn't surprised by their reaction, even though most New Zealanders outside of Gita's predicted trajectory didn't care.

'We're urging campers to move away from the waterfront by tomorrow afternoon. We're expecting gale force winds, and up to 200 millimetres of rain.' Lachlan gestured to the sea and then the ranges in the distance. 'We don't know if there will be a tidal surge, or what might wash out of the mountains.' Lachlan pointed south, beyond the headland. 'Over at Goose Bay they had a surge of almost seven metres after the earthquake. A cyclone is different from a post-quake tsunami, but we think you'll be safer inland.'

The implications for the group were swiftly debated in a mixture of German and English. Lachlan was peppered with more questions about secure destinations. Two vans were heading for Nelson and Golden Bay.

'Away from the waterfront in Nelson should be safe enough,' said Lachlan. 'Personally, I wouldn't go near Takaka before the storm. There's only one road into Golden Bay. If there are slips or washouts, you could be stuck there for days. Even weeks.'

That caused more yabbering, mostly in German. A Welsh accent sought Lachlan's attention from over his shoulder.

'Excuse me officer. Is there anything that we need to know about?' It was a middle-aged couple from a Britz motorhome. Curiosity and the German's consternation had drawn them outside.

'I'm warning people about Cyclone Gita which is due to charge through here on Tuesday and Wednesday. Are you aware of the danger it poses on the coast?'

'Ah, yes. We know about the storm officer.' The grey-haired male looked smug. 'We're driving to Hanmer Springs tomorrow. We hope that should be out of range.'

Lachlan nodded. 'It will get wet there, but I'm sure you'll be safer than on the coast.'

The content Brit waved goodbye and shut the door of the rental motorhome. The couple had views of the rocky beach, but Lachlan wondered why they weren't outside. It was warm, with enough clouds to shield them from the sun. To Lachlan, it was like watching the sea on the internet.

A breeze from behind the seafood caravan provided another reason to be outdoors. It also reminded Lachlan he was hungry. A seafood chowder would fix that. His mission with the campers was almost done; they were aware of the storm, and most were planning parks. Two of the men were adventure junkies and wanted to experience the storm in Nelson.

Lachlan left the tourists to their planning and retrieved his wallet. It would be the last seafood treat for a while, depending on whether the café survived the tempest.

BLENHEIM

Laughter and chatter swirled around the tables at Cloudy Bay, the fourth and final vineyard on their Marlborough tour. Kim was engaged in conversation with a European couple. Secondary school French lessons weren't enough for Jo to keep up. She drifted away with a bottle to find a shady tree.

Few tourists were worried about the approaching storm. Jo topped her glass and surveyed the valley. It was a dry, rocky landscape compared to the North Island. She had been dreaming of this winery experience since Christmas – but now she struggled to enjoy it.

She looked across to an animated Kim. Her friend had been sent away to overcome trauma, depression and paranoia. The tactic had worked. Kim was laughing and chatting, no sign of the nervous scalp scratch, nightmares, or grumbles about Stephanie Grant scooping all the exclusive stories.

Ironically, as Kim's mood soared over the past week, Jo found her spirits sliding. She tried to hide the emotional dip with wine, travel adventures and banter. Jo knew it hadn't fooled Kim, but she'd brushed aside her friend's attempts to explore any demons associated with Byron's death.

The Kaikōura visit was always on the agenda. Jo thought that she was emotionally prepared to visit the beach where Byron died. That fragile confidence had been fractured when she'd seen his killer in Auckland. She had no doubt and then her father's contact had confirmed the bastard had been released.

The revelation had come just before the kayak trip. Jo couldn't explain why she hid that bombshell from Kim. Or the reason for the second troubling weekend call. The police had no idea where Byron's killer was. It was attributed to bureaucratic friction between departments. Again, she didn't share that with Kim. Jo had disguised it before climbing into the motorhome with a segue to her father's concerns about the cyclone. Some personal things could never be shared, even with friends.

Jo turned towards the distant hills as moisture welled in her eyes. It annoyed her. She was known for being feisty and passionate, but public tears were rare. She swiped them away between rapid sips of wine.

KAIKŌURA

Wiremu Henare approached the backyard barbecue with two rump steaks on a tray. Spike Maloney nudged a dozen sausages aside with tongs. He was about to be entrusted with the main course.

'Four minutes each side, no more.'

Spike saluted with his beer bottle as the thick beef was laid on the grill. 'Who decided that was the correct time for a good steak?'

'My dad.' Wiremu inhaled the aroma of summer. 'If Mum was cooking, he'd tell her when to turn the meat, when to take it off. Never used a watch. Judged it perfectly every time.'

Spike nodded, turned the sausages. They never received the same attention. Wiremu sat and rested his back against the wonky picnic table. It had survived dozens of larger and more robust barbecues at the rented bungalow. A sparse salad – lettuce, tomatoes, avocado – indicated they were the only two for dinner. The meal would be supplemented by supermarket potato wedges, currently in the oven, a loaf of white bread and a bottle of tomato sauce.

Wiremu sipped his beer, resisting the urge to check his watch. His father had an extra three decades of experience around the hotplate. Thirty seconds later he looked at the G-shock: short by 10 seconds. He counted down from five for Spike.

'Ok, turn those beauties. I'll get the wedges.'

The two-bedroom house was remarkably tidy for bachelors. Charter work taught them the value of being organised on the water and at home. The lounge suite, dinner table and chairs were hand-me-downs, or bought at the second-hand shop. The only art on the walls were rugby posters: the 2011 and 2015 World Cup winning All Blacks and the Crusaders. Twenty-five-year-olds without steady girlfriends didn't need elegance. Besides, they wanted to accumulate wealth, not spend it on furnishings. Apart from the massive 4K television with the Sky Sport subscription. That was a must-have accessory.

Wiremu returned to the barbecue on cue. 'Take the steaks off and let them rest for five minutes.'

'Yeah, yeah. Mate, you tell me the same thing every time.'

Spike went back to rotating the sausages. 'What are we going to do about Gordie Tulloch?'

Wiremu chewed a crispy wedge. 'We're going to sweat him tomorrow.'

'You reckon he's going to do the pick up before the cyclone?'

'He can't do it during – or after. The shit will either be at the bottom of the sea or halfway to South America.'

Wiremu portrayed the strong, silent type to most people: the muscle behind Spike's mouth. But it was the 120-kilo Wiremu who was really the thinker and planner. His subtle observation of Gordie's boatyard activity led to one conclusion: *WOFTAM* had been commissioned for drug smuggling.

Gordie couldn't fish, couldn't take charters. There was no other reason for his boat to have full tanks. The Marlborough sale story was bullshit. Not even JAFAs were that stupid. They knew about Gordie's excursions away from the charters and whale boats. Nothing had returned on *WOFTAM*, apart from Gordie docking with a rare smile.

The meeting with the Australian at the pub, gleaned from one of the barmen, indicated it was likely to be a drug shipment. Kaikōura seemed a strange and risky location to bring in millions of dollars of coke, heroin, meth or whatever. Especially ahead of a cyclone. That wasn't Wiremu's concern. They had to know when Gordie would make the pick up and intercept him before the handover.

Wiremu had no doubts he could flatten Gordie with a couple of punches, if necessary. He outweighed the seaman by more than 30 kilos. Sure, Gordie might have learned a few dirty tricks in prison, but it had been a dozen years since Wiremu lost a fight. That was to three Christchurch teenagers who later needed urgent dental work when Wiremu took his revenge at secondary school.

The plan was to *join* the deal, with a view to being involved in future operations. It was unlikely to be an isolated drop. Wiremu believed the Australians wanted a new backdoor into the local drug trade.

The pair were confident that Gordie would eventually understand the wisdom of having partners. If not, it might have to be a *hostile takeover*. Wiremu loved those corporate terms. Gordie would be relieved of the goods and his contact details; the young entrepreneurs would present themselves as the reliable bagmen. There was nothing Gordie could do to stop them. Smashed teeth and a broken nose wouldn't earn Gordie any sympathy from the local plods. Not that Wiremu thought the dumbass would complain.

'Everything points to the pick up being in the next 24 hours.'

Wiremu speared a sausage from the barbecue and smothered it in tomato sauce. 'We're going to do shifts in the truck at the bowling club. Gordie has to drive past to get to the marina.' Wiremu chomped half the sausage.

'Shit mate.' Spike threw the tongs on the hotplate. 'I'll go out of my mind sitting there all night.'

Wiremu chewed for half a minute. 'I said we'll take turns.'

'What about during the day? Okay, we don't have a charter tomorrow, but we'll look suspicious hanging around the bowling club. Those old bastards play every day.'

Two more bites finished the entrée. 'We'll move to the marina after dawn. We can find enough work around the boats to keep ourselves busy. We'll be waiting for Gordie's return.'

Spike shrugged and turned off the gas. Dinner was ready.

'You still reckon he'll take the shit home? Arrange the handover from there?'

Wiremu piled the largest steak, half the wedges, four more sausages, a lettuce leaf and tomato on a plate. 'It makes sense to me. Gordie doesn't have a lockup and he can't leave the stuff on the boat. If it looks like he's driving straight out of town from the marina, we'll go to Plan B.'

'Run him off the road?' Spike filled his own plate.

'If necessary. But I think Gordie will realise he's been rumbled if we're sitting on his bumper. His ute and Land Rover are crap, but he won't want to end up in a ditch. Especially when he knows there could be a few broken bones to go with the mangled metal.'

Silence descended as the pair attacked their meals.

The Bruisers emerged from the fish restaurant on the main street satisfied with their meal. They had flirted with the fried chicken shop next door, but fish and chips won again. Leighton Conroy fancied a sweet finish to the evening. Alcohol was off the menu until the job was finished.

'Fancy an ice cream mate?' Conroy pointed to the parlour across the road.

Fetu Leota patted his trim waist. 'You trying to destroy this temple? I had a double scoop last night.'

'You could eat half the Tip Top factory and not put on a kilo. Not the way you train. Come on.' Conroy moved to the edge of the road to wait for three motorhomes to pass.

Fetu joined him. The tall, athletic duo in polo shirts and denims attracted admiring glances from the tourist convoy. 'Did you notice that Highlander with tinted windows parked across the road?'

The motorhomes were followed by another half dozen cars and camper vans.

'Yeah.' Conroy checked his watch. 'One person behind the wheel. Could be listening to a news report.'

'Maybe,' Fetu said. A break in the traffic opened. They crossed without glancing at the vehicle again. A Westpac ATM provided a convenient stop. Conroy inserted his card and tapped in the minimum cash withdrawal: $20.

'Driver still inside?'

'Yep.' Fetu wandered in a small, impatient circle. 'I don't think it's that pensioner who clocked us yesterday. I can't imagine her with an SUV.'

Conroy snorted as he pocketed the card and cash. 'More likely to see her on a bike – or a broomstick. Could be nothing.' He took the receipt and shredded it. More time for observation.

'Could be.'

'But you've got that feeling of being watched.'

'Yep. It's never failed me.'

'Okay.' Conroy walked to the souvenir shop next to the bank. They spent two minutes browsing. Even that was about 60 seconds more than the tourist items warranted. The ice cream parlour was another two doors around a slight bend. 'You hang on the street while I get you a super-duper cone.'

'Just a single, Leighton. I hate to waste good food if we have to ditch it for a chase.'

Conroy entered and waited in line behind a Spanish couple. He was back on the pavement with the treats within five minutes. 'Any movement?'

'Nope.'

Conroy licked his double chocolate. 'I had a thought in there. I wonder if that's the watcher. He's a pro – always on the lookout for anything different. We might stand out to a guy with more than a decade on the job.'

'True.' Fetu slowly consumed his single cone while keeping the Highlander in view.

'He knows not to compromise us, or himself. Perhaps he saw us coming out of the restaurant and decided to wait until we're clear.'

'That would make sense,' Fetu said. 'No one else in town should know about us.'

'Let's head back to the motel. If the vehicle follows – we'll stop them for a polite inquiry.'

'Does that mean I get to smash a nose?' Fetu licked spillage from his fingers.

'Only if I don't like their answer. For all we know, it could be the vicar's wife wanting to shag me.'

The Bruisers chuckled as they walked towards State Highway 1.

The seven o'clock radio news sting started on the SUV radio as the Bruisers exited the restaurant. Heath could afford to wait for them to leave the area. They looked big and tough; he didn't want a bad report from them to the bosses in Auckland. Heath turned up the volume.

'The latest MetService modelling has ex-Tropical Cyclone Gita slamming into the upper South Island and lower North Island on Tuesday.

'Civil Defence and council officials met this afternoon to plan their response. They urge residents to use the remaining time to prepare their emergency kits, fill up gas and water bottles, tie down or remove outside furniture. Wind gusts are expected to exceed 120 km per hour.'

Heath tuned out the rest of the report as he watched the Bruisers loiter. One stocked up on cash before they bought ice creams. Heath couldn't see the shop, but a week in Kaikōura was enough to identify all the important food locations.

'You guys must be sick of waiting.'

There was only so much television or reading you could do on a mission, especially for the Bruisers. Heath had spent years following and watching targets. He had learned to switch on for the job, then relax when opportunities allowed. Two colleagues from the academy who were also shoulder tapped for undercover work never developed that knack. They became like over-wound watches. He heard they imploded on drink and drug binges. They joined to serve the community; instead, it ruined their lives. Heath had encountered misfortune but survived.

Heath watched as the blond-haired Bruiser presented a smaller cone to his mate. They appeared to be a tight unit: experienced, strong, composed. The second Bruiser – a Samoan – looked like he could crack walnuts with his biceps.

'Maybe you guys don't need guns after booting down doors.'

The rough side of the job never interested Heath. He guessed these Bruisers would get a kick out of breaking bones during a takedown. They finally disappeared around the bend. Heath switched off the radio and left the SUV.

He could afford the luxury of a sit-down meal and not worry about Gordie Tulloch slipping out to sea. The inside source had come through with fresh information: the drop was going to be after midday on Monday. The bosses had conveyed that information two hours ago. They had also given Heath a number for a burner phone with the Bruisers.

The approaching cyclone was likely to hasten the handover schedule. They couldn't afford for any delays in the communication chain after Heath reported Gordie's arrival on shore with the merchandise. Gordie might dump the shit in his Land Rover or ute and race to a rendezvous with his contact. Heath could follow, but if the Bruisers were left behind in Kaikōura, there might not be a chance to intercept.

The aromas of fish and fried chicken battled for Heath's attention. It had been a high cholesterol week; could the arteries survive another night? Coopers Catch won; he could get a salad with the fish and pass on the chips. Maybe.

FIJI

'Your eyes are on the television Semesa, but I think your mind is elsewhere,' said Joeli Naitini.

The former team-mates were watching their first Super Rugby replay of the season, usually an occasion for high spirits and chatter. There had been no reaction from Semesa to a gravity-defying try in the corner by a South African player.

Semesa tuned back in for the replay. 'Ah. That was incredibly good. These professional players are so agile. Almost like acrobats.'

Joeli passed a bowl of potato chips. 'Normally you would be grabbing a ball Semesa and trying to copy that try on the sofa. You have worries at home, my friend? At work? With the church?'

Away from his wife's gaze, Semesa was brave enough to scoop a handful of salty goodness from the bowl. 'No, no, no Joeli. All is wonderful with the family. Everything really is good. I have been preoccupied with Cyclone Gita. She has been such a bad girl. And now I think she is about to deliver a final sting to New Zealand.'

Joeli retrieved the chips and claimed a bigger handful. 'You are so serious and caring with your work Semesa. I can sympathise. You know how dangerous these tropical storms can be, even when they descend into colder climates.'

The try conversion missed from out wide, the match resumed with a bone crunching tackle on the flyhalf. The former players winced.

'Our lives are shaped by the fickleness of the weather, Joeli. It has always fascinated me. I get strong feelings about some of these storms – which will be mild, which will be bad. A few which will be truly terrible.'

'And you think Gita is in the third category?'

Semesa shrugged. 'Her power is waning, but her tentacles are wider. Gita can do much greater damage over a wider area. New Zealand has stronger housing and infrastructure than the islands. But at times, there is nothing we humans can do to defy nature at its fiercest. I will pray my concerns are not realised.'

The conversation returned to rugby matters as another try was scored.

FEBRUARY 19

BLENHEIM

Kwozzimoto was humming on State Highway 1 when Jo's mobile rang. She checked the caller ID before thumbing the reject icon. Kim glanced but didn't comment. Much of the trip had been spent without chatter. They were half way between Blenheim and Kaikōura. The turquoise sea was a stunning contrast to the dark shore.

'That beach looks weird. Can we pull over?'

It was an kilometre before they found a safe and suitable park. Kim guided the motorhome close to the dunes where they had the seascape to themselves. Jo flung the passenger door open before the engine stopped. Her thongs were left behind – that was a mistake.

'Ewww. Shit!'

Kim had to shout. 'Black sand too hot for your toes?'

More swearing prompted Kim to investigate. She found Jo rubbing her feet furiously with grass.

'Damn horses. They shit all over the place.'

Jo had tromped on a pile of fresh dung, leftover from someone's morning canter. Kim was tempted to take a sneaky photo to share with the *Spotlight* crew. Jo's darkening mood kept the phone in her pocket.

'Phew! That smells awful. I'm not letting you back in Kwozzi stinking like that. You'll need to wash your feet.'

The ineffectual grass was flung away. 'Brilliant! Whole bloody sea probably smells of horse shit. Why can't they clean up after themselves like dog owners?'

Her muttering continued all the way to the Pacific for a proper cleansing. Kim rested her back against Kwozzi's warm bonnet. The view reminded her of the Great Ocean Road at Fairhaven. The ranges on her right looked like the Otways. However, there was no comparison with the sand; Australian golden sand had more allure than this black stuff.

Kim suspected the stink might not wash away in the sea. She tipped dishwashing liquid into a bucket of water and prepared a towel by the front step. Five minutes later more curses heralded Jo's return.

'I still bloody smell of horse shit; if I could find – oh!' Jo sat on the bottom step and plonked both feet in the bucket. 'Yow! That water's colder than the sea.'

'Stop your whining and hurry up. We've got a busy day.'

Jo swirled her hands through the water to create froth. 'We've made good time. It's not even nine o'clock.'

They had left the overnight camp at the Blenheim racecourse before eight, which was an early start for them, but they wanted to reach Kaikōura for the Byron tribute and to prepare for *Spotlight*. Neither was convinced they could make the pre-cyclone story dramatic enough. The sky was overcast, the sea more agitated than the crossing of Cook Strait, but there wasn't much else to indicate a cyclone was about to ravage New Zealand.

'We still have to get through the roadworks. That French couple at the winery said there are several choke points. We'll be doing well if we're in Kaikōura by 10.30.'

Jo hauled sudsy feet from the bucket and sniffed. 'I think I've got rid of the pong. Chuck me my jandals please.'

'Jandals? Are you turning Kiwi?'

'Nah. I got sick of men looking at my crotch when I asked where my thongs were.'

Jo ditched the water and returned the bucket to the garage as Kim woke up Kwozzimoto. There was only a slight shudder as they exited the layby. Much the same as when they left Blenheim. Not as bad as Sunday's stuttering start.

Kim joined the main highway behind another motorhome. 'Should we call Declan? Give him a warning there might be something wrong?'

Jo snapped a photo of the mountains and sea. 'I think it might be better to wait until Christchurch. He might get spooked and want it checked out immediately. We could be stuck there for the rest of the week waiting for a mechanic to say Kwozzi was being temperamental. It's only as he starts – the rest of the time he's a champion.'

'Fair enough. Look out for seals. Apparently they love this part of the coast.'

'It's hard to believe this was uplifted by two metres.'

'Scary thought. I hope this cyclone doesn't have the same impact as the earthquake. Look at those workers and the machinery – they've been repairing the roads and rail for 15 months. And it looks like they have a lot more to fix.'

Kwozzi stopped behind a Maui motorhome. Ahead of it were several trucks, campers, cars and a smiling woman in a fluorescent jacket with a stop sign.

KAIKŌURA

Gordie searched the freezer for bread without mould. There were only two crusts and a slice left in the week-old packet. They would be enough for breakfast: toast, fried eggs, all covered in baked beans. A big can of Heinz because it was going to be a long day. That was why he was trawling the frozen offerings for something else to sustain him during the afternoon and evening. He wasn't likely to leave the boatyard after midday – except in *WOFTAM*.

The kitchen radio had been silenced after the third cyclone warning. The bitch was a day away, the first rains and gales arriving in a few hours.

'Fucking brilliant!'

Gordie defrosted the bread. There wasn't much to make sandwiches with: the cheese was rock hard, the ham past its use-by date. An American introduced him to the combination of peanut butter and jam a few years ago; lucky they were both in the cupboard.

'Next week beef steaks for breakfast, lunch and dinner.' That thought cheered Gordie. He would have the money to eat anything. If he could be bothered going to the supermarket. Maybe he would eat at the pub for the week instead.

The day had started early, by the fisherman's standards. A text woke him at seven o'clock.

letterbox

The number was blocked. Gordie wondered if it was the handover man. It took him another 10 minutes to obey the command. That was part belligerence, mostly the time it took to roll and inhale the first cigarette of the day.

He found a courier pack at the gate; there was no sender name. Inside was a cheap phone.

'Another phone? What's wrong with the bloody one I've got?'

Gordie had shrugged and powered it up: another text was waiting.

> text when return

It had been too early for the neighbours to be on their way to work or school. Was the phone delivered by van, or hand? Was it another layer of security? The models were cheap, no expense to ditch them after a few messages or calls. Or was this something else? Could it be the dude sneaking around the house? Were Spike and Wiremu getting sneaky?'

The new phone was a change from the plan agreed with the Sydney guy at the pub. Maybe that's the way the drug gangs rolled; always keep the worker drones off-guard. He shouldn't worry; it meant there was nothing incriminating on his own mobile. *Do I have to bin both phones after the job?*

Gordie wasn't concerned that breaking the gang connection would jeopardise future contracts. They knew where he lived. If he did a good job, the Australians should organise more shipments. There should be no stress about the payment. It was agreed the contact would hand over the cash when the shipment was delivered. If there were no dollars in hand, Gordie wasn't going to give the shit away. He had some firepower to protect his sea booty.

The new drug phone sat on a bench near the kettle as Gordie completed his ration pack. He'd found A box of chocolate-coated muesli bars behind the baked beans in the pantry. A few beers would be welcome, maybe a few swigs of rum if it got chilly bobbing around on the waves. But Gordie decided that could be too risky in an approaching cyclone. He would go dry for a day.

An unexpected sensation surged through Gordie as he made the final preparations. It had been a long time since anything created such a buzz. He could understand people getting addicted to the adventure.

MELBOURNE

Spotlight's program producer sprawled in his chair, mulling the dismal offerings available for the show that night. They had good mid-program stories, but no strong lead. He sipped coffee from a chipped Collingwood mug; it was cold.

'I hate the silly season. Nothing happens between the end of the Big Bash League and the start of the footy.'

Mac's complaint was missed by the fill-in PA. Carla was gathering copies of the rundown from a printer in News. The *Spotlight* machine had run out of toner.

Stephane Grant was on the phone at her desk; Dugal Cameron fiddled with a camera nearby; Pete Benson and other crew members were discussing their weekends in the conference room; and senior producer Curly Rogers was pounding his keyboard at the back of the office.

'What are you up to Curly?'

'I spoke to Kim on the way into work. I'm making some notes.'

Mac's chair sprang forward.

'The cyclone's arrived at last? Is it smashing the crap out of the poor Kiwis?'

'Nope. Kim says there's not much evidence – apart from grey skies and more wind.' Curly stood, gathered his clipboard and coffee for the production meeting.

'Jeezus. We hammered the promos all weekend. Our girl Kim in the eye of the storm!'

'And the news boys gave it another boost last night. Must have been a quiet day for O'Malley to dredge up the Samoa footage again – and give us a back announce about a special report from Kim Prescott.'

'We have to run a story. It can't be ignored after that publicity.' Mac found his pen; only black, any other colour jinxed the day. 'Can Kim find us a tearjerker? Sandbags being filled and laid in front of shops and homes? Windows being boarded. Do the Kiwis go feral like the Americans in a hurricane? How about the gun stores – do they stockpile assault rifles and ammunition?'

Curly ushered his boss ahead of him at the conference room doorway. 'I told Kim we're desperate and how to inject drama into the story. We'll focus on the battered town syndrome. Kaikōura was smashed by the earthquake – now another natural disaster is about to descend. She can get a few interviews; we'll mix it with the quake damage from the library and the cyclone footage from a few weeks ago. Before you know it – we'll have a masterpiece. It's still a toss-up whether we do the live phoner to the pub. If the wind and rain arrive, we'll get Jo to shove her out the door.'

Mac slapped his second-in-command on the back. 'Tell Jo to find some thick rope to wrap around Kim's waist. It will look even better!'

KAIKŌURA

Spike chatted to other deckhands as he wandered the marina at South Bay. Everyone was in storm preparation mode: securing boats, ropes, ladders, squabs. The vessels were out of the water, but anything not tied down could end up at the Chatham Islands by the end of the week.

Wiremu worked steadily around the company vessels. He was pacing himself to ensure the duties lasted long enough to keep an eye on Gordie. Their target wasn't on *WOFTAM*, which indicated a late afternoon or evening pick up. Wiremu wanted to know when Gordie went to sea.

There was more urgency around the other boats; an early finish meant a longer afternoon in the pub. No charters would be booked in the next few days, possibly even a week or more. Whales were Kaikōura's stars. They weren't going to hang around in storm-tossed seas: all the marine life would scatter.

Normally Wiremu would have grumbled at Spike's socialising. Not today. He watched his mate approach their charter boat on his third circuit of the yard.

'The boys reckon they'll be in the pub by three o'clock.' Spike glanced at the nearest vessel, lowered his voice. 'It might seem strange if we don't join them.'

Wiremu coiled some more rope. 'Yeah. I've been thinking about that.' He secured the rope in a locker, and found another length to slowly repeat the exercise. 'No sign of Gordie yet. My bet is on an evening exit.' He looked at the darkening clouds and white caps. 'It won't be fun out there by dusk.'

Spike climbed aboard the boat and lounged on a bench. 'You sure it's going to be today? I wouldn't want to be out there. Maybe his bosses will want to delay. Nobody would want to risk losing the merchandise.'

Wiremu reached for his water bottle. 'Gordie's at the end of a long chain. The delivery ship will be working to a schedule that started weeks, maybe even months ago. They'll dump the stuff overboard at the designated spot. Gordie knows he'll lose both his balls if he's not there to pick it up – regardless of the weather.'

Spike sat up. 'Hello. Here comes the Bounty.'

They watched as Gordie's ute rolled through the yard and stopped beside *WOFTAM*.

'I think you're on the money, Wiremu.'

They both drank from water bottles and watched the seaman haul a day pack from the ute's cabin.

'That's unusual,' Spike said.

'Yeah. The only person in the yard to be putting provisions on board today.'

'What's he got inside there? Food, booze – a gun?' Spike laughed at his own joke.

Wiremu paused before answering. The thought that Gordie might have access to a weapon never occurred to him. He was a sneak thief; everyone knew to keep anything valuable locked down. Gordie never broke into boats or sheds, but items left loose on deck soon disappeared. There had been lots of accusations, and a few punch-ups over the years, but no one had ever caught him with stolen goods. Most at the yard believed the prison sentence was well-deserved. It wasn't long enough, although it didn't relate to Gordie's pilfering.

'A gun might be worth considering Spike.'

'Shit!' Spike's eyebrows lifted. 'You really think so?'

'There's a lot of money at stake. Drug shipments get ripped off by other gangs – and entrepreneurs. The Aussie guy might have slipped Gordie a pistol – or taser – to defend himself until he makes the handover. Maybe even some pepper spray? We can't be overconfident with him.'

Spike scratched his bristles. Shaving had been shelved until the charter work resumed. 'Yeah. He was cocky the other night at the pub. He was still spinning the boat sale bullshit. Then told me to fuck off.' Spike looked across to *WOFTAM* where Gordie showed the only seagoing activity. 'He's a mean bastard, but rarely arrogant.'

'We'll bear that in mind tonight.' Wiremu stood. 'It might require a sneaky entrance – then some shock and awe tactics, like the SEALs.'

Wiremu went to the cabin to retrieve a tool kit. 'I'm going to tinker with the port engine for a while. That will give us another excuse to keep an eye on Gordie.'

'But what about the pub? It will look strange if we're the only ones who don't join the session.'

The tools rattled as Wiremu rummaged. He lifted his head. 'Now that's a thought.'

'What?'

'We do need to go to the pub, even if it's slightly later. But what if we brought Gordie with us?'

'Eh? He's never invited. He might join an occasional session – but nobody ever asks him.'

Wiremu found the wrench he required. 'We're going to mend some bridges. You'll offer to buy him a beer for being a prat.'

'But he's got a drug shipment to pick up. He won't want to go to the pub.'

The lid to the engine compartment was lifted. 'He's being offered free beer. It would be too suspicious to knock that back – not after we've already told him we suspect he's doing something illegal.'

The big man eased to his knees. 'I think he's smart enough to go for a couple of drinks – then slip away when everyone gets pissed. Gordie's spent half his life on the water around Kaikōura, much of that with a belly full of booze. He'll be able to handle his beer and the boat. Once he leaves the pub, that's our cue.'

Wiremu focused on the engine tinkering that would occupy him for as long as required.

Saffron Fernsby absorbed the energy of the approaching cyclone from atop the Kaikōura Peninsula Walkway. There was no sign of whales or dolphins as lines of white caps grew with every passing minute. Overhead, seagulls drifted on the freshening wind, screaming for tidbits that would become scarcer. Saffron sent them into a frenzy with a handful of bread scraps.

'Make the most of it, my darlings. I don't think I'll be back this way for a while.'

In fact, Saffron was certain she wouldn't be on her favourite path for many days. Every instinct told her that terrible times lay ahead. Her new temporary home had suffered so much after the quake. Now, nature was about to make life miserable once again.

It wasn't only the storm that made Saffron uneasy. There had been a long build up; Cyclone Gita gliding inexorably around the South Pacific, island nations powerless to stop her destructive path. Yes, there was reason to be concerned and fearful for her fellow residents. Homes and livelihoods were going to be battered, some destroyed. Possibly a few lives taken. Brick and timber should withstand the worst of a waning cyclone. Yet, Saffron couldn't shake that feeling of foreboding. That forces beyond the natural world were also gathering for a reckoning.

A cheeky gull snatched the plastic bag from Saffron's hand, the final crumbs scattered with the wind. The bag itself was soon discarded, allowed to blow out to sea. There was nothing Saffron could do to retrieve it from the cliff, which grieved her. She hoped no marine life fell victim to her inattention.

There were few walkers on the path. The seal colony was still busy with tourists snatching selfies with mammals before they slipped away into calmer waters to ride out the storm. She decided to return, rather than going all the way to the marina. The reconstruction after the quake should ensure the sea walls and vessels survived. She held onto her floppy hat as she turned into the wind to retrace her steps. Perhaps a seafood chowder at Jimmy Armers Beach would settle the uneasiness. A rare treat.

Walking was always time for reflection. The return journey past Point Kean brought back memories of the *suspicious* man dancing around the main street to avoid Gordie Tulloch. And those two musclemen. They could have been innocent tourists, but she didn't get that feeling. Saffron wondered if she should mention those gentlemen to Constable Naismith if she saw him before the cyclone.

No doubt his hands would be full when Gita descended. These new thoughts might see her dismissed as a conspiracy theorist. Still, she couldn't shake the feeling that those three gentlemen were connected to her general apprehension.

LYTTELTON

Rafael Serrano could feel the vibrations of a ship preparing for departure. The maintenance crew were almost ashore, it was the Captain's job to complete the paperwork for departure. They were six days behind schedule, but on track for the predicted drop-off time delivered to the gang on the weekend. Perhaps slightly earlier, depending on the skipper's eagerness to push his repaired vessel.

It was a pity the handover couldn't happen in port. That would have eliminated the risk of a sea drop. The contact could have been told to drive to Lyttelton, or somewhere nearby in Canterbury. Rafael could have hired a car for a few hours and the job would have been completed. But it was the gang's consignment, and they wanted to do the drop at sea.

Rafael didn't need to leave the bridge to announce the *Hoplite* was underway again. The text was already prepared.

Leaving. Arriving 9pm

The message was innocuous. How many couples announced their work movements in abbreviated terms? Millions, Rafael was sure. He would tap send once they were clear of the dock, sometime in the next few minutes. There would be a solo final text.

Home

Rafael went to the bridge window. Below, his smiling Filipino conspirator waited for the command to haul in the ropes. In a few hours, he would be on standby for a more important directive to drop their consignment.

KAIKŌURA

The mood on Kwozzimoto was sombre as Kim carefully reversed out of the motorhome park near the tourist information centre. Thank goodness for the rear camera, as she had mere centimetres to glide between two campers. Not even the giant crayfish pod on the council office could elicit a smile or comment from either traveller. The day had a shitty start, courtesy of the horse manure on the beach, and it hadn't improved.

Curly had rung twice; the first call to confirm they were committed to a story. The second chat involved instructions for the pictures he needed for Kim's story. He'd even emailed a rough script. Jo would be pressganged later as mobile phone camera operator. That didn't help her mood, given the emotional baggage that was peaking in Kaikōura. Their Aotearoa adventure was on hold for a couple of days.

Road works to mend the quake damage squeezed their timetable for story production and a suitable homage to Byron. Then came the accident at Clarence. It was barely a one-horse town: half a dozen houses, a rafting/kayak business, a T-intersection. That traffic challenge was too much for a French tourist in a camper. He joined the main highway on the wrong side of the road, hitting another van filled with German tourists.

The collision was a glancing blow; fortunately, none of the six travellers were seriously injured. Their vehicles, on their 10th or 20th journeys around New Zealand, would never complete another circuit. The discussions to determine costs and removal were likely to last much of the day. Jo directed Kim to skirt the carnage and drive on. She hated the unnecessary reminder of the next stop on their itinerary. At least no one was dead at Clarence.

Jo held a bouquet in her lap as Kwozzi took them along The Esplanade. The flowers were bought at a drab dairy near the supermarket. Norfolk pines lining the beach side of the road were a visual improvement, but not a mood enhancer. Beyond, the shingle sloped steeply to the water. A mixture of community facilities, houses, motels and a couple of cafes were on the other side. They held no interest for Jo. Kim remained quiet. A fierce shore break pounded the pebbles.

Dozens of campers and motorhomes lined the road. Several had washing lines strung between their vehicles and the pines. Not a good look for travellers – or residents. The craggy ranges were behind them, ahead were low chalky cliffs compressing the town against the sea.

The road forked at the grey two-storey pub. A few hundred metres to the left was the century-old New Wharf. Jimmy Armers Beach was to the right. As they entered Avoca Street, Kim noted their next campsite – a grass section behind the hotel – was already full of vans. They would look for alternatives later; the site where Byron died was a few hundred metres away.

A narrow footpath flowed to the right of the bitumen. It was empty. A handful of pedestrians in t-shirts, shorts and daypacks risked the gravel verge where tourist traffic passed within a metre. Probably like Byron on that fateful night. The road snaked through a mixture of new-builds and humbler cottages with million-dollar views. Kim pointed to a pink 19th century house on a sweeping bend.

'There's Fyffe House.'

They'd read an online article two days ago about Kaikōura's oldest structure and the last remnant of a pioneer whaling station. Oil from the southern right whale was shipped from these rocky shores to light homes around the world. There was no time, or inclination, to stop for a history tour.

'We must be close now,' Kim said.

Jo didn't reply. They were abreast of two ramshackle green sheds which marked the entrance to the old wharf. Ahead was the shack which housed the winch. Kim eased Kwozzimoto out of the traffic, finding barely enough space to park beside two rusting boat cradles. The flower stems twisted in Jo's grip as Kim switched off the engine.

The road ahead weaved around a rocky shoreline. Half a dozen campers were parked near a public toilet block. The footpath had disappeared before the old homestead. The verge optimistically displayed a painted bicycle symbol beside a 50 km/h sign. The road between the cliff and coast wasn't wide enough to warrant a centre line. Motorhomes had to take turns to navigate the gap, or risk losing wing mirrors. Cyclists would pedal at full speed through the choke point; wiser walkers scampered over the rocks. Byron had chosen to stay on the bitumen on that February 19 night two years previously.

'Do you know the location to lay the flowers?'

'Yes.' Jo jumped out. Kim followed through the passenger door as Kwozzimoto blocked part of the cycle lane. 'Dad said it's the third bike symbol after the winch shed.'

Kim grimaced as a 10-metre motorhome filled the choke point as it returned from the seal colony. 'I think we should go over the rocks.'

Jo didn't listen. She set off along the cycle lane, the flowers clutched close to her chest.

Kim looked over her shoulder. 'Jo. There's another camper coming.' She gestured for the driver to slow down. 'I think we would be safer off the road.' She scurried after her friend.

Jo kept teary eyes on the unbroken white line as she marched. A toot from the angry driver earned him a middle finger. Kim caught up after 60 metres, when Jo stopped at the symbol which couldn't portray anything about her loss.

'Come on Jo.' Kim wrapped an arm around a shoulder and guided them onto the rocks.

'Are you girls bloody mad? Get off the– oh!' The abuse from an

English passenger was clipped as their van drew level. The flowers and tears were universal signs of bereavement.

'Sorry!'

He was ignored, as was the next convoy of cars, campers and motorhomes. Jo stood wrapped in Kim's arms; the tears flowed as her body convulsed with grief.

They stood like that for 10 minutes, a curiosity to a silent procession of tourists: no words were shared.

Kim broke the embrace to recover a packet of tissues from her shorts. The sobbing had reduced to an occasional sniffle. Jo lowered the bouquet to the rocks, then gratefully took a handful and wiped her eyes.

'Thanks Kim.' She dabbed again. 'I… never expected it would be so tough.' Jo looked from the road to the beach. 'It's such a bloody silly place to die.'

More tissues were offered, but not required. 'I get the feeling that Byron was much more *important* to you than you've told me.'

Jo laughed, then wiped her eyes again. 'Typical bloody journalist. Always reading between the lines.'

'Sorry Jo. I don't want to upset you – just trying to understand your bond with him.'

Jo knelt and adjusted the flowers; they should be a proper tribute for the few days of their existence. There had been nothing to mark Byron's death before – and there wouldn't be anything in the future. Melissa would never travel to New Zealand; Jasmine had moved on with her life and Jo knew that she could never come back to experience that pain again.

Jo kept her eyes on the bouquet. 'We were lovers.'

'Oh Christ!'

A yellow rose petal dropped. Jo sighed and stood to share the story for the first time.

'We met at university – I was first year; he was about to graduate.'

Kim frowned. 'Was he your stepbrother then?'

'No. Not when we first met. Everyone was single. Dad and Melissa were away – separately – on extended holidays in Europe. They were on the rebound from broken marriages and hooked up on a ski field in the Austrian Tyrol.'

'They never knew about you and Byron back in Melbourne?'

'No. Not that Byron or I ever shared details of relationships with our parents. We might concede to seeing someone. But we were never going to admit we'd met the love of our lives.'

'Shit!'

'Yep. We clicked straight away. We were inseparable for the summer. We were bonking our brains out at his place, my flat, the beach – anywhere we could. We didn't know that Dad and Melissa were doing the same in every ski chalet.'

'I remember you saying that your Dad's second marriage followed a whirlwind romance.'

Jo flicked a pebble towards the incoming tide. 'Yep. He proposed at the top of the Eiffel Tower. They were married at a registry office in London a week later. They're both English-born, which helped with the paperwork.'

'Jeezus. And their relationship has lasted okay?'

'Surprisingly well. No marry in haste, repent at leisure. They were a perfect fit.'

'But that ruined your chances with Byron?'

Jo bent down to find another projectile. 'Totally destroyed us.' The stone went further into the waves.

'I'm not sure of the law. Can step-siblings … do anything?'

'We never checked. It grossed me out when we found out. I left my lover's bed in the morning. That night, Dad *introduced* me to my new stepbrother.' Jo shuddered at the memory.

'Did your Dad and step-mum ever find out?'

'Nope. We hid it well on the few occasions we were all together. It was tough. Byron and I really connected. It took a long time to get over him.' Jo shuffled on the rock. 'Maybe I never did.'

'That's heartbreaking Jo. No wonder there's tension between you and Melissa.'

Jo shrugged. 'It didn't help.' She looked down at the flowers. 'I thought that pain was in the past. And now the bastard that killed him is free.'

'Are you certain it was him in Auckland?'

'Yeah. Dad reached the cop who handled the case. All they can say is that he is out of prison – but for privacy reasons, they can't tell us where or what he's doing.'

She felt Kim's arms envelop her again. The moment was tarnished by a laughing yobbo in a noisy Holden.

'Get a room ladies!'

Heath was certain he could smell whitebait fritters at South Bay marina. The seafood van was on the other side of the peninsula; surely the aroma couldn't carry that far on the wind? He looked through the tinted windows at the northerly flow of the darkening clouds. Maybe it was proof of the cyclone's power and imminent arrival. Heath's stomach growled. There were sandwiches, chocolate bars, water, and a thermos of tea on the passenger seat. That would quell the hunger pangs but didn't compare to the offerings at Jimmy Armers.

He looked across to the hardstand which had been busy all day. Boaties were securing their vessels against the coming storm. Several had driven away, to the pub most likely. They would share tales of surviving bigger storms until the current threat passed. Gordie Tulloch's WOFTAM was still on the trailer, no indication it was about to be hooked to a tractor for launching. Was there time for a run around the peninsula for a treat? Heath stifled the temptation by reaching for a Mars bar; chocolate and caramel would have to suffice.

Moving the rental car could draw attention to himself. The seafarers at South Bay were focused on their boats. An SUV wasn't likely to make anyone curious – unless it drove away and returned, the driver not emerging from behind the wheel. Stationary, with tinted windows, it was another parked vehicle. Ample food and an empty 2-litre plastic milk bottle made Heath self- sufficient until his target went to sea. He settled back into his next book on the Kindle.

MELBOURNE

'They're bloody marvels.' Mac watched as Curly swiped through stills and videos of Kaikōura on his mobile phone. 'Dugal Cameron and Kenny Withers will be shitting themselves. If The Hatchet finds out our lead story tonight was produced by a camera on a mobile phone, they'll be out of jobs by Friday.'

'What about the picture and story quality? The boys will argue a case for sequences and their professionalism.' Curly flicked through a short clip of Japanese tourists posing by a slumbering seal. It was representative of the tourist destination; but didn't highlight the drama about to descend. Curly wanted menacing clouds and churning seas. Kim texted her best offerings were at the end of the file.

'Look what you did with your mobile on the Great Ocean Road. You pulled on a thread that unravelled Tugga's Mob.' It set us on the path to booming ratings and greatness. The only downside was that Amy Stewart didn't finish the job on The Hatchet with the crossbow.'

Curly grunted, then smiled when he found the ocean scenes he needed. Kim must have waded into the water up to her thighs. The low elevation contrasted the white surf with dark skies and craggy rocks. The waves might only be a foot high, but Kim made them look threatening.

'Good one Kimbo.' Mac smiled. 'The one-woman band is another step closer.' Mac looked across to Stephanie Grant's latest cosy chat with Dugal. 'Maybe we shouldn't show that to our head camera op – I don't want him to panic and retrain as a manicurist.'

Curly laughed as he shunted the footage to an editor. Next would come four interviews in one-minute chunks.

'Kim says they can't stay by the pub tonight. The camping area is full – they'll have to drive to a place called Goose Bay, about 15 km south of town.'

Mac shrugged. 'They can always drive back in the morning.'

'Yeah. But they asked if we could record the cross to Richard Templeton, instead of going live. They don't want to be on slick and windy roads in a big van when darkness falls.'

Mac clicked his fingers. 'Of course – the two-hour time difference. Yeah. That makes sense – we need them alive to report when the storm really hits town.'

Curly shook his head, picked up a clipboard and headed for an edit suite. 'I won't tell our new foreign correspondent and fledgling camera op how concerned you are about their welfare.'

'By the way, how did Jo's tribute to her stepbrother go this morning?'

Curly paused in Edit 1's doorway. 'Emotional, Kim said. Extremely emotional.'

KAIKŌURA

There were Six burgers and four cups of chips on the motel room dining table overlooking The Esplanade. The view couldn't overcome Fetu Leota's disappointment.

'This place is uncivilised.'

Leighton Conroy retrieved two cans of coke from the fridge. The box of 18 was down to four – enough to finish the job. He knew the source of his partner's ire – the lack of a McDonalds or KFC in Kaikōura.

'How can any town survive without the essential food groups?'

Conroy held up the classic Kiwi burger he was attacking with gusto.

'Mate, this is better than anything you'll get from under those arches.'

'But can you drive through and pick that up at three o'clock in the morning?' Leota paused to demolish half of his first burger in one bite. 'Why should you have to drive to Blenheim every time you want to finger-lick the chicken? It's not right.'

The conversation withered as they devoured burgers and fries. Conroy had heard the same complaints on other jobs where their skills had been required in the wop wops. A four-day mission the previous year had been dire for their professional and personal friendship – there wasn't a takeaway shop within 50 km.

Normally they ate healthier at home under the scrutiny of their partners. Quick carbs were the fuel to get them through long operations in the field. It was likely to be their last meal until the takedown was complete.

Leota and Conroy were as prepared as they could be for that aspect of the job. Their weapons were cleaner than when they came out of the factory. There was nothing else they could do except wait. The shipment had to be collected and brought ashore. Leota and Conroy would then go into action. It was standard practice. Experience was important in their profession – but it didn't ease the boredom. Especially in towns without Maccas and KFC.

SYDNEY

Bondi Beach was a balmy 27 degrees as Sterling Trescowthick paced the embankment behind the lifeguard tower in a grey summer suit. He was occasionally buffeted by children with boards eager to find waves after school. Sterling was focused on a mobile call that went to a message box – again.

'You've reached Jo. I'm away for two weeks playing with cute Kiwis.'

The double entendre had waned for Sterling after the third repeat since lunch. Sterling made two requests for a call back from his typically irreverent daughter: nothing. He knew cell phone coverage was reliable along the coast road around Kaikōura. The extended silence was annoying, especially when Sterling had more difficult news to convey.

His ex-wife's mother had suffered a fall. It wasn't life-threatening, but at 85 a broken hip was life-altering. The independent NanaJo and his daughter shared a special bond beyond their names. NanaJo enlisted Sterling to inform the favourite grandchild, and to extract a promise that Jo wouldn't abandon her holiday.

Sterling should have been peeved the duty fell to him. His first wife was at a spiritual retreat somewhere near Mullumbimby, beyond reach of modern communications. The medical mishap had added to a stressful day. Jo was visiting the site where Byron was killed. It would have been an emotional experience. She was already upset by the chance encounter with Byron's killer in Auckland. Now he was adding to her problems with the news about her grandmother.

Perhaps she was caught up with the TV story of the coastal town preparing for the cyclone. Jo had reassured him Mac's weekend promos were a beat up, trying to draw an audience during the silly season. Hopefully she was simply too busy helping Kim's production to return his calls.

KAIKŌURA

The bar and restaurant at the pub were packed by late afternoon. The veranda tables were also full, along with the beer garden under the trees beside the main building. It wasn't raining, but the pine tables across the road were mostly empty of free-range drinkers. Patrons either wanted a barrier between them and the approaching storm, or they feared getting drenched when the heavens opened.

Gordie rolled a cigarette, his back against the bar wall. He watched a tall, attractive mid-20s brunette dash across the road with a phone to her ear. Apparently, she was an Australian television reporter doing a story on the cyclone. *What a load of shite.*

The completed rollie was tucked behind his right ear. It wasn't wise to leave them lying around on this side of the road. They would be in someone's gob in seconds if he turned his back. He set about balancing the other ear with rollies.

The reporter looked tasty. She was as lean as a whippet and could sit down anytime for a photo shoot with a woman's magazine. Her mate inside was cute too. A wee thing – but scary. She had an aura that kept the local peacocks at bay. She was filthy about something, so the lads were focusing on her mate. It was laughable watching them fall over each other to create space for 'the media'.

Gordie sipped, rather than gulped, his beer; an unusual approach to a second freebie, courtesy of Spike and Wiremu. He was wise to them though. They wanted to get him pissed, so he need their help at sea. The wankers didn't know he could sink several pints and still be fit enough to pilot *WOFTAM* in a storm. The only issue was making sure the cops were not doing breath tests between the pub and the marina. That was unlikely with Gita a few hours away; they'd have way more importatant things to care about.

He'd paid Wally Ferguson to launch *WOFTAM* while everyone was at the pub. Gordie could jump on and cast off before Spike and Wiremu knew he'd slipped away. Wally was happy with $20; there was no one else at the marina to know about Gordie's strange adventure. The idiot would forget he'd done the job by the morning. And Gordie would be armed and ready for Spike and Wiremu when he returned from sea. That would make them back off.

'You all good there, Gordie?' Spike asked. 'Need another beer?'

'I'm sweet bro.' The latest rollie went behind the ear. 'Tell me again – who won the lottery?'

Wiremu joined the duo against the wall. 'One of the Whale Watch guys. Works in the office. He wants to get onto the boats, so he's greasing the boys. They keep asking him for more pints and he keeps paying. No one's working for a while – it's time to enjoy ourselves.'

Gordie nodded, took a deeper gulp of his beer to reassure the lads. He couldn't resist another jab at the morons. 'Did he win first division? I didn't hear anything about a big local win.'

'Nah,' Spike said. 'Nothing that big. Enough to buy his way out to sea with a few beers.'

The irony didn't escape Gordie. He watched the reporter run fingers through her shoulder length hair as she returned to the bar. It revealed a small bald patch above the right ear. *Wonder what caused that injury?*

'Just popping out for a ciggie, boys.'

He knew Spike and Wiremu would follow as he eased through the crowd. He lit the rollie by the front door, inhaled deeply and looked left to the wedge car park. It was full. He was still annoyed that a motorhome was parked in his favourite spot close to the fence. Gordie was tempted to key the camper: the park was for locals.

Gordie watched a man turn the corner and do a double take when their eyes briefly locked. He was a fit bugger: lean, average height, dressed in jeans, a dark tee shirt. Why was he spooked? The man hurriedly pulled coins from a pocket. He ignored Gordie and his shadows as he walked into the pub. There was something about the man's profile that niggled. *Shit. He's the intruder.*

Gordie took two deep gulps from his pint. How many people knew about his drug deal? Did everyone want to rip him off. Or was that guy working for the Aussies – wondering what Gordie was doing at the pub a few hours ahead of an important pick up? He tuned out Wiremu and Spike's Super Rugby chatter as he considered the implications.

'I've gotta take a piss.' Gordie flicked the rollie away and followed the intruder indoors.

The confined interior made Kim's denims oppressively hot. But she was grateful for the layer of protection from wandering hands as she squeezed through sweaty bodies to the public bar. She couldn't tell if it was the same hand that molested her twice, or if two patrons would later boast about groping the Australian reporter. She found Jo in her own space.

'Curly said they'll be ready to record in 20 minutes, Richard's on his way to makeup.'

Jo nodded. Kim reached for a chilled coke. Their interviewee, chopper pilot Mason Barnard, was at the bar talking to an elderly woman. Mason had previous experience of natural disasters and was better talent than the local cops. He wasn't likely to be flying until after the cyclone, no one begrudged him what might be his last beer for a few days.

Kim looked at her colleague. Recording videos and arranging talent for the story had temporarily distracted the PA from her morning grief but it looked like Jo was back to thinking about her former lover. That had been a revelation. Kim missed Nathan since their split, but she never considered him the love of her life. After witnessing Jo's misery, she wasn't sure she ever wanted to reach those emotional depths.

'Are you okay? You've gone quiet again.'

Jo sighed. 'This day is absolute crap. Dad's been trying to reach me while we were filming. I finally called him back.' She took a slug of wine. She didn't have to talk or appear on camera, just hold it.

'What's happened?'

'It's NanaJo. She's had a fall and broken her hip.'

Kim instinctively reached out to comfort her friend. Jo ducked away.

'I think we've used our female hug quota for the day.' Jo looked at the mostly male patrons. 'That idiot who advised us to *get a room* is probably drooling already.'

'I'm so sorry. How bad is it?'

'She's in surgery. Dad says she was sparky on the phone. NanaJo made him promise that I wouldn't rush home to help her.'

'Well, it would be at least 36 hours before we could get anywhere for an international flight. We can reassess on Wednesday, after the storm has passed. Is your Mum with her?'

Jo snorted, took another draft. 'Mum's at a hippy retreat in New South Wales. Dad's in Sydney on business. He's rallying the family to support NanaJo.'

'That's tough – sorting out the former in-laws.'

Jo's reply was cut off by the chopper pilot. He was accompanied by the short, elderly woman. Kim was immediately struck by her serenity.

'Hi ladies. How long before you need me?'

'About 15 minutes thanks Mason,' Kim said.

'I'm ready – although you might have a more interesting conversation with this woman. This is Saffron Fernsby, a former Oxford don. She predicted the cyclone was going to hit Kaikōura – almost three weeks ago.'

'Wow! Really? Are you a climate scientist Professor Fernsby?'

The credentials demanded respect, but Kim was bemused that anyone could have predicted the wild trail of Cyclone Gita. Even her final left turn to New Zealand seemed random. Meteorological maps Kim had studied showed Gita was charging towards Australia. Why the sudden late shift to smash the Kiwis – and how could this little woman predict that? Kim was curious; but needed to know more if she was going to change her on-air talent minutes before recording.

'I was actually a lecturer in Ancient and Modern History for 40 years.' Saffron gestured to the nearest table of pub veterans. 'But these gentlemen prefer to call me The Witch.'

Saffron smiled at the drinkers; they were too smart to be baited in front of a TV reporter.

'A witch?' Kim didn't think the elderly woman looked crazy.

'You could say I am in tune with the natural world, have been since my childhood. At times, I can sense approaching danger – such as storms. Not that I promote these skills – unless it could save lives. Society is quick to pillory anyone with special gifts they don't understand.'

'And you knew the threat that Cyclone Gita posed long before the weather services?'

'Yes. I felt her dangerous energy from the start. I alerted the police.' Saffron smiled sheepishly. 'It took them a while to accept.'

Kim nodded, trying to think what else she needed to know before committing to the switch. Saffron provided it.

'I'm afraid this cyclone hasn't run out of puff. Kaikōura is about to suffer another severe blow.'

'Are you certain about–'

Kim's question was aborted as she watched Jo launch herself across the room and smash her hand – the one holding the wine glass – into the head of a stranger.

'You bastard!' No one moved. 'You killed Byron.'

Jo flailed at the man with both fists as wine and blood dripped from his face. A tall man nearby reacted first, sweeping Jo away without spilling a drop from his pint.

'Why didn't you stop, you prick?' Jo swung wildly, not even close to reaching her target. 'Byron could have been saved. You were a cop, for Christ's sake.'

The referee holding Jo stopped mid sip and turned towards the victim, as did the whole pub. Heath Michel held a handkerchief to his face, backed through the silent crowd and disappeared.

MELBOURNE

Spotlight presenter Richard Templeton hummed *Ode to Joy* as he attached a lapel microphone. Beethoven's ninth symphony was the last tune on the car radio as he arrived at the studio. Next, he attached an earpiece and studied the one-page script for the two-way with Kim Prescott. Curly Rogers interrupted his thoughts from the control room.

'Richard. We've got some problems in New Zealand.'

Templeton rested his arms on the desk. Gremlins loved to play with television services. 'Technical issues? I thought she was going to be on the phone?'

'No. And yes. She will be. There's something else happening. I've got Kim on the phone. I'll have an update in a minute.'

Templeton looked up through the lighting grid. Behind the glass he could see Curly with a phone to his ear. The other hand was furiously rubbing his shaved head. Then he saw Mac enter the control room.

'Morgan. Do you know what's happening?'

The question was for the director, sitting a metre from the intense conversation.

'I'd better let Curly tell you, Richard.'

Templeton was bemused. Normally Morgan Gardner was the biggest gossip in the station. He put a hand over the microphone and called out to the camera operator. 'Bluey! What are you hearing? Is it something that *Spotlight's* executive producer should be worried about?'

Bluey Reynolds nodded. 'Sounds like one of your girls has glassed a copper in a pub then done a runner.'

Templeton never swore around microphones. He choked the first response. 'Was it Kim?' Everyone at Channel 5 knew she had biffed a cop while running the other week. Post-traumatic stress was blamed. The New Zealand holiday was supposed to be therapeutic.

'No. It was Jo. Apparently she accused the cop of killing her brother.'

'Jeezus.' Templeton's sangfroid failed him. He pondered whether to join his producers in the control room. The cross was unlikely to happen; they didn't need to film their PA being arrested. What made Jo go troppo?

'Richard.' It was Curly on the earpiece. 'Mac's on his way down to explain everything. Kim still wants to go ahead with a cross. Mac's keen, but I'm not so sure.'

'Is it true – Jo attacked a policeman?'

'We're not sure he's a cop. Kim says Jo punched a man and accused him of killing her brother. Another punter hauled Jo off the guy. The victim ran off.'

'What about Jo? What does she have to say for herself?'

'We don't know – she scarpered as soon as she was released.'

Templeton's head dropped as Mac entered the studio. The PR implications had to be reported to Channel 5's chief executive, Reg Bradley, ASAP. His father-in-law wouldn't be happy.

'Change of plans Richard.' Mac's smile portrayed no concern about his PA smacking the Kiwi constabulary. 'The heavy rain's started in Kaikōura; it looks like a storm set. Kim's dropped the chopper pilot – you'll be joined by a witch who predicted the cyclone.'

KAIKŌURA

Gordie struggled to keep his anger in check as he pushed through the crowd, away from the wild bitch. The *intruder* is a cop. Good on her for belting him. Gordie hoped the glass split his head open. The bastard had been snooping around Gordie's home. That meant the cops knew, or at least suspected, Gordie was involved in the drug drop.

'Shit, damn, buggery. He's trying to fuck my payday.'

No one paid any attention to Gordie's mutterings, the boozers on the periphery wanted to know about the fight. A little Aussie TV star bashing a Kiwi cop was going to be a legend. Gordie reached the front door. Spike and Wiremu weren't propping the outside wall. They must have been drawn indoors by the stoush.

Now was a good time to slip away: it was pissing down, the pub was crowded, the drinkers distracted. Those assholes wouldn't know he was gone. But what to do? Gordie needed time to think. Was the drug pick up blown? Would Gordie cruise back into the marina with *WOFTAM* full of cocaine or meth to find the cops waiting?

Why did the fucker come at night?

The cops hadn't snuck around when Gordie was arrested in his bed. He was still hungover, barely aware that he'd smashed into a car on The Esplanade. Baz McCullers and the boys from Blenheim kicked his door down. Apparently, there had been a couple of teenagers shagging in the back of the Ford. Not that Gordie could see anything after a night at the pub. He staggered home; unaware the cops would soon give him a wakeup call.

The young lovers were not badly hurt. But the judge treated Gordie's mishap like attempted murder. A previous drink-driving conviction did not help during sentencing. The prick had given Gordie 18-months in Rolleston. He served eight.

Prison time for drugs would be much longer if Gordie hauled them from the sea. But what would the Aussie gang do if he let them sink? Kill him – or maim him? He would never be able to convince them the cops were watching. Gordie was on his first contract, no credit in the crime bank. He was fucked.

Gordie ducked left from the veranda into the waterfall from the roof. Every part of him, from the beanie to his boots, was drenched before he reached the car park where the ute faced Avoca Street. The motorhome was still parked beside the fence. Gordie reached for his keys to teach the tourists a lesson. He paused; a solution to his problems was leaning against the motorhome.

Kim was wracked by guilt inside the pub. The interview with Saffron Fernsby was brilliant. The concern that Cyclone Gita would be a damp squib was swept away by the Oxford don and the timely torrential downpour. An articulate explanation of her extra sensory perception kept the pub audience spellbound. Kim was certain it would be the same for Victorian audiences when the story was broadcast in an hour.

The clincher for Saffron's credibility had been recounting the Great Storm of 1987. It struck Britain, France and Belgium at night in mid-October. Wind gusts exceeded 200 km/h, causing £2 billion damage and 18 deaths. Saffron had alerted several friends in its the path; they fled their cottage minutes before an oak tree destroyed it.

Luck had turned a half-baked story into a must watch. The Australian audience would tune into *Spotlight* on Tuesday night to see if The Witch was correct. More likely, Kim reasoned, they wanted to see a reporter blown out to sea.

To record the interview had been the professional thing to do. Mac was ecstatic, even Curly had dropped his misgivings. They promised to call after the program. It should have been a euphoric moment after weeks of dud performances. Yet, the primary emotion for Kim was guilt: she had not followed her friend after the pub attack.

The reporter was shocked by the assault even though she had inside knowledge about the reason – the death of Jo's former lover. It was a day of revelations, but Jo didn't tell her the driver had been a cop. Their recent history in the *Spotlight* team had shown they were both good at keeping secrets.

Initially Kim expected Jo would return within a few minutes; turned back by the heavy rain and a desire to apologise, perhaps explain her actions. There was no sign of Jo by the start of the interview. Mason Barnard offered to fill the role of camera person despite being dumped in favour of Saffron. His job was to hold the phone close and steady. News and current affairs could bend the broadcast quality rules in a crisis. Get the vision and sound was the mantra – anyway you can.

Kim felt a delicate touch on her elbow. Saffron offered a white wine.

'I thought you might need this, my dear. It was an interesting 15 minutes of fame.'

'Thank you Saffron.' Kim enjoyed the first sip. 'I like the variety that my job offers – but even that was unusual by our standards.'

'Do you know why she attacked that man?'

'Jo's stepbrother was killed in a hit and run accident near Jimmy Armers Beach two years ago. Today was the anniversary.'

'Ah. An extremely emotional day. They must have been close.'

Kim didn't feel compelled to reveal the depth, or complications, in Jo's relationship.

'Yes. It was a terrible shock. In fact, it's been a tough day for poor Jo. She stepped in horse droppings at the beach, saw a road accident on our way to pay tribute to Byron, then she learned her grandmother was in surgery for a broken hip. That would upset anyone. To cap it off – she finds her brother's killer in the pub.' Kim shrugged, then drank more wine.

'Oh dear. Most people would understand her flying off the handle. I hope she is all right.'

'I thought she would be back by now. That's why I went ahead with the interview. Maybe she's sulking in Kwozzimoto.'

'Pardon?'

Kim pointed to the front car park. 'That's our motorhome. We were always coming to Kaikōura – for Byron. Then our bosses heard about the cyclone and wanted a story.' She waved an arm. 'Here we are.'

The congested pub showed no sign of emptying. Kim wondered if that was typical for an approaching cyclone, or a normal Monday in the fishing town. 'Do you think the man Jo attacked went to get help? If they're as sensitive as the Victorian cops, Jo might be arrested!'

Saffron stared at her half full sherry glass. 'I don't think he will complain.'

Kim assessed her first witch. 'Is that local knowledge – or your special gift?'

'A bit of both.' A stray strand of grey hair was brushed aside. 'I've seen that man acting strangely around town.'

'Oh? As in anything illegal?'

Saffron looked around the room. 'Not that I witnessed. I saw him trying to avoid someone. He dashed down a lane when he spied an awful local fisherman called Gordie Tulloch. It was strange behaviour, so I tried to be an amateur sleuth.'

Kim raised an eyebrow. 'I'm intrigued.' She claimed two empty stools at a nearby table and invited Saffron to sit and fill her in on the ex-cop and the seaman. The tale included the two muscle men who made Saffron's heart flutter in the main street. They were an anomaly, like the pub victim.

'Something is out of kilter with all these men. I don't have the skills to make sense of it. But I have a feeling that something is wrong. They're dangerous – just like this cyclone. Powerful energies are converging in Kaikōura.'

Wiremu held two pints as he returned to the veranda of the pub.

'Gordie's gone. Must have slipped away during the fight.'

Spike Maloney looked at the downpour. 'He's a mad bastard going to sea in this weather. His handlers must have threatened him.'

A third of Wiremu's pint was consumed in one swallow. He looked wistfully at the rest. 'Yep. Enjoy your last beer. We'll go wait at the marina.'

'Can we grab some burger and chips in town first?'

'Yeah. I'm sure he'll be a couple of hours.'

The pair drank in silence. Dark clouds smothered the ranges across the bay, waves smashed onto rocks in front of the pub. It was a captivating performance by mother nature, viewed from the safety of shore. Kaikōura had seen many storms. How would Cyclone Gita be measured against them? Wiremu knew those answers would come within hours. His empty pint was left on a table.

'Come on, drink up, Spike. It's time for some tucker – then a takedown.'

The bridge of the *Hoplite* rolled more than a Saturday night drunk. It wasn't the roughest passage that Rafael Serrano and his shipmates had endured, but it was close. Experience taught them to keep a firm grip against rogue waves; broken bones in a cyclone would be agony.

The navigation system was Rafael's eye in the storm as the sea ahead was like a frothing mass. The skipper had ignored the engineer's advice to treat the repairs carefully for the first day. There was time to make up; the *Hoplite* surged towards Cook Strait and, hopefully, calmer waters off the North Island's east coast.

Rafael couldn't argue against the philosophy, but it did mess with his timing for the drop. There was nothing he could do about it. The Lebanese gang knew the *Hoplite* was racing a cyclone and trying to get back on schedule. It was Rafael's job to drop the stuff in the right place, the collection was down to the go-between.

There was no sign of Datu Aquino on the deck. It would be madness to spend unnecessary time outside. The conspirators had planned the quickest and safest dump: less than 30 seconds to open the hatch, biff the stuff and the beacon out. Datu had used his seniority to ensure the rest of the crew would be busy elsewhere.

Rafael looked at his watch. He would text Datu in 15 minutes, the drop to follow five minutes after; half an hour earlier than forecast. White spray splattered the bridge windows.

Good luck to the fool who ventures out to find it!

Water puddled around Jo's feet in the pub entrance. Her short dark hair was plastered to her scalp, and her blue cotton top and tan shorts hung like sodden rags. She was the most miserable sight in the South Island. Jo didn't say where she had been for the last hour.

'I need to get away.'

'Let's go to the van and get you dry.'

'I mean it Kim. I can't stay here. Too much bad shit's happening – we have to get out of Kaikōura. This place is jinxed.'

'For Christ's sake Jo – look at it?' Kim waved at the deluge. 'This is only the start – the worst of the cyclone is yet to come. I don't want to drive Kwozzi in that. The publican said we can stay in the car park.'

'I'll drive then.' Jo turned and marched into the downpour.

'Here Kim.' Saffron Fernsby had watched the standoff. 'Take my umbrella – you need to stop her.'

Kim shrugged away the offer. 'Jo's too stubborn. She'll be trying to start Kwozzi – even though she can barely reach the pedals. There's a campsite about 15 k's away at Goose Bay. It might be far enough to satisfy Jo – and close enough to return to the pub tomorrow for a live cross.'

Kim looked at the darkening sea. 'Hopefully Jo will be calmer by the morning – or I'll leave her on the coast! Thanks for your help Saffy. See you tomorrow.'

She was saturated within half a dozen steps,.

White caps stretched in every direction; rain and seawater lashed the wheelhouse of *WOFTAM*. Conditions were tough, but Gordie had survived bigger seas when fishing with his father two decades ago. Cyclone Gita's peak was still a day away. It was manageable if Gordie kept calm. A couple of beers had increased his bravado.

The marina was lost from sight within a few minutes. There was no fear of colliding with other boats, every intelligent skipper had secured their vessels behind the seawall, or tied them down on the hardstand. Most larger vessels would have scurried out of the cyclone's path, apart from the damaged international trader from Lyttelton. It was one of two boats that had a reason to risk the wild seas.

Gordie was exhilarated. Sure, there was drama and tension ahead. He had to find the drugs before they were swallowed by the waves. Technology would do its job. The co-ordinates should be arriving on his phone soon. He could have waited in the marina for that critical information, but that would have given Spike and Wiremu time to catch up. He didn't want to reveal his firepower before going to sea. Gordie would chug steadily towards the expected drop zone and still be within cell phone range.

The return would be interesting. The young dumbasses would be waiting, expecting Gordie to panic and hand over the gear. *Fuck off!* The big turd would go down like a bag of spuds with two slugs in his gut. Gordie imagined stepping closer and giving Wiremu the *coup de grace.* His silly mate with the yappy mouth would be too shocked to run; a double tap would sort him.

'Bang, bang – problems solved.'

Nobody would be around the marina to witness the shootings. Should he just kick the bodies into the water? Or hand over the drugs to the gang's contact, take the bodies out to sea and feed them to the sharks. Gordie snorted at his musings between *WOFTAM*'s pitching. That's all it was – wishful thinking. The silly pricks would run a mile as soon as Gordie pulled out the Sig Sauer.

A wave tilted *WOFTAM* to port. The vessel slowly corrected. It looked ungainly, but the former charter and fishing vessel was built to handle rough conditions. Gordie checked the mobile: bingo, the drop had happened. He transferred the details to his own system, adjusted the helm a few degrees to starboard and cranked up the revs. He should be close within 10 minutes. Gordie looked at the glowering sky; it obscured any sign of the vessel that delivered Gordie's cargo. He smiled. Finally, good things were coming his way.

Kwozzimoto rocked as the wind buffeted the vehicle. His wipers blinked at warp speed, yet Kim struggled to see the traffic control woman in the fluorescent jacket 20 metres away. She had never experienced such heavy rain. They were midway between Kaikōura and their overnight campsite on the coast. The rising swells made Kim wonder if it was a wise choice. She looked across at Jo who hadn't said a word since leaving the pub. Both had changed into dry clothes, yet Jo shivered under a thick beach towel in the navigator seat.

Kim turned on the heating and boosted the fan. Her friend's emotions were scrambled by the day's shocks. The warmth might provide some cheer. The sauvignon blanc would stay in the fridge until they found a site to park. Jo had a lot of explaining to do about the pub attack.

Finally, they were given the cue to enter the southern one-lane traffic, the controller still smiling and waving despite the tempest. Thoughts of the Great Ocean Road at home returned as the quake-damaged road here clung to the cliff side. They passed a campsite at Peketa that would have been perfect for the night but Jo nixed that idea; it was too close to Kaikōura – the cursed town.

Kwozzimoto was second in line behind a Volvo SUV, Kim couldn't count the headlights behind because of the curves in the road. There was no concern about delaying traffic as the maximum speed was 30 km/h. They negotiated the second choke point in the same way but then Kwozzimoto himself warned them of trouble to come.

'Oh, oh. I think we have a problem,' Kim said.

Jo stirred from her cocoon. 'What's wrong?'

'A transmission warning light just came on.'

Jo slipped the towel from her shoulders and checked the dashboard. 'What does that mean?'

'It says to pull over and check the manual.'

They were in a queue of cars, campers and trucks in a storm, the road was restricted to one lane. Stopping was not an option.

'He sounds okay – the engine's still going.' Jo scanned for a few metres of dirt that might serve as a layby.

'Shit. If he breaks down – we'll block the main highway.'

'We have to keep going. Pray for a parking bay.'

The hammering rain drowned the motorhome's engine noise. They sweated through the next kilometre. A roadside shed and fence indicated the end of the road works, to the left was a storage area for road crews and trucks. It was empty.

'Thank Christ,' Jo said as they edged out of traffic. They made it 10 metres before Kwozzimoto shuddered to a halt.

'That's not good.'

Kim was surprised the co-pilot didn't flip out. 'Should I turn it on again – or will that do more damage?'

'You have to try.'

They held their breath as Kim turned the key. Kwozzimoto burst into life but the transmission warning light reappeared.

'See if you can find a gear.'

Kim flicked the shift to drive and stepped on the accelerator. Kwozzimoto shuddered for a metre and shut down again.

'Oh good. This truly makes my day. Kwozzi spits the dummy with a cyclone bearing down on our heads.' Jo looked at the pounding surf 40 metres away. 'And he picked such a lovely coastal setting. We are fucked.'

They sat in silence until Kim switched off the headlights. Ahead was a wall of froth. Normally, Kim loved pounding waves and driving rain. They were snug inside the motorhome – but how safe were they going to be when Cyclone Gita arrived in all her fury? Jo rummaged in her handbag and pulled out her mobile.

'Who are you calling?'

'Declan. Kwozzimoto's his baby – he needs to get us out of here.'

They looked at the screen: no service.

MELBOURNE

Five pairs of anxious eyes stared at the phone in *Spotlight's* conference room. The second number they dialled also went to voice mail.

Jo's mobile hadn't been the first option; after all, she was the cause of the angst for Mac, Curly Rogers, Richard Templeton, Dugal Cameron and Ken Withers. The two cameramen didn't need to be involved; an employee glassing a cop in a pub should be a management issue. Jo was often a pain in the ass for Dugal and Withers, but she was part of their *Spotlight* family. They wanted to help.

Stephanie Grant hovered in the doorway. 'No answer?'

'No. We tried Kim's phone three times before Jo.' Curly said.

'Maybe reception isn't great at the cop shop.' Stephanie missed the collective grimace as she hoisted a bag onto her shoulder. 'I have to dash. Text me if you hear anything tonight.'

Five heads nodded as they stared at the phone. 'Do you think the cops arrested them both?' asked Dugal.

'No. They wouldn't have let Kim do the interview if it was serious,' Mac said.

'That was a cracker interview, by the way,' Withers stood. 'Rain pissing down, wind howling – and The Witch predicts it's going to get worse. We'll have most of Victoria watching tomorrow night – if Kim doesn't get locked up with Jo.'

'No, no, no.' Mac shook his head. 'I'm sure she's okay – and Jo. I don't know what made her go troppo. But if anyone can talk themselves out of gaol, they can.'

'They do have a talent for finding trouble.' Templeton prepared to leave as well. 'At least there's no body this time. Send me a text if you hear from them before midnight.' The executive producer waved goodnight. Dugal and Withers did the same.

Curly's finger hovered over the redial. 'Should I try one more time?'

'Nah, mate.' Mac pushed away from the table. 'They've got our messages and know we're anxious. They'll call when they can. It's possible the cyclone's already stuffed communications.'

'Should we contact Jo's father?'

Mac slumped into his seat again. 'Not at this stage. If the girls can sort it out with the New Zealand cops, maybe the family doesn't need to know.'

'But if Jo is sitting in a cell right now, facing assault charges, she might appreciate some legal help from home.'

'That's fair. But until we know exactly what's happening, I don't think it would help to worry her parents.' Mac yawned as he stood. 'I'm getting too old for this drama.'

He waved his senior producer ahead into the empty office. Both would be back by 8am to start again. 'Mind you, I didn't know Jo had so many skeletons. There must be more history with this stepbrother than we ever knew.'

SOUTH PACIFIC OCEAN

WOFTAM pitched and rolled in the wild seas with no hands on the helm. The boat was on auto pilot, but technology couldn't help Gordie secure the drugs. He held the railing with one hand and lunged at the blue barrel with a hook: missed again.

'Fucking arseholes!'

The recovery would look farcical if Gita hadn't ensured there were no other lunatics on the water to witness Gordie's humiliation. He was lucky to even locate the bobbing bounty. The GPS was supposed to put Gordie within five metres of the beacon. For 15 minutes the navigation system indicated *WOFTAM* was on top of the drugs, yet there was no sign of them. Gordie was terrified his propeller had punctured the bin and they were slowly sinking to the bottom.

It was the first time Gordie appreciated the marine regulations for safety harnesses. A spinlock tether kept the seaman attached to the mother ship as he groped beneath *WOFTAM* with the hook. The incessant wind, waves and rain threatened to sweep Gordie away; he was saturated, but still in the game. When the the 20-litre barrel finally surfaced near the stern, he couldn't align *WOFTAM*, himself and the cargo.

His futile efforts made Gordie wonder if it would have been wiser to enlist Wiremu and Spike for the mission. He briefly flirted with the idea of rushing back to the marina and collecting them.

Gordie glared at the taunting blue bin. It would be impossible to see in another 10 minutes. There was no time for plan B. It was up to him to land it – and protect it from pirates.

He established a routine by the fourth run at the barrel: position *WOFTAM*, engage autopilot, scramble to the rails, lunge. The fifth and sixth efforts came up empty as well.

It was the lucky seventh that snared the prize; Gordie always used that number in his Powerball selections. This was going to pay more than he had ever won in the lottery. The hook found the rope attached to the barrel, but he still had to get it onboard. *WOFTAM* rose and fell on two enormous waves as Gordie clung grimly to his boat and treasure. He braced to haul it over the side. The 20-litre barrel was smaller than he expected, but it would still require all his strength.

WOFTAM tilted heavily to starboard. Gordie anticipated the physics, released the boat, heaved on the line – and tumbled backwards onto the deck. There wasn't anything like 20 kilos of drugs in the barrel, maybe not even half that weight.

Gordie frantically checked the container for a severed rope or chain. Had the other half, third or three quarters of the shipment floated away – or sunk? There was no evidence of a broken line. The container was sealed, there was just one rope to the beacon.

There was no time to think about half-full or empty drug bins. *WOFTAM* pitched sharply to port; Gordie could see a bigger wave about to broadside them. He flung the barrel into a corner of the wheelhouse and grabbed the helm. Gordie gunned the engine and powered through the wall of water, avoiding death by a few seconds.

It was going to take all his skills to reach the marina safely. The adrenalin that had been pumping through his system since leaving the pub wasn't likely to wane at the dock. He knew Spike and Wiremu would be waiting; there was going to be a confrontation and the need for some firepower. He might have to fire a shot, or two, at the pesky bastards without fear of being heard by residents: rain and wind would smother any noise. The thought of using the Sig Sauer in battle made Gordie smile as he surfed a wave towards the marina.

GOOSE BAY

Kim left the dry motorhome to find an easy-fix button for the broken engine, using a golf umbrella to shield herself as she prodded beneath the bonnet. Jo meanwhile was dealing with Kwozzimoto's owner but the phone signal was intermittent, so it took six attempts to reach Declan.

He was upset the breakdown ruined their trip – and most likely his next rental contract, but promised to organise a tow truck from Christchurch in the morning. The motorhome was still under warranty: the Fiat dealer could sort out the problem. It was Kwozzi's location that caused the most agitation.

'You mean you're right on the water edge? Are the waves breaking over Kwozzi?'

Jo looked at the rolling walls of foam. 'Not quite – we're about 40 metres away.'

'But that's the cyclone zone? The TV forecaster says it's going to get wilder.'

'Thanks for your concern Declan. But we feel safe – there's a few rocks between us and the waves.'

'Oh. Right. Right. Yes. I'm glad to know that.'

Jo was bemused. 'Is there something else worrying you Declan?'

'No, no. I wanted to make sure you and Kwozzi are safe. It's most unusual for a new motorhome to have a transmission problem – he's not even two years old. I'm sorry you've been stranded.'

Jo sighed. 'It's been an awful day. I need a wine and you need to find a towie. Send me a message when you do.'

It was going to be a mission to find a truck big enough to haul the seven-metre motorhome three hours south to the city. Not many drivers would want to brave the conditions; the cost was likely to double – or triple. That was Declan's problem.

Jo plugged her mobile into the charger. Everything else was still functional, especially the fridge. When she looked out the windscreen the umbrellas had multiplied. She didn't care who was holding the second brolly, unless it was a mechanic. Wine was the priority. She retrieved a bottle of sauvignon blanc and briefly debated whether to get a third glass. She took two from the cupboard over the cooker; the good Samaritan had to earn his vino.

The umbrellas exited stage left as Jo swivelled the navigator seat towards the table. A few seconds later, half of Cyclone Gita came through the door with a bedraggled Kim.

'Goodness, I've never experienced rain like that.'

'Did you find a go button?'

'No.' Kim peeled off the sodden jacket and dumped it on the step. 'It sounds like the clutch plates have jammed.'

That analysis was absorbed with a healthy sip. 'Did you work that out – or was that the verdict from the mystery umbrella holder?'

'That was James. He's one of the road crew in the traffic control station.' Kim reached for a towel in the bathroom. 'He thinks we've had a slow leak in our hydraulics. We must have finally run dry.'

'That doesn't sound like an easy fix.'

'No. We'll need another motorhome for our last few days.'

Jo rubbed a hand over the leather armrest. 'I've got used to this luxury. Don't think I can go back to being a pleb.'

Kim hunted for dry clothes from the cupboard over the bed. 'There should be thousands of motorhomes for rent in Christchurch. We'll get something similar.'

Dry and dressed, Kim swallowed the chilled wine gratefully. She checked her phone: messages from most of the *Spotlight* crew. They could wait. The breakdown had been a welcome distraction. But the elephant in the motorhome could not be avoided any longer.

'We are assuming we'll be able to continue our journey – that the cops won't lock you up for bashing a stranger.'

'You should talk! You hit a cop and walked away – thanks to Nathan.'

'That was a reflex action! I thought I was about to be attacked!' Eyes locked over the small table. 'You *attacked* him. With a glass!'

Jo broke first, spilling wine as she gulped. Her shoulders slumped. Still no confession.

'The victim runs from the pub – you follow. What happened Jo? You were gone for an hour? Did you chase him? Is there anything else I need to know?'

'No!' Jo's cheeks were bright red. 'I didn't go after him. I was running *away* from him. I was shocked. Horrified to see him – and then embarrassed that I hit him. I ran down to Jimmy Armers Beach. I sat there in the rain and cried… for Byron.'

'That was the man who killed your stepbrother?'

'Yes.'

'I thought he was in Auckland.'

'He was.'

'And you're sure that was him at the pub?'

'Yes.'

'And he was a cop?'

A sullen nod was the reply.

SOUTH BAY

The marina lights could not be seen through the downpour. The wind and seas wanted to push him south, towards Goose Bay. Gordie contemplated running with the tide. There was a ramp he could divert to. It hadn't been used much since the quake because of the coastal uplift. Gordie didn't want to beach the boat; the rock shelf would provide shelter until the morning. He could text the contact, direct him to the location, the barrel could be handed over, Gordie could collect his money, and the boys at the marina would be none the wiser. He could wait until the waves settled, return to the marina, haul *WOFTAM* back onto the trailer and go spend the cash.

Gordie considered that option as he surfed the massive waves. He believed *WOFTAM* was heading for the airfield at Peketa, although the coastline was merely a dark mass. The seas eased closer to shore, and that inclined Gordie to turn the helm towards the marina.

An occasional wave broke over the seawall as *WOFTAM* motored to the jetty closest to the hardstand. The water inside the marina was churning but he swiftly lashed a rope from behind the cabin. Two more lines were flung onto the decking and Gordie scrambled to secure both. The bow was tied first, then the stern. Gordie looked up to see Wiremu and Spike huddled beneath long jackets.

'Awful weather to be out testing the engines, Gordie,' Spike shouted.

It was the moment of truth for Gordie. He knew the young buccaneers would be waiting. Did he have the balls to produce the gun? He slipped a hand behind his back.

'It's none of your fucking business what I do with my boat.'

'We don't care about that rust bucket, Gordie.' Spike inched closer, leaning into the wind. 'It's what you have on board that interests us.'

Gordie gripped the Sig Sauer. It was wet, but reassuring. He knew it would still fire. *Bang, bang.* Both fuckers would be blown into the water. Not a soul would hear the shots. With luck, they would wash out with the tide.

'I repeat. My boat is not your concern. Now fuck off.'

Wiremu nudged his mate aside. The movement was confident, he outweighed Gordie by half a rugby team.

'What the fuck?' The appearance of Gordie's gun stopped Wiremu two metres away. 'Is that for real?'

Gordie tilted the Sig slightly to the seaward side of the jetty and squeezed. The muzzle flash was more frightening for the raiders than the noise.

'Fuck!' Spike held up two hands and retreated. 'Come on now Gordie. No need for anything stupid.' He didn't take his eyes off the gun as he edged behind his larger companion.

Wiremu surrendered the jetty more gracefully; slowly easing back with one hand raised in reassurance. 'You be careful with that Gordie. We just wanted to be partners.' He pointed to the dark wilderness beyond the marina. 'You were out there a long time. You were bloody lucky to get your cargo and make it back safely. We just wanted to offer a partnership.'

Gordie waved the pistol. 'This is all the help I need boys.' It felt sensational to watch them back away. He noted Spike kept the former rugby prop in front of him all the way to the shore. Gordie followed. 'If I can beat a fucking cyclone, I don't need any help from dickheads like you two. Now fuck off – or the next bullets go into your guts. That's a slow, painful death.' Gordie had no idea if that was true, but it sounded tough.

'Okay, Gordie,' Wiremu said. 'We're out of here.'

Spike ran to their ute. Wiremu's exit was more dignified, although he regularly checked over his shoulder that Gordie was still on the jetty. The wheels spun furiously as Spike fishtailed onto Moa Road.

The barrel of the Sig still felt warm as it returned to his waistband. The expense was worth it for the protection – and the thrill. Those fuckers would never bother him again. Word would spread. Gordie would be untouchable in Kaikōura: if no bastard told Baz McCullers.

He had the shipment, had beaten a cyclone, and was now safely ashore. Next step was to arrange the handover. Gordie closed the cabin door and retrieved the dry mobile from a drawer near the helm. He texted the agreed code.

home safely

It was a perfect message for a dangerous night. Families and friends navigating flooded roads and relentless winds, would be reassuring each other about completed journeys. He glanced at the blue barrel and hoped that was all the contact expected. Gordie figured it was small enough to ride with him in the cabin of the Bounty to whatever rendezvous site was chosen. The fuel tank was full, but he hoped the meeting point would be close. The incessant rain would be loosening shingle in the ranges. He couldn't guarantee how long the roads would stay open. The barrel was hoisted, ready for transfer to the car park, when the reply came.

meet at home

There was no need to haul *WOFTAM* onto the hardstand. Nobody else was stupid enough to launch for a few days. He would be home in 15 minutes. He could greet the contact with a beer – and the Sig Sauer if the cash payment had been skimmed.

GOOSE BAY

It was a challenge for Jo to pour wine with the motorhome rocking and rolling from the wind and rain. There was also the worry that a wave might sweep them into the South Pacific. But Jo noted a flock of seagulls sheltering behind the rocks. If they disappeared, then it was time to worry.

'How did you find out the driver was a cop? I gather that wasn't revealed during his court appearance?'

Jo carefully brushed several crumbs from her sweatshirt before she was ready to answer. Neither felt like cooking. Dinner would be potato chips, hummus, wine and chocolate.

'No. Dad hired a private investigator.' Her friend waited patiently across the table as Jo sipped more wine. 'The whole court scene didn't seem real to Dad. The guy drives away after running over Byron; yet pleads guilty at the first appearance. The judge sent him down for four years. All done and dusted within a few minutes. To Dad, it appeared a deal had been made before the guy appeared in court.'

'What did the private eye find?'

'An enigma. We had a name from the court appearance. But Troy Michaels had no history: no social media accounts, no credit ratings, no car licence, no power bills, no partners, or family. No tangible sign he existed.'

Kim nodded. 'What happened next?'

'Dad paid more money and the investigator dug deeper. He was an ex-copper too. The grapevine finally bore fruit. Not much, but they confirmed the driver was also with the New Zealand police.'

'Was he on duty the night of the accident?'

'We never found out. Every attempt to get confirmation from headquarters – and via the old boys' network – came up empty. Our gumshoe was good, but he was a former South Island cop. We wondered if even he was protecting old mates.'

Kim shook her head. 'Byron's death keeps getting weirder. I'm sorry you've been carrying this burden. Well, two of them – your forbidden love and his mystery killer.'

The sympathy was dismissed with a shrug.

'What about your stepmother?' Kim retrieved their last chilled sauvignon blanc from the fridge, although there was another case in the garage. 'Did she go ballistic?'

'We never told her. Dad and I saw how badly Byron's death hit Melissa. Telling her that the driver was a cop would have caused a bigger meltdown. We kept it as our secret. It took a year to find out he was a cop. By that stage Jasmine had drifted out of our lives.'

'But the pain was still raw for you? I wonder why the cops hid his identity and profession? He still received four years gaol, which sounds about right for a hit-and-run offence.' Kim held up her hands to ward off Jo's glare. 'I'm just looking at it from a legal point of view. It's been two years – it's possible he was released early for good behaviour.'

Jo shrugged. 'That's if he ever went to prison.'

'What? You think the cops did a deal with the judiciary? Go through the façade of a court appearance for the grieving family?'

The emotions and tiredness made Jo's shoulders sag. 'I really don't know. But when I saw him in the pub, so close to where Byron died, I just wanted to smash him.'

'You did smash him, Jo.'

For several minutes the wind, rain and sea were the only sounds. The battery was fully charged, but they only had one light switched on. There wouldn't be any sun tomorrow for the solar panel, and they might need to ration their power if a rescue truck didn't arrive before the cyclone. The half-bottle of wine was returned to the fridge as another economy measure. Jo lowered her penthouse bed as Kim climbed into her own at the rear. Kwozzimoto rocked violently as another gust hit them broadside.

'This is getting creepy.' Kim pulled the duvet closer to her chin. 'That moaning wind almost sounds human.'

FIJI

Semesa Bari marvelled at the sight on his computer screen. He didn't mind the overnight shift, not when a phenomenon like Cyclone Gita was running rampant. The data revealed that Gita's harmful reach would extend from Taranaki to Christchurch.

The wind would remove a few roofs, but it was the rainfall that would cause the most damage. Semesa always felt conflicted by the dual emotions: awe and fear. They encroached on his duties with every new tropical disturbance that could grow into another problem child.

The cooler waters of the Tasman Sea marked the final days of Gita's run. She would roll over New Zealand and wither away, but not before delivering a final wallop.

FEBRUARY 20

KAIKŌURA

Fingernails drummed a military beat on the table, not that Fetu Leota could hear his fidgety mate over the downpour on the motel roof. It even drowned the rugby commentary on the sport channel. The television provided the only illumination.

'Something's gone wrong,' Leighton Conroy said. 'It's well after midnight.' He looked through the rain-streaked window. 'If the skipper hasn't hooked the catch by now, he's probably sunk.'

Leota rose from the couch and stretched his massive frame. 'What do you suggest? We don't have a number for the watcher – and we don't know the skipper or his boat.' He shrugged. 'That's the problem with our bosses – they love to compartmentalise.'

Conroy slipped his Glock into a shoulder holster. 'We'll check the marina. If he made the pick up, I'm sure the boat's tied to a jetty. He wouldn't risk trying to haul it out with a tractor tonight. The rest should be on the hardstand.'

Leota grabbed the two oilskin coats draped over armchairs and threw one to his partner. 'A boat might prove the delivery. But it won't help us unless he's waiting for his contact. We don't know where the rendezvous is.'

'If there is an old shit-can boat at the marina we'll investigate. If no one is on board, we'll call the boss. It will cover our arse in case something has happened to the watcher. We don't want them thinking we've run off with the stash.'

Leota checked his weapon would be dry and accessible. His denims and boots might get soaked, but that didn't matter. He scooped the car keys from a coffee table. 'I'll drive. You palagis wouldn't know how to handle a cyclone.'

Conroy cuffed his shoulder, pulled on a dark blue cap and dashed into the deluge. The rental car was 10 metres from the unit door. The windscreen fogged within seconds from the drenched coats and body heat; it took a minute for the demister at full blast to provide a partial view.

Leota had to divert onto the wrong side of the road several times to avoid mini lakes. It wasn't a risk as Kaikōura was empty. They went up Killarney Street past the cemetery.

Conroy snorted. 'Hope those bodies don't wash down to the sea.'

Leota ignored the comment, he needed all his concentration for the road. Visibility was about five metres in front of the headlights, which restricted them to mobility scooter pace. It was only a few hundred metres from the top of the hill to the marina turn at the trotting club. It took almost two minutes to reach.

Conroy used a hand towel to clear a persistent fog patch on the windscreen. 'Christ, I can't believe that skipper went to sea. He's either brave – or broke.'

'Let's hope he made it home.'

The car park in front of the marina was empty. Waves crashed over the seawall, spraying the whale watch vessels inside. They had to leave the safety of their rental car to check the other berths. They found a 12-metre charter boat tied to a jetty close to the hardstand.

'I think that's our answer right there Fetu.' Conroy held the cap to his head and turned his back to the wind to be heard. 'The prick made it back. The watcher either missed him – or he's in trouble. We need to call the boss.'

The tin roof of Gordie's villa threatened to rip free with every gust. Nature would decide, so he swigged more beer while lounging on the Chesterfield in the kitchen. Two bottles of Monteiths had already been biffed into the bin beside the oven. The bourbon and cola would wait until after the handover. He wanted to keep a clear head.

There was still no sign of the contact. The Sig Sauer had slipped from Gordie's waist band. It was wedged between the cushions beneath him, close enough to reach if required. Gordie was too tired to worm it back into his butt-crack.

He was surprised by the level of exhaustion. Adrenalin had sustained him through the ferocious ride at sea, and during the confrontation with Wiremu and Spike. That prompted a smile. He was sure Spike pissed himself when he proved the Sig was no fake. Gordie wanted to put the bullet into the timber jetty, but a fresh gouge might set tongues wagging.

The energy had seeped from him on the drive home. It was a slow trip from the marina, the conditions restricting him to 15 km/h. There was a brief surge of adrenalin when he arrived at the villa to see the rear light on.

Had the contact made himself at home, or had he left his own light off after a nocturnal piss? That happened often enough. He took a precautionary look through the window, saw no lurking danger, stepped through the back door and turned on on the kitchen light. He raided the beer fridge.

His stomach growled but it wasn't going to shift him from the sofa. Besides, there were no snacks in the cupboard, and he couldn't be bothered cooking bacon and eggs.

'Fuck this. Just get here and give me my money.'

Gordie stared at the blue barrel which sat on the oak table in the centre of the room. Was that all the contact was expecting? He hoped so because there was nothing else floating at sea. And Gordie was *not* going back. At least not before that bitch Gita passed.

He reckoned the barrel contents weighed only about 12 to 15 kilos. That wouldn't be much cocaine, meth, heroin or whatever to warrant Gordie's $50,000 pay packet. Sure, it was dangerous hauling it in during a cyclone. But the gang didn't know about the weather conditions when they hired him.

It was summer in New Zealand, just like Australia. They expected it to be a milk run: motor out in the twilight, hook the goodies, hand them over, count the cash. Easy peasy. Anyone could have done it – until the cyclone loomed on the horizon. Maybe the Aussies had some inside intelligence? If everything turned to shit, they wanted a skipper with balls – like Gordie.

That thought made him happy. Another beer would make him happier; if he could be bothered walking to the fridge. He let his eyes close, just for second. Gordie had to be alert when the contact arrived.

The slamming backdoor jolted him awake. 'Fuck!'

A man in a drenched, hooded black raincoat dripped water from the doorway to the table. He laid a canvas backpack on a timber chair.

'Time to wake up Sleeping Beauty.' The accent was American.

'Who the fuck are you?' Gordie assessed the man as he folded back the hood. It revealed short, blond hair that was called a crewcut when he was a kid. The man looked military.

'Don't you Yanks know common courtesy? It's polite to fucking knock first in New Zealand.' Bolshie was good; it helped Gordie cover getting caught off-guard with a drug shipment in his house.

The American unzipped his oilskin; but didn't remove it. His hands returned to the jacket pockets. Water puddled on the chipped vinyl. Neither man was concerned.

'I think you'll find that *our* business is best conducted without much fuss.' He looked at the barrel on the table. 'We don't like to draw attention to ourselves.' He walked a circuit of the table, examining, but not touching the barrel.

'You know my name, what do I call you?' Gordie remained seated, close to the pistol. It would look awkward trying to slip it into his trousers. His senses were humming. It might have been the shock, or something more primal. The Yank was a tough-looking bastard.

He was mid-40s, about six-foot, built like a front rower and blessed with a confident air.

What the fuck is an American army officer doing in the drug trade in Kaikōura?

Gordie could never voice that thought, lest it be his last dealings with the cash cows.

'You can call me Oliver. Oliver Wendell.'

It sounded fake to Gordie, but he wasn't going to object. 'Okay Ollie. I risked my fucking life for that barrel. There was only one out there – so it better be what you're expecting?'

'We're about to find out.' Wendell's right hand emerged from the pocket; a soft snick followed – the blade of a flick knife appeared.

Gordie's throat went dry. 'What the fuck?' He was too shocked to grope for the gun.

'Chill Gordie.' Oliver attacked the waterproof seal around the barrel lid. Inside 30 seconds he was twisting it free. The barrel was tilted, and he reached his meaty hand inside. Gordie watched it emerge – with a bag of *gravel?*

They were chunky stones, not the usual size poured onto roads and driveways. It didn't look like any sort of product you wanted to snort, inject or inhale. Was it a new precursor for a super drug? Perhaps they had methods to grind it to powder? Oliver pulled another two from the bin. The yank didn't appear upset by the quality, which helped Gordie relax, slightly. He knew he should be wary until the exchange was complete, but he slipped a hand behind his back to grasp the pistol while Oliver's attention was on the booty.

'What kind of drugs are they?'

Six bags were laid out on the table. 'These ain't drugs.' Oliver smiled. 'These stones are much more valuable than a couple of kilos of coke.'

Gordie wanted to take a closer look, but that would reveal the weapon in hand. His position on the Chesterfield kept everything on an even keel. 'There's not much more than 10 kilos there. What *stones* could be more valuable than coke or heroin?'

Wendell lifted a bag and fondled it; the contents tinkled. 'Have you heard of conflict diamonds?'

'Conflict? That rings a bell.'

The American laughed. 'Maybe you know them better as blood diamonds. You might have seen a movie about them with Leonardo DiCaprio?'

That caused a spark in Gordie's brain. 'They're from Africa, right? Warlords use them to pay for their guns?'

'You got it buddy.' Oliver held up approximately two kilos of uncut diamonds. 'Not just warlords. Any wannabe dictator who wants to overthrow a government uses these babies to buy all the weapons and armies he needs.'

'What's the trade worth?'

'About 80 billion dollars. It's smaller, but not as dirty as the drug business – for me.' He placed the bag on the table. 'And they're much easier to hide from border patrols. My fellow citizens are the biggest consumers of diamonds in the world.'

The military bearing of Oliver Wendell made sense. The Americans had a permanent base at Christchurch airport for the Antarctic Program. Air force planes regularly shuttled between the United States and New Zealand. Gordie could see the connection – a few bags of stones could easily be stashed by a loadmaster. There would be nothing to make a drug pooch sniffle on either side of the Pacific.

Gordie's moral compass was always off kilter. Drugs or blood diamonds, he didn't care what was being smuggled, as long as he was paid. The client was happy with the product, everything was hunky dory. Almost – he needed to see the cash.

'I've done my work. You've got my money?'

'I do indeed have your pay off, brother.' He lifted his backpack from the floor and reached inside, pulled out a black pistol instead of a handful of cash.

'What the fuck are you doing mate? We had a deal! I risk the worst storm in a century to get your fucking diamonds. You owe me my $50,000.'

Roofing iron clanged in the wind as sweat broke out all over Gordie's body. He had a weapon, but it was tucked behind his back. He was an amateur against a military shark in any quick draw. He had to stall, find an advantage to free his arm.

'Shoot me and every cop is going to come after you. You'll never make it back to the States.'

Oliver snorted, waving at the storm raging outside. 'Nobody's going to hear anything. Plus, you're not the most popular man in town. That's why you were chosen. Your body can rot here for weeks before anyone might investigate. You're just a patsy.'

'But don't you want to do this again? You'll need a reliable skipper to pick up the stones. I showed I can beat a cyclone. No one else has the balls around here to do that.'

'I'm grateful you were dumb enough to go out. But it was a oncer.' He held up another bag. 'My friends and I are getting out of the air force – but not with a pitiful military pension; these are going to set us up for life. We have contacts in Manhattan who will pay millions, even without the correct certificates.'

The gun was aimed steady on Gordie's chest. Oliver showed no sign of nerves – or regret.

'What about the Australian gang? Are you ripping them off as well? They'll come after you. Why kick over a wasp nest for the cops to point them in your direction. You don't need to kill me.'

Oliver shrugged, 'We need a clean trail. The deal with the Aussies was done at a distance. They were paid well, but they sniffed a rat. That's why the drop happened at sea – they didn't want to expose their regular connections. The cyclone caused us some nervous moments. But thanks to your *balls,* we've got our nest egg.'

The Chesterfield rested against the second bedroom wall, opposite the table and sink. Oliver levelled the pistol from less than two metres away; Gordie wondered if the bullet that killed him would smash his beer stash behind the sofa. It was a weird, random final thought.

He raised his eyes, ready to unleash a tirade, when the cracking sound of the winds snapping a macrocarpa branch outside drew both their attention to the kitchen window.

The bigger surprise was the shocked wet face staring in through the window. Oliver instinctively swung his pistol towards the new threat. Gordie knew it was his last chance. He freed the Sig Sauer, then pulled the trigger: once, twice, until a gut punch smacked all the air out of him.

The Bruisers huddled by Gordie's front gate. Fetu Leota and Leighton Conroy had ditched their caps in the rental car, which they'd reluctantly left close to the main highway. They didn't want any connection to the property in case the takedown went bad. There was no sign of neighbours, but the bowling club and church they passed on their reconnaissance might have security cameras. The stormy conditions ensured they would merely be shadows in their dark jackets.

Wind gusts buffeted them as they trudged to the fisherman's home. They were wet and grumpy, although pleased the watcher had revealed a possible rendezvous site before going off the radar. The Auckland bosses were angry about his disappearance, but not concerned about his welfare. Unless the watcher had gone rogue and scooped the drugs himself. That might be the next job for Conroy and Leota if the fisherman's house was empty.

A battered ute and a dark Mazda sedan in the driveway offered some hope they were not too late. There was also a decrepit Land Rover in the backyard. Conroy cupped a hand and leaned closer to Leota.

'That car looks like a rental. I think it's likely to be only two people inside – the collector and skipper.'

Leota didn't waste more words on the wind; hand signals confirmed their next moves. Conroy tapped his chest and pointed to the right side of the villa, which left the driveway to his larger mate. They separated, Glocks in hand inside their jackets.

Conroy stepped carefully past the veranda and bay window as water gushed from the holed spouting. There was no alternative as the front yard was a minefield of junk. There was no light coming from the front rooms, so he assumed the handover was happening out back. There was little concern about security cameras on the edge of the building or hidden in the trees. This home owner usually had nothing to protect.

Light spilled from what he guessed was the kitchen window ahead. He paused as macrocarpa branches twisted and strained threatningly against the roof. They were probably more than half a century old, and had survived fiercer storms than this, so weren't a worry either.

Conroy eased up to the window. The blind wasn't down. He could see two men: the closest, standing with his back to the window; the other, wearing an All Blacks beanie, and sitting on a leather sofa. The seated man looked terrified, and then startled at the sound of a large branch crashing to the ground.

The broken limb missed Conroy by a metre. But the bullet smashing through glass a second later struck him above his nose.

Fetu Leota propped by the weatherboards at the end of the driveway. Paint flakes stuck to his oilskin; it would need a thorough clean after this job. His night vision was good despite the gloom cast by the shelter belt of trees. The rear of the property was full of rubbish, and some kennels. The latter didn't bother him, the Auckland bosses said the watcher confirmed there were no dogs.

To Leota's right was a rickety, open porch and the doorway to what he presumed was the laundry and toilet. He had been in enough old villas to know the layout. A door, flush with the rear wall would take him into the kitchen. Not yet though. He would wait to hear what Conroy had seen or found on his scouting run down the right side. His partner should reach the laundry in the next minute, unless he was gaining valuable intelligence via a window. Patience had saved Leota's life several times on missions, he would wait despite the rain dribbling on his head from the broken spouting.

The great crack of a snapping branch followed by four gunshots changed that plan. Leota kept his gun on the back door: anyone exiting would be treated as hostile. He knew Conroy wouldn't come out that way, not just because of their shared ingrained survival skills, but also because his partner would never have entered the villa and initiated a gun battle. Leota expected Conroy to silently join him and take up position near the laundry wall.

It didn't happen. Two minutes Leota waited. There were no more gun shots, no sign of his mate. The adrenalin that surged with the first sounds of battle hadn't dissipated. It was controlled, keeping him alert in god-awful conditions. He checked down the driveway; there was no sign of neighbours coming to investigate. Leota doubted if the gunshots would have carried to the nearest house.

It was time to move. First, check Conroy's route. His first fear was that a branch might have fallen on his mate. That was a better alternative to Conroy getting drilled by four bullets. Leota shook his head as he glided past the laundry. That thinking didn't add up. The shooters should check who they had shot. Unless they were still cowering inside.

Leota reached the end of the house. A foul odour confirmed the toilet was the other side of the wall. He peeked around the corner; his heart sank, Conroy was crumpled on the ground. No heads poked through the shattered window, no voices or noise came from inside. He had to risk checking for signs of life. He crabbed towards his mate. Blood and water mingled on Conroy's face. A bullet had struck him in the forehead. It was a waste of time, but Leota checked for a pulse: nothing.

'Fuck! Sorry mate. I'll make them pay.'

Carelessness might have cost his mate his life, but Leota still needed to know who was inside the villa. It was too dangerous to barge in the back or front doors with his gun blazing. The only way to assess the situation was to peep through the window. Carefully, very carefully.

Leota held his gun ready and edged an eye to the frame. It was only a split second, but it was enough to reveal a body on the floor near the table and a man on a couch. Had Conroy shot them both, but caught a final bullet himself?

Leota picked up the Glock next to his partner's body, checked the magazine: full. Conroy hadn't fired. He must have been killed doing what Leota just did.

But why were there two bodies in there? Was there a third person?

That complicated matters. Leota still had the mission to complete – get the contents of the sea drop. But now he also had to clear Conroy's body from the scene. Without knowing if there was a twitchy gunman nearby. Given the stakes involved, they should've considered the collector might have a partner. Leota needed to check the house perimeter again; the inside gunman could be stalking him.

Another rain squall smashed onto the roof, pouring down onto Leota as he cautiously circumnavigated the villa, checking the windows and front door; everything was locked. He reached the Land Rover in the driveway without seeing evidence of a hasty exit from inside. It felt like forever but had only been a few minutes since the gunshots, yet Leota knew his time at the location was running short. There were no sirens in the distance, but that didn't mean a neighbour hadn't alerted them.

Leota peered in the kitchen window again: no movement from either body, no sign of a prowling gunman. There was no other alternative: he had to act, or his career with the Auckland gang would be over. Leota returned to the back door, calmed his breathing, then opened it with the gun ready.

It was like stepping into a 1960s slum, apart from the two bloodied bodies. The portrait of the merciful Lord on the kitchen wall couldn't help these men. The man close to the table had been shot in the face. The second victim – the skipper judging by his grungy clothes and beanie – had been shot in the stomach. He was barely breathing.

Leota kept his Glock on the skipper as her scouted the room: two bodies, one pistol, a blue barrel, six packets of stones, a backpack. The gun was an M9 – US military. Defence force weapons ended up in the strangest places when money was involved. But one gun and two bodies didn't explain the scenario at his feet – unless a third person was hiding.

It took Leota five careful minutes to clear the bedrooms, lounge, bathroom and hall cupboards: there was nobody else. Had the two men been fighting over the gun? Was that how Conroy was shot? His mate knew well enough to keep his head down when bullets were flying.

The carnage might never be explained, particularly if the guy on the sofa didn't survive. He hadn't moved, the breathing was ragged. Leota wasn't inclined to question him. It was a risk to leave the M9 in place, but Leota was confident the guy would be dead before any police arrived.

Leota holstered his gun and checked the crystals. What high would they produce? He examined them closely. It didn't look like meth, not that he was an expert on drugs. He slipped the bags into the pack and slung it over a shoulder. A grunt from behind chilled him. Leota turned slowly, the guy on the sofa was pointing a bloodied Sig Sauer at him.

Gordie's guts had been ripped apart. Every breath felt like a double-bladed knife gouging deeper. The American prick was dead, lying on the floor with a bullet hole where his eye used to be. That had been sheer luck.

Oliver had fired the first shot out the window. That gave Gordie a chance to fire his own gun. The bullet clipped Oliver's shoulder, throwing him off balance. The next two bullets were fired simultaneously; one was fatal, the other doomed Gordie to a slower death.

But now now some big Polynesian bastard was at the table stealing everything he'd risked his life for.

'Fuck off, you prick.' The challenge was barely more than a whisper. 'That's mine.'

Gordie was fortunate to have hung onto the Sig Sauer when he was shot, but his gun hand wavered.

The new intruder held both arms wide, no sign of a weapon. 'Take it easy mate.' He eased the pack onto the table. 'I thought you were dead.' He pulled out two bags. 'I was sent to do a pick up – not kill you.' The hand went into the pack, two more bags were retrieved. 'He shot you. I didn't.'

Gordie's eyes and brain struggled to focus. The pain was nothing like he'd ever experienced, not even a stab wound in his 20s felt this bad. He watched the big guy return another bag to the table. How many was that? The man was moving again, the pack on his shoulder.

'You can live well on that. There's no need to shoot me.'

Gordie was struggling to think. He was probably dying, yet he couldn't let this thief walk away. He gripped the gun with two bloody hands; it helped. The guy was almost at the door. Two steps and he could fling it open and flee. Without all the diamonds?

Gordie finally grasped the reality; the guy would wait a few minutes, then sneak back and shoot him. Then it would be simple: grab the stones and slink away as a multi-fucking millionaire. Life was so unfair. Gordie watched the bastard reach for the handle.

But his hand wasn't on it when the door opened.

'Fuck it.'

Gordie pulled the trigger until the fireworks stopped; the Sig Sauer slipped from his hand.

'Who would have thought that Gordie had a gun?' Spike swigged more beer as he circled their lounge. It was the fourth bottle on the 78th circuit. A change of underwear and denims had been required before the pacing started. 'And the arsehole fired it!'

Wiremu had matched his mate in consumption, but from the comfort of the armchair. Brooding was more his style than venting. The pistol made sense to him, now. Gordie had sent Spike off at the pub with a flea in his ear, and he wasn't daunted by Wiremu's intimidation. Initially, that had been put down to *braggadocio,* survival skills learned in Rolleston prison where the weak were squashed. It turned out Gordie had the firepower to back up his confidence. To have been outplayed by a half-wit wounded Wiremu's pride. He wanted *utu:* payback.

The bungalow shook as the approaching cyclone tried to shunt them closer to the South Pacific. It wasn't sensible to venture outside, yet Wiremu felt compelled to check Gordie's house. It was possible the drugs handover hadn't happened yet. The weather was feral, perhaps the contact wanted to wait until morning – or even Wednesday? It was far-fetched, but Wiremu couldn't rest knowing that Gordie Tulloch got the better of him. And a stinking rich pay-off.

'I'm going to Gordie's.'

Spike paused mid sip and stride. 'What the fuck, mate? He's got a gun – and he's happy to fucking use it.'

Wiremu went to the closet by the front door and retrieved his sea jacket. 'It worked because we didn't know. Now we do. If the handover hasn't happened, we might catch him unaware. If it has, Gordie will be rolling in cash.' He reached his big arm to the top shelf and brought down a wicked hunting blade. This thing had gutted a dozen wild boars.

'You're taking a knife to a gun fight?'

'It's a weapon – and he won't be expecting us.'

Spike made no move to claim his jacket.

'Well, I guess Gordie won't be expecting *me.'*

The veranda did nothing to protect him from the drenching rain when he opened the front door. A plastic bucket cartwheeled down the road before jamming under the fender of a Suzuki. Other debris was likely to be flying around town; Wiremu didn't want to risk damaging the precious truck. It was only a few minutes to Gordie's; he leaned into the wind and walked.

Tree limbs were scattered across roads and properties. Wiremu wasn't a homeowner – yet. But if he could get his hands on the drug shipment, or Gordie's cut, he might soon be able to afford one of Kaikōura's fanciest houses.

Would he offer a share to Spike even though the dipstick wimped out? Probably. He wasn't surprised that his mate pissed himself when Gordie fired a round into the water. They both knew Wiremu was the brains and the brawn of their association. It suited him to let people think that mouthy Spike was the organiser. Being underestimated worked to his advantage: Wiremu could watch, learn, analyse. Until Gordie outsmarted him. That hiccup was about to be corrected.

Wiremu passed the Catholic church. Ahead, was Gordie's hovel surrounded by a belt of swaying macrocarpa. Branches were creaking under the strain. The lashing rain had seeped down his collar and chilled his back. It was annoying, but not a hindrance after a dozen years learning to cope with southern winters in the hills beyond Kaikōura. Wiremu was comfortable on the land and the sea, just like his ancestors.

A dark Mazda was parked behind Gordie's Bounty. That was promising. It looked like a rental car, which meant the bagman was still there. Maybe Gordie offered him a bed for the night because of the conditions? Wiremu looked at the debris strewn around the front yard and wondered if any guest was that desperate for lodgings. There were no lights in the lounge, or front bedroom.

He pulled out the knife and eased down the driveway. It had been a long time since the blade had been used in anger. That was not on a boar's throat. It had been five years previously when a smarmy Christchurch dealer tried to sell a bag of grass. Literally it was grass, not weed. The con was a proper tinnie to establish the bona fides. Wiremu insisted on checking the full ounce, which made the dealer nervous. He bolted, but not before his arm was sliced. Wiremu wasn't scared of blood.

The trees at the rear of the property provided little shelter from the wind. The thrashing branches made it impossible to hear if anyone was still awake. He shifted the knife to his left hand, ready to intimidate. Wiremu slowly turned the kitchen door handle and nudged it forward. He was easing into the gap when a voice croaked, 'Fuck it.'

Next came a volley of bullets.

GOOSE BAY

Kim rolled to the left of the sleeping compartment and lifted a blind: the sea was a white mass of foam, the sky grey, the rain unrelenting. There was some positive news; their early warning system – the seagulls – were still between the rocks.

She squirmed across to the driver's side and repeated the process. The highway was busier. Three traffic control vehicles had arrived in the layby. Six men in orange waterproofs were huddled by the fence that marked the boundary of the roadworks.

Kwozzimoto had been shunted closer to a low embankment the previous night to make room for the new vehicles. Puddles formed around anything stationary. Kim rolled back to the left and opened the window. A lake had formed under their stranded motorhome.

'Damn! Jo – you awake?'

There was a grunt from beneath the duvet on the dropdown bed.

Kim scrambled into yesterday's tee shirt and shorts. No need to waste clean clothes, they were going to be sodden soon. 'Get up. We're surrounded by water. It's about a foot deep already.'

'Oh Christ! I was listening to the rain, hoping yesterday was a bad dream.' Jo yawned and sat up. 'I think I saw a spade in the garage under the kayaks.'

Kim slithered into her damp jacket, found a cap. 'Come on – get dressed. We have to drain it before it reaches floor level.'

'Shit!'

Kim ducked under Jo's dangling feet and opened the door. The wind wasn't as fierce as she expected, the hills provided some protection, but the rain soaked her before she'd waded to the back of the motorhome.

It was safer to open the garage door on the seaward side. She hoped it was unlocked as the keys were still in the kitchen. They had been neglectful about security for most of the trip; New Zealand seemed such a friendly and safe country. The water was shin deep as she clasped the top and bottom latch and swung the door open.

'Oh my God!'

The spade was forgotten – because of the body.

There was a body in Kwozzi's garage.

It was a man. The same man last seen by so many witnesses in the pub the previous evening getting attacked by Jo. He was now crumpled on top of the inflatable kayaks and barbecue, the left side of his face and hair a bloodied mess. The damage was more severe than the glassing her friend had dished out. The guy had run away from that. As Jo had. Hadn't she? Or did she follow Byron's killer – and finish the job?

But how? Jo was half the size of this guy; she was angry, feisty, upset yes – but she wasn't a killer. Surely not?

'You ladies have got a serious problem.'

A contractor in a white hard hat approached. Kim looked at him, back to the body, thought of her mate – then shut the door.

'Yeah. We've broken down and can't drive out of this puddle.'

'That's an understatement. I'm Derek Dobell.' He stayed at the edge of the water, which suited Kim. 'Not a great place or time to break down.' He assessed Kwozzi. 'It looks like a new motorhome.'

'It is. Just one of those things. The owner is trying to get a tow truck to take us to Christchurch before the worst of the cyclone arrives.' She gestured to the expanding lake. 'If we're still above water.'

'Sorry. That's not going to happen. We've closed State Highway 1 south of the Hundalees.' He jerked a thumb over his shoulder. 'The checkpoint is closing as well – just our crews allowed on the road.'

Kim's shoulders sagged. Their cyclone experience was going to be longer and more dangerous than they wished for. 'Can you help us drain this water? We don't have a shovel.'

'Yes, we do.' Jo sloshed through the water from the front of the motorhome. It was almost to her knees. 'I saw it under the kayaks.'

Kim turned from the worker and winked twice at Jo. 'No, you were wrong, Jo. Nothing there. If these men can't help us, we'll have to use our hands to scrape a trench.'

'Oh. I see. Okay. Yes.' I guess we'll have to do that then.' Jo shrugged when the worker disappeared around the other side of Kwozzi. Kim stalled further comments with a finger to her lips.

Dobell returned a few seconds later. 'We can help, but you'll have to wait until we get the road signage and other bits and pieces sorted.'

He walked 20 metres behind the motorhome. 'We can breach the embankment here – that should fix the flooding problem.'

He walked back. 'I can't do anything about the sea though.' High tide is at nine o'clock tonight – that's when the worst of the cyclone is due to pass over. The campsite's a few hundred metres down the road – they might have an empty cabin. If they're full, I've got a mate and his wife who usually have a spare bedroom. I can give him a call if you like?'

Jo brightened at the offer of a dry haven. 'That sounds like a–'

'That's very kind,' Kim interjected. 'But we need to stay with the motorhome. The owner is nervous about leaving it alone.'

Dobell shrugged and turned for the road. 'No problems. I'll send a couple of guys over in about 10 minutes.'

'Thanks Derek.' Kim held up a hand to stop Jo's outburst until the good Samaritan was out of range.

'What the hell is wrong with you Kim? Okay, smart move to get the men to drain the swamp, but why knock back a safer bed for tonight?'

'Because of this.' Kim opened the garage door.

'Oh. Shit. That's–' Jo's knees buckled, she slumped into the water.

KAIKŌURA

Saffron Fernsby allowed herself a rare extra half hour in bed listening to rain thrum on the tin roof. Her small, one-bedroom cottage in Oxford was stone and clay tile; it cushioned the sounds of heavy downpours. Nature always made an impression in New Zealand.

It was going to be a day spent indoors: reading, baking, following the news service for Gita's progress across Aotearoa. The cyclone was almost upon them; only the foolish would venture outside in the next 24 hours.

It was a small apartment, tacked on the end of an established home two decades ago to cater for an elderly parent. There was even a front garden where Saffron had dabbled with a rockery over the summer. It was an easy construction: shingle, timber, any interesting detritus collected from the beach and her walks. Betty Quayle, the owner in the main house, approved of the landscaping and provided a plastic chair and table. Traffic noise was never an issue away from The Esplanade; it was a sunny nook out of the wind that frequently provided an opportunity for chats with pedestrians.

When Saffron opened the curtains, she found one of those neighbours slumped over the brick front wall. It was Wiremu Henare; he shared a house with his crewmate two doors away. The lads held the occasional noisy Saturday night party; but were always polite when greeting Saffron. Was he drunk, or injured? Whatever, he needed help. Saffron scooped a hooded jacket from a peg and rushed into the downpour.

'Wiremu.' Saffron touched a wet shoulder. It was bloody. His knees were on the footpath, his torso and arms inside her garden. He had dropped a pack. Had he hurt himself while trying to retrieve it? 'Wiremu. Can you hear me?'

No response. She checked for a pulse: he was alive, but too big to lift or move by herself. The landlord was in her 80s, far too frail to help. Saffron could call an ambulance, but that would leave Wiremu exposed to the elements until they arrived. Already his pallor looked terrible.

His mate Spike should be at home because the charters were cancelled, that was the best option. He could help drag Wiremu to shelter. Saffron ran to the bungalow front door and knocked; rain and a tin roof smothered her best efforts. Her knuckles ached as she continued to pound while holding a finger on the doorbell. A sleepy, bedraggled Spike finally appeared in the doorway.

'Professor. What's wrong?'

Spike looked like he had slept in his clothes.

'It's Wiremu. He's bleeding in my garden. I need help getting him to shelter.'

'Shit. I've been worried about him. Is he all right?'

'*No!*' Saffron was worried the drinking had dimmed Spike's brain. 'I just said he's lying out in the rain. He's deathly pale. We need to get him inside. Come on.'

Saffron charged back to the footpath, hoping that would motivate the sluggish mate. She stopped at the gate, Spike was hauling on a jacket. Forty metres down the road there had been movement; Wiremu was lying on his back. It was going to be a mission to get the big lad inside either property.

Spike caught up as Saffron knelt beside Wiremu. They both saw the source of his affliction: wounds in his left wrist and shoulder.

'Christ, mate.' Spike slumped to his knees. 'I told you not to go. He already tried to shoot us once.'

'Shoot you?' Saffron gingerly peeled part of the jacket sleeve away. There was a raw gouge through the wrist, but not much blood. It had probably been washed away by the rain. 'You're suggesting these are bullet wounds Spike?'

'Yeah. I'm sure it was Gordie Tulloch. We're all screwed now.'

'Well, put that aside for the moment. Let's get him under cover so I can call an ambulance. And the police.'

MELBOURNE

The morning production meeting at *Melbourne Spotlight* was a small affair with only three attendees: Mac, Curly, Richard. The rest of the crew had been ordered from their seats while Curly set up a conference call. Mac could see his staff were miffed, they hovered around the command post. No doubt they were curious – and concerned – about the new drama engulfing Kim and Jo.

'Hello. Mac?'

'Hi Kim.' Mac hovered over the speaker. 'I've got Curly and Richard with me. The rest of the team are out of the room. They're not happy – but we think it best for the moment. Okay, Curly knows part of the story, Richard is totally in the dark. Better start at the beginning.'

The executive producer nodded as he raised a mug.

'We have a body in the garage of the motorhome.'

Mac and Curly were sprayed with coffee.

'You what?' Templeton raised a hand in apology as he passed paper towels to his senior producers.

'I opened the garage door this morning – looking for a shovel – and there was a body inside.'

Templeton's perplexed expression almost made Mac laugh. 'No, boss. They weren't trying to bury the body – they had to rescue the motorhome from a flood. But that's the small bikkies. Go on Kim. You know who the victim is.'

'Yes. It's the guy Jo, um, hit in the pub last night.'

Templeton laid both palms flat on the table. 'This is the guy who was jailed for killing Jo's brother in a hit-and-run two years ago?'

'Yes.'

'And now he's dead – in your motorhome.'

'Yes.'

'Where's Jo?'

'She's listening.'

'What do you have to say, Jo?' Templeton looked at Mac and Curly. 'Did you kill this man?'

'No!' It was emphatic. 'How could you ever think that?'

Curly doodled on a notepad. Mac twirled his Collingwood mug. Never had any of them encountered a situation where a colleague might be accused of murder.

'I'm sorry if that offended you, Jo. But the question had to be asked,' Templeton said. 'How do you think he got there? And how did he die.'

'We think it might be head trauma,' Kim answered. 'His face and hair are covered in blood. Far more than anything Jo did to him in the pub. As for getting in the van? We're guessing whoever killed him dumped him while I was waiting in the pub for Jo.'

'Could it have happened during the night – while you were sleeping?'

'Impossible. They close the coast road each night for repairs – plus we didn't know we were going to get stranded here at Goose Bay. No, it had to be at the pub. The motorhome was parked outside.'

Mac raised a finger. He needed to state the obvious. 'Which, from a police perspective, makes Jo their number one suspect.'

'That's what we're thinking, Mac.'

Silence settled on both sides of the Tasman. It was Curly who initiated the next phase.

'Time is getting away from us. How long ago did you discover the body?'

'About half an hour.'

'Did anyone see you opening the garage door?'

'Yes. One of the roadworkers. They're digging a trench to drain the swamp around Kwozzi. It's bucketing down, we're up to the axles.'

'Did he see the body?'

'No. Just that I was looking for the shovel.'

Mac picked up the baton again. 'Okay. You can't afford to delay much longer before notifying the cops, Jo. Use your mobile to do that. Don't give them much detail. Say you're tourists who found a body in your motorhome and give your location. Hang up after that. You can always blame a dodgy phone signal. Kim, we need to–'

'Hang on, Mac. There's a worker at the door. Give us a second.'

The line was muffled, the speaker presumably covered by a hand.

'Christ. This is serious guys,' Templeton said. 'The cops are going to arrest Jo as soon as they arrive. We need to find out where she's likely to be taken and get her a lawyer pronto.'

'Agreed boss,' Mac said. 'What about her family? We probably need to get them involved, in case her father wants to fly over to help.'

'Mac!' Kim's tone was urgent. 'The road workers heard *moaning* from the garage.'

'Moaning?'

'Yes. Jo's gone out with them to check. And yes, of course they're probably suspicious – they saw me standing there with the door open.'

'Shit,' Mac said.

'The road to town is closed because of the cyclone, so they're trying to get a rescue chopper. We'll get back to you soon with an update.'

'Wait Kim,' Mac shouted. 'Take the phone off speaker.'

'Okay. What?'

'Kim, you need to film everything. Especially the guy in the garage.'

'Understood Mac. I know it's a bigger story than the cyclone.'

'It's more than that Kim. The cops are likely to arrest Jo. She was seen assaulting him – now he's found half-dead in your motorhome. They won't accept Jo's denial that she's not responsible.'

'But when he wakes up, he'll tell them who attacked him.'

'What if he doesn't? He's likely been comatose for at least 12 hours. That's not a good sign. We need to get on the front foot – we *must* present Jo's case tonight. The New Zealand networks will pick up our story. You need to record an interview with Jo ASAP. There might be a cop on the rescue chopper. Once Jo is in police custody – we lose control of the message.'

'Okay boss. I'll talk to you once the guy is on his way to hospital.'

The line was disconnected, two producers and their executive slumped in their seats. Briefly. Mac was first to feel the energy building for a major event day.

'Let's hope he survives – at least long enough to tell the cops who thumped him.'

KAIKŌURA

A shooting was the last call out Lachlan expected during a cyclone. Car crashes, property damage, looting, maybe even runaway pets would be on his list. Not a shooting – and not in Kaikōura.

Wiremu Henare and Spike Maloney were considered thicker than thieves – according to pub gossip – always ready to protect each other. Lachlan never seriously considered Spike as a suspect during the five-minute drive to the crime scene. And now he had a more likely candidate: Gordie Tulloch. Spike was convinced Gordie shot his mate.

Lachlan and Spike were sheltering from the rain on the veranda of the bachelor bungalow, where Spike had dragged his wounded mate. It was easier than lugging him inside the professor's small flat. The paramedics were grateful for that decision. They had cut away Wiremu's jacket and shirt to reveal *three* bullet wounds in the arm, chest and shoulder. Within minutes, Wiremu was on his way to the hospital up the hill. There was no prognosis on his condition. Lachlan arrived as the ambulance departed with lights and siren.

'Okay Spike. Why would Gordie Tulloch shoot Wiremu?' It was too wet to take notes. Lachlan's main concern was finding out if there was a deranged gunman loose in Kaikōura. 'Was it personal – or has Gordie gone psycho?'

Spike looked at the bandage wrappings and bloody dressings on the ground. He sighed. 'It was personal.'

'Why?'

'Gordie did a pick up at sea last night.'

Lachlan was stunned. 'He went out in that *storm*? What was the pick up?'

Spike shuffled his feet. 'We think it was drugs – coke. Or ecstasy. Something like that.'

'And Wiremu went around to *relieve* Gordie of some of his goodies?'

'Yeah.'

'So Gordie objected to that and put three bullets into your mate.'

'I think so.'

Lachlan was worried, but also partially relieved. A man had been shot, but he didn't think the gunman was crazy, or likely to cause more mayhem. Unless more locals resorted to piracy. Gordie had been protecting his illegal haul. So this violent reaction was understandable if you followed a criminal code rather than the law. He had to talk to Baz McCullers about organising an Armed Offenders Squad to disarm the disgruntled fisherman.

'Was Gordie at home or on the boat?'

'Home. Wiremu tried to intercept him at the marina.'

'Just Wiremu? Not you as well? You two are joined at the hip most of the time.'

'Nah. I'd never do anything like that. It was all Wiremu's idea. I told him he was crazy – that Gordie might shoot him to protect his stash.'

'How did *you* know Gordie had a gun?'

'Oh. Um. Wiremu said Gordie used it at the jetty. He fired into the water to prove he was serious.'

'Yet your big mate still went sneaking around Gordie's place?'

'He came home and brooded for a while. He reckoned Gordie would be so exhausted after battling the sea that a couple of beers would knock him out. He was going to slip in, grab the shit and boogie.'

'He was going to do that unarmed – and by himself?'

'Yeah. Wiremu's a brave bugger. Maybe silly, but never scared.'

Lachlan knew that was bullshit, but he didn't have the time or patience to break Spike's story. He pulled a mobile from his pocket. The next conversation with his senior sergeant shouldn't be heard by morons like Spike, or anyone who scanned police frequencies, but he needed to get the ball rolling. Baz McCullers was at the station.

'Baz. You need to call HQ and get an Armed Offenders Squad.'

Curtains had twitched in several nearby homes when the ambulance arrived and departed. Normally the bells and whistles attracted an outdoor audience but not in a cyclone. The only ones to venture out into the cold relentless rain had been Saffron, Spike and the paramedics who tended to the shooting victim. And Constable Naismith had sent Saffron home to shelter, when he arrived, saying he would get a statement later.

Saffron held a mug of hot relaxing chamomile tea to one cheek then the other to help thaw her face and hands. She stared at the wet garden; there was no evidence of the dramatic morning. The wounded man was gone. She'd give his pack to Spike the next time she saw him.

It tinkled as she placed it on a chair by the door. Saffron suppressed her curiosity, with difficulty. She wanted to know why Wiremu was shot, and the bag might provide a clue, but her moral code would not let her look. It was bad manners to pry. The bag would taunt Saffron until Spike could take it away. On the other hand, perhaps the police should know about the bag? The contents might have caused the shooting. Was it her civic duty to search it?

Saffron sipped, stared at the grey skies and decided: it was time to leave Kaikōura. She had enjoyed her stay and learned much about the Māori. However, there were too many bad vibes. The town was going to be hammered by the cyclone and the clean-up would take weeks, possibly months, to fix. And now there was another complication – residents being shot in the streets.

She suspected Wiremu, and his friend, were engaged in criminal activities but shootings were a sign that in the world of ordinary crime, things were out of control. Was it a gang problem, or an issue at the marina? Spike had kept mumbling about Gordie firing a pistol.

Saffron had many questions and few answers. The only certainty was that the events of the past few days had ruined her South Island idyll. The Pacific Ocean was vast. Saffron would spend the afternoon plotting her next adventure. She really wanted an island-hopping expedition to Hawaii. There were many communities to explore and people to meet. Sadly, her pension would determine the extent and comfort of that journey. New Zealand's high cost of living had depleted her bank balance significantly.

There was no lease on the apartment. Saffron could be on her way to the Cook Islands, Fiji or Samoa within a few days – if a cheap airfare was available.

'Wouldn't it be nice to travel first class for once?'

Saffron giggled at the thought. Before she tackled the future, she wanted an update on the troubled Australian tourists. She hoped their night at Goose Bay was more tranquil after a traumatic Monday. Saffron paused with a finger over the speed dial. Hmm, should she tell the reporter about the drama in her front garden? Her eyes drifted to Wiremu's pack.

GOOSE BAY

'There's no chopper available to pick up the victim,' said Derek Dobell.

They huddled close to the seaward side of the motorhome. It provided a little protection from the wind, but nothing from the downpour. Everyone was soaked. They had agreed it was safer not to move the man until the experts arrived.

'We can open the road to Peketa for an ambulance, but the paramedics are worried about slips. They can't afford to lose a vehicle or crew during a crisis.' Dobell looked at streams of water gushing off the hills. 'I don't blame them. But we need to get medical care for this guy. By the way, do you know his name?'

'No,' Jo said. The tourists had agreed it wasn't wise to reveal any connection to the victim. That info would be saved for the police.

Several workers were busy re-directing some traffic that had slipped through the southern roadblock, and another gang was draining the layby of water. Nobody had questioned Jo or Kim about the injured man in their garage.

'We can't afford to leave him any longer.' Derek called to his crew on the road. 'Jimmy! Get your Hilux over here.' He turned to Kim and Jo. 'We'll lay him in the back. One of you can ride with him, make sure he doesn't roll around.'

'No,' Jo said. 'We can't leave the motorhome.'

Dobell stared at her.

'We're not being callous.' Jo pointed to the turbulent seas. 'The owner is a family friend – we promised him we wouldn't abandon it to the waves.'

Further discussion was interrupted by the reversing Hilux. Dobell took charge of the extraction, calling in another three beefy workers to gently transfer the victim. The rain washed some of the blood from his injuries. He was deathly pale but he made no further sounds even as they wrapped him in a tarpaulin. It was a 15 km journey into Kaikōura; if the road wasn't blocked by a slip.

'I'll drive, Jimmy. You sit in the back and make sure he doesn't suffer any more injuries.' Dobell looked at Kim who was recording everything on her mobile phone. He shook his head. 'Okay ladies. We'll get on the road.'

'Good luck,' Jo said.

Dobell paused at the driver door. 'You know I'll have to tell the cops about this, don't you?'

'Yes.' Jo shrugged. 'We don't know how he got into our motorhome. But we're happy to help the police any way we can.'

'Well, they won't be here today. Let's see what the road is like after another 12 hours of rain.'

Dobell waved and shut the door. Seconds later the Hilux was slicing through mud to reach the bitumen. The barrier lifted and the vehicle disappeared.

'I hope this phone camera is waterproof,' Kim said. 'I've recorded all the shots we need for a story. But it better be dry for the program tonight.'

Jo closed the garage door, relieved the water had been drained from the layby. But mother nature would decide in a few hours if she wanted to breach their small barrier against the sea.

'What a mess. What do we do now?

'Get inside, dry out and call Mac. We won't have to worry about you getting arrested today – let's focus on getting your version of the story to the public.'

'I'm struggling to see how an Australian current affairs program can convince New Zealand cops of my innocence.' Jo wriggled out of her wet jacket and clothes. Their towels were still saturated. Fresh clothes felt just as clammy.

Kim fillled the kettle and ignited the gas. 'It's about getting our story out first. It creates the right impression. The New Zealand media can't contradict it – not without us or the victim.'

'But what if *they* talk to people at the pub? They'll say I smashed the guy in the face with a glass,' Jo said, spooning some instant coffee into two cups. She'd kill for a real coffee but the cafes were beyond reach.

'We broadcast your *confession*,' Kim said. 'You admit to hitting him, because you were in shock that your brother's killer was out of prison. We provide the backstory that no one else knows. And you declare no knowledge about the next stage – the more extensive head injuries and the dumping of the victim in our motorhome.'

Jo found a packet of Tim Tams in the cupboard and wondered how long they'd have to last? The kettle boiled. Kim's phone rang.

'Oh. Hello Saffron. Yes, we're okay – but there has been a wee bit more drama, as the Kiwis might say.'

Derek Dobell was worried about the water pouring from the ranges. The deluge was predicted to last through the night. How long would the shingle hold in place under this onslaught? He believed they would make it to Peketa, getting back might be more difficult.

Dobell knew he wouldn't be able to make an immediate return to Goose Bay. Delivering an injured man to the hospital without explanation would be suspicious. Even for a respected official with the North Canterbury Transport Infrastructure Recovery. That was why he wanted one of the Australian women to accompany him; it was their motorhome where the victim was discovered. Dobell was certain they knew more about the attack than they revealed.

He had a hands-free phone kit on the dashboard. It would be quicker to call Baz McCullers direct at the Kaikōura police station, rather than going through the emergency line. The number was on speed dial.

A harried voice answered the call. 'Kaikōura Police. Unless this is an emergency, can you please...'

'Baz. It's Derek Dobell. I've got something for you guys.'

'Mate. Unless it's a body – I really can't deal with it right now. I've got a rogue skipper with a pistol and a wounded Māori who tried to pinch a drug shipment. I'm trying to get an Armed Offenders Squad together.'

'Well Baz. My body is still breathing – but I don't know for how long. I'm a couple of klicks short of the hospital now. Coming in from Goose Bay.'

'Christ! Has he been shot?'

'I don't think so. Looks like he's been bashed.'

'Is he one of your blokes?'

'No. A couple of Australian tourists found him in the garage of their motorhome. Been there all night – until one of my boys heard him moan.'

'Are they two women? TV journalists?'

'Yep. They claim they don't know who the guy is – or why he was dumped in their motorhome. Not sure that I believe them.'

'Shit! One of them glassed a stranger in the pub last night. The victim and the attacker disappeared. I only heard about it this morning.'

Dobell felt his stomach lurch. 'Well, there is some good news Baz. They can't run any further – they've broken down at the Goose Bay checkpoint. Transmission problem: you can arrest them anytime you want after the cyclone.'

MELBOURNE

Mac was grim-faced. 'He doesn't look healthy.' He stood behind Curly Rogers as they viewed Kim's video files from Goose Bay. The killer of Jo's brother looked like a cadaver. There was no police officer to hold back the media – *Spotlight's* crew was living in the crime scene.

'These are great clips Mac.' Curly opened another file. It was a wider shot of the road crew removing the man they understood to be Troy Michaels from the garage. The shots were five to 10 seconds, alternating between close ups and wider.

'Nice work Kim.' Mac said. 'Blur the guy's face and we won't have to worry about viewers barfing in their dinners. Send a clip to the editors. Someone from News will come running within a few minutes. Grab Stephanie Grant to do a short story for them. Tell her to emphasise we will deliver the full story during our live cross to Kim and Jo.'

Curly smiled as he copied several clips to the senior editor's bin. 'That's going to make Steph happy – promoting an international exclusive for Kim Prescott.'

Mac glanced at Stephanie's desk where her fingers danced across the keyboard. 'A bit of rivalry doesn't hurt. If no blood gets spilled.'

The veteran producers chortled quietly, lest Stephanie learn the source of their mirth.

'Okay boss. How do we want to play this?'

'The package will deal with the mysterious victim in their motorhome and the efforts to get him treatment. Thankfully, there's vision of Jo being supportive as they move him.'

'Then, if Kim still has battery life on her mobile, Richard can segue to Jo's connection to the victim via her dead brother. Kim picks up the story again, revealing there was a confrontation in the pub last night. The road killer ran away. Kim explains that was the only time they saw him – until this morning.

'She introduces Jo to declare her regret about the pub incident. Kim will need to build the case that the first *minor* incident was witnessed by dozens of people. That suggests someone with a grudge against the victim used the stoush to falsely set up the girls. The guy was probably whacked again in the carpark, then stashed in the motorhome knowing police would target Jo. That tugs at enough heartstrings for the first night.'

'Yeah, but it will be Australian tears.'

'Not for long. We'll tip off the Kiwi networks we have a cracker story in their backyard that's even better than the cyclone. They'll record *Spotlight* and turn it around for their late news and breakfast programs. It might make the cops think hard before they arrest Jo – and possibly Kim.'

'Christ. I almost forgot about the cyclone. That's going to be at its peak when we go to air.'

'Let's hope we can retain mobile phone coverage. It's an isolated part of the country, I'm surprised the signal has been so good.'

'The girls had a bit of luck there. The road crew at the checkpoint gave them the WiFi access code – we should be sweet. Unless the sea swamps them mid-program.'

'Tell Kim to keep the camera rolling for the whole show!'

KAIKŌURA

Lachlan Naismith's patrol car rocked constantly as it blocked half the road in front of the Catholic church. Constable Sebastian Twomey's vehicle formed the other half of the barricade. They were the front line against Gordie Tulloch whose house was 100 metres along the road. Another police vehicle was parked 60 metres behind them.

Strategically, the constables should have been standing on the road with Bushmaster rifles in case Gordie decided to run amok with his pistol. Neither officer thought that was likely to happen; it was wiser to stay inside and wait for the Armed Offenders Squad. Their own Glocks were handy, in case the unlikely happened.

They had been on guard for several hours. The first mission was to move nearby families out of the firing line. They presumed Gordie was at home; cars were in the driveway and there had been no response on his phone, not even an invite to leave a message. Two households were reluctant to depart, until they were promised free meals at the pub. None had reported anything unusual during the night. Most slept soundly as ferocious storms were not unusual on the coast.

Normally the senior sergeant would be in charge at the scene, until an inspector arrived with the AOS. A difficult day for Kaikōura was complicated by a NCTIR supervisor arriving at the hospital with an assault victim. Lachlan was on his way to the shooting scene when that news lobbed on Baz's desk.

From the brief reports passed over the radio, the victim could be the person allegedly assaulted by one of the television crew. Lachlan heard about that drama when he arrived at his lodgings ready for sleep. No complaint had been filed by the victim, the women had departed in their motorhome, therefore Lachlan decided it was small fry compared to the harm that Cyclone Gita was delivering. He decided not to complicate the senior sergeant's day with more paperwork.

Macrocarpa branches were flaying Gordie Tulloch's home like they were angry with it. Several limbs had been torn free; the greenery and twisted timber now rested against the house and in the front yard, destined to lie there until they rotted away. Their demise would be quicker than the rusting cars.

'This sucks.' Twomey's call came over the secure radio channel from a few metres away. Neither was keen to get soaked to state the obvious.

'Yeah. There's been no movement all day. He's probably dead drunk by now, regretting he plugged Wiremu.'

'Or dead.'

Lachlan bit his tongue. The channel was supposed to be police-use only, but you never knew when nerds were listening. 'Do you think he's holding the driver of that rental car hostage?'

'Or vice versa?'

Frustration and a sore back niggled at Lachlan. There was no ETA for the AOS; it was a slow process getting them down to Kaikōura in a cyclone. And it could all be for nothing. What if Gordie was sleeping off a hangover? Or had fled with the drugs after fighting off Wiremu?

Lachlan admitted that didn't look to be the case; the Land Rover and ute were blocked by the Mazda.

A tearing sound drew his attention back to the property – a two-metre branch hung limply over the driveway. Another decent blow would send it crashing onto the rental. Surely that would motivate the driver to move the car. A minute later the inevitable happened, the bough crashed onto the bonnet. No response from inside. Not even a twitching curtain.

'Did you see that, Sebastian?'

'Yeah. I would expect someone to peek from inside. Gordie must know our shooters are on the way. It could have been them smashing the door in.'

'Yeah. It doesn't feel right.' Lachlan reached a decision; he didn't share it over the radio. He had a pistol and a ballistic vest. A helmet might help but, again, Lachlan had a feeling it wouldn't be necessary. He left his cap on the passenger seat, exited, locked the car and ran to Twomey's vehicle.

The tap on the window shocked his colleague whose eyes were on the villa. Water streamed in the small gap in the window.

'Shit Lachlan. Warn me next time you come calling with a pistol in hand. What are you doing – going for a piss?'

'You could say that. Look after my keys for a moment.' He pushed them through the narrow gap.

'Why do I need–'

Lachlan hoped Twomey would stay off the radio as he dashed down the right side of the lane for the nearest macrocarpa on the boundary. It wasn't a blind spot, but the nearby paddocks were too sodden to wade through them. Within 15 seconds he was backed up against the trunk. The run was 100 metres but he panted like it was a kilometre.

A glance along the fence revealed a gap between the palings; yard maintenance hadn't been a priority for many years. Wind destroyed another branch towards the rear of the property; it crashed into the backyard. The trees could prove more dangerous than Gordie's gun. Lachlan ran to the fence; the opening was large enough to put his head through. Every rule in the book told him not to do it; adrenalin and instincts gave him the courage.

He was halfway down the villa. He peeked right for the kitchen window; there was a body. The man lying on his back wasn't his target, but someone had scored a bullseye. Sightless eyes stared into the branches above, blood and water mingled around a bullet hole in his forehead.

Shit!

Did Gordie shoot him, or someone else? Lachlan should have backtracked, relayed that information to his sergeant. It might hasten the formation of the AOS to know they had one wounded and one dead. And possibly more inside. Lachlan couldn't help the guy on the ground, but there might be more injured.

The jacket hood barely kept the rain out of his eyes. He shivered, gripped the Glock tighter and pushed through the gap in the fence. Five steps put him beside the body, out of sight of any sentries inside.

Lachlan checked for a pulse for confirmation: nothing. A Glock lay on the ground close to the right hand.

Looks like a service weapon.

That complicated matters. Was there an undercover narcotics operation underway? The local station would never be informed. Lachlan remembered that a pub patron said the guy who was attacked was a cop. It sounded far-fetched. At the time. Maybe Lachlan should have added to Baz's paperwork this morning.

That was irrelevant; there was a dead man at his feet, Lachlan needed to check inside for more casualties. Slowly, he edged up to the window. The lights were on, that could help his view, or expose him. He counted silently to three, then peeked. Two more bodies.

Lachlan ducked out of sight. There was no sound or movement from the kitchen, no shouts or bullets flying in his direction. One man was face down near the open back door, the other was on his back near the table. It was a fleeting scan, but neither looked like Gordie Tulloch. Had he killed three men, wounded another, then fled into the hills? Or in another vehicle? Anything was possible.

It was four minutes since he left Twomey in the patrol car. His colleague would be getting twitchy, contemplating a call to base. The lack of gunfire might give Lachlan a few more minutes. He had important information, but no location for the man with the pistol. He stepped around the body, approached the rear of the house. It was a junkyard, covered with fallen branches, but no more bodies scattered around. That was good. The laundry window was too dirty to reveal anything. A few steps later he was at the back door.

Cyclone Gita wanted to enter with him. She hammered against the bullet-riddled door; her progress blocked by the body on the floor. The gap was wide enough for Lachlan to risk another peek: body at doorway, body near table, body on couch – Gordie. Lachlan withdrew his head, breathed deeply, then carefully stepped over the large dead Polynesian. Surprisingly, there was a hunting knife beside him as well as a Glock.

Gordie was still wearing his All Blacks beanie. The only difference to his standard uniform was the blood stain on his plaid shirt and trousers. Lachlan knew it was several hours old, the left hand over his stomach was mostly dry. Gordie's right hand was draped over a cushion. On the floor was a pistol. Possibly a Sig Sauer; at least it wasn't a Glock. Gordie's head was tilted towards the painting of Jesus.

'Too late for prayers, Gordie.'

Death occupied the villa, but Lachlan went through the motions of confirming no other bodies were in the bedrooms, bathroom or lounge.

Twomey would be having kittens, or about to burst through the back door. Lachlan didn't want to become part of the body count. He pulled out his phone; this was another call that shouldn't be overheard.

'Sebastian.'

'Christ, Lachlan. You've had me worried. I was about to radio Baz and hurry the gun squad.'

'You can tell Baz to cancel the AOS. But he'll need a big forensic crew. There's four bodies in here.'

Lachlan disconnected to let his colleague stand down the cavalry and order up the investigators. The scene of crime people would be grateful that three bodies were inside the house; rank would be pulled on the officer sent to examine the victim outside the kitchen window. Maybe it would require danger pay; Cyclone Gita was still working up to full fury.

He needed to leave the crime scene without disturbing anything. Lachlan checked the man near the table as he passed. He appeared to have been shot twice: through the shoulder and the left eye. There was no way to tell how many bullet holes were in the guy at the door; he was face down.

Spike Maloney provided a clue for the shootout: drugs. And there was the evidence on Gordie's table: a plastic barrel and bags of crystals. The dirty, gravelly substance was not something he'd encountered before. But Gordie had risked his life to collect this stuff during a cyclone. It must be valuable for such a foolhardy mission.

Lachlan pondered the cliché about no honour among thieves. What went wrong during the handover? Four men were dead, a fifth was fighting for his life. That was a conundrum for the detectives to solve. So was the empty barrel. Had it only contained five bags?

GOOSE BAY

The road supervisor returned late afternoon. He didn't leave the Hilux cab, obviously not prepared to get wet just to update them on the victim. Or so Kim presumed. Unless the news was worse: and he was dead.

Most of the crew had been aloof during the afternoon. The drainage trench kept Kwozzimoto above the rainwater, although there was nothing that could be done if Cyclone Gita sent them a tidal surge. Traffic on State Highway 1 had withered to nothing. It was to be expected the crews might huddle in their vehicles or in the checkpoint office. Derek's arrival was the signal for the convoy to depart south, beyond the dangers of the slip zone. Kim looked at the rivers pouring off the hills and wondered when they would be seen again.

Two workers remained in the shed. They were employed on rotating 12-hour shifts to manage the checkpoint. The night crew had the easiest job: the road was closed; they could read, stream programs on their computer or play games.

Kim was grateful for the generosity of the lads. They offered a laptop for Kim to use during the *Spotlight* program. It saved Kim and Jo the dilemma of doing the live cross on a mobile phone. They were surprised by their motorhome's solar panel though. It continued to charge the battery without a hint of sunlight through the grey, wet mass that stretched across the horizon. At times, the clouds almost skimmed Kwozzimoto's roof.

Everything was ready to go for *Spotlight*, although Jo's phone needed a top up. She had been talking to her father for half an hour. Kim had tuned out the conversation, not sharing Jo's confidence that she was unlikely to be arrested; or charged with murder.

'Mac is convinced this is the best way to declare my innocence Dad.' Jo rolled her eyes. 'No. I won't be jeopardising my legal defence. I'm going to tell the truth – exactly what happened. I would say the same in any court case. Not that I believe it will happen. If anything, I might get a warning. Once people hear the full story – they'll be saying I should have whacked him a few more times.'

Kim doodled on a pad, not daring to raise an eyebrow at that assessment. The motorhome rocked continuously. She looked for the seagulls among the rocks: still grounded, still safe.

'Look Dad, I have to go because this is draining the phone battery. We don't have any sun to charge the solar panel, so I'm not sure when we'll be able to talk again. We're totally safe from the cyclone. If anything happens with the cops tomorrow, Kim will give you a call. But I'm pretty sure we'll be home on Sunday. Toodle pip.'

Jo sighed heavily. 'Parents are such worriers.'

'With good reason – in our case.'

They laughed, which eased some of the tension.

'I would love a wine, but I guess you won't let me before the program.'

'Good guess.' Kim fiddled with the Skype settings on the borrowed laptop.

'How come we pour booze into guests in the green room before our shows?'

'Because we want some people to relax so they'll spill their secrets. With you, we're presenting your case to the court of public opinion. You need your wits.'

Jo grumbled and foraged for snacks in the cupboard. It was getting darker, the barrage from the skies was intensifying. The danger period for them was high tide at nine o'clock. If Kwozzimoto wasn't swept away, the worst of the cyclone should be gone soon after midnight.

Those concerns had to be put aside, the program was the immediate focus. Mac and Curly had rung several times to discuss the format. *Spotlight* would open with Richard Templeton revealing the crew was in the middle of a breaking story that was almost secondary to the cyclone. He would throw to Kim's package about the body in the garage. Next would come the live interview between Kim and Jo, detailing the backstory with her stepbrother to explain the pub assault.

It wouldn't include the whole story – that Jo and Byron were lovers before their parents married. That might be too much for a television audience to comprehend. It was easier to pitch Jo going ballistic when she found Byron's killer close to the death scene.

The Skype connection had been tested. Everything was fine. Kim would record 30 seconds of cyclone footage from the motorhome 15 minutes before the program started. It would be rolled in as overlay to set the mood.

Jo returned to the table with grapes, cheese, crackers and two cans of coke. 'I wish there was Bundy in that.'

'Save me some. I'm going to call the hospital and see if I can get an update.'

Kim listened to the dial tone through her speaker for 30 seconds. Small hospital, weather emergency, they were going to be busy. She was on the verge of hanging up when a clipped voice answered.

'Hello.'

'Is that the Kaikōura Hospital?'

'Yes. Sorry, we're extremely busy. How can I help?'

'I know about the medical emergencies. I'm a journalist after an update on the assault victim and the man with the gunshot wounds.'

Saffron Fernsby had given Kim the background on Wiremu Henare collapsing into her garden. That prompted more Trans-Tasman calls with the producers on how it might fit into their story. Mac finally ruled it didn't. Their focus was the Australian angle: Jo, Kim, the hit-and-run driver. He didn't want to complicate the story with a drug crime wave in Kaikōura. The hunt for the shooter was a New Zealand problem.

'Which shooting victim?'

Jo stopped eating.

'Pardon? You've had more shootings?' Kim said.

'I know I shouldn't be telling you this, but I know you will insist on talking to a doctor and they are too busy. If I give you information off the record, can you attribute it elsewhere?'

'Certainly.' Kim was grateful she hadn't identified her media organisation. One of the Kiwis could take the blame if she had to break the confidence. Bad form, but it might be necessary.

'We admitted three serious casualties today. The assault victim is still unconscious and can't be moved to Christchurch. Two men were admitted with multiple gunshot wounds. One is in a stable condition. He might be transferred to the city tomorrow – if the road isn't cut by the cyclone.

'The other man died on his way to hospital. He couldn't be resuscitated.'

Kim scribbled on a notepad. 'That's terrible. Was it the Māori man, Wiremu Henare who died?'

There was a pause. 'We're still off the record?'

'Yes.'

'No. The man who died hasn't been identified. Apparently the first people on the scene assumed that everyone was dead.'

Kim watched Jo mime *everyone?*

'You poor people. What a terrible day. There's the cyclone causing chaos, now you have a bashing, and the shootings. Have the other bodies been moved to the hospital?

'No. The other three bodies will remain on site until the forensic examination is completed. That's standard.'

Jo counted the fatalities on her fingers. *Four!*

'Of course. You have been a great help. Thank you and good luck getting home safely. Are you in any danger from the killer.'

'Thank you dear. We're okay. The police believe the shooter was a local fisherman – Gordie Tulloch. He's one of the dead.'

The name rang a bell. Kim pointed to a phone number on the pad: Saffron Fernsby. Jo dialled while Kim ended the fortuitous hospital call.

MELBOURNE

Mac McKenzie leaned against the rear wall of the cramped studio control room at Channel 5. Normally he watched the *Spotlight* broadcast from the office, with a beer in hand, trusting Curly to orchestrate another seamless production. The sudden twist in the story with the multiple shootings, and the possible link to the ex-cop Jo bashed, required an overhaul.

Most of the crew were news and current affairs veterans, they took the late changes in their stride. A new rundown was circulated, vision recut, a dozen studio and VT operators brought up to speed. It should be fine. But with so many links in the chain, Mac knew it was possible one small mishap could turn the whole show to crap. That was why he loitered at the back: watching, listening, trusting, praying.

Mac could see his reporter and kamikaze PA shoulder to shoulder at the dining table in the motorhome. The lens range on the laptop just covered them. Mac was pleased to see they were relaxed, chatting quietly and responding to prompts from the director or sound engineer. Kim had both hands clasped on the table. There was no sign of the fidgeting and nervous tics so evident in the weeks before the holiday. She was confident and focused.

Jo smiled occasionally, possibly buoyed by the latest news of the multiple shootings. The police would be too busy to worry about a minor scrap in the pub. Still, it was important to get their version of events on the record. Lay out their narrative, then get the girls home again ASAP. That executive plan hadn't been shared with the travellers. It could wait until after the program – and maybe the cyclone.

The vision of Kim and Jo rocked constantly, it looked like Cyclone Gita was directly over their stranded motorhome. On another monitor was the vision shot from their window a few minutes ago. It was cued on the first frame: a tempestuous sea, dark clouds, sharp rocks dotted with white specks.

'That's our early warning system. When the seagulls take flight, so do we.'

Jo's flippant comment caused a ripple of nervous laughter. Nobody had done a program from the middle of a cyclone in a tourist town where the murder rate had spiked 400% in a day.

'Five minutes to air,' the director's assistant called over the comms. Curly swivelled in his chair and gave the boss a thumbs up.

KAIKŌURA

Windows rattled and the whole Kaikōura Police Station shook as Cyclone Gita vented her final fury. Reports were arriving about damage to roofs, homes, sheds, businesses. How bad wouldn't be known until morning. The fire brigade was the front line for lives in danger. The small police team was scattered throughout the town in support. Several motorists were encouraged to return to their homes.

Lachlan was in the station alone. Baz McCullers and Sebastian Twomey were still at Gordie's hovel where three bodies waited on the forensics team. The men were basically guarding the scene as nobody else was likely to reach Kaikōura before dawn.

One detective from Blenheim had beaten the first landslip north of the town. He'd been on a case near Clarence, but was diverted soon after headquarters heard about the multiple gunshot victims. That had taken a weight off the senior sergeant's shoulders.

Baz wasn't happy with Lachlan's lone wolf efforts which broke too many procedures to count. Hence Lachlan's banishment to the station to write his report. No amount of creativity was going to save him from an arse-kicking. It wasn't just the fact that he risked his life at a scene where an active shooter was contained, but he stupidly hadn't checked for signs of life in all the bodies.

When Baz visited the crime scene, after calling for the senior investigators, he did inspect the victims – and found a faint pulse. The big Polynesian guy was still alive, barely. So questions would now be asked about whether he would have survived with earlier treatment. He'd also been their best hope for an explanation of what went down.

Wiremu Henare's injuries were painful, but not life threatening. Lachlan had a suspicion that Wiremu was a latecomer to the shootout. The wounds were all down his left side. The bullet holes in the door, and his escape, indicated that Wiremu's life might have been saved by the timber. A detective might learn more tomorrow. Lachlan would not be part of the investigation.

He returned to his keyboard, adding to the chronology, trying to explain his reasons for not wanting to contaminate the crime scene. His mobile phone rang. It was another constable from the Nelson office who was on holiday in Australia. The distraction was welcome.

'Flynn! Shouldn't you be in a nightclub instead of annoying me?' Lachlan tucked the phone against his ear and filled a kettle with water. Coffee would sustain him through the long night ahead.

'Hey Lachie. No one goes out here before bloody midnight. I'm getting too old for that.'

All the coffee cups were in the sink waiting for a conscientious washer. He rinsed his favourite Crusaders mug.

'So, the rest of Melbourne is that boring you want to ring me? Or you want the gossip on the shootings? I'm guessing you picked it up online.'

'Yeah. I was flicking through the Kiwi news sites and found it. Most of the Aussie media doesn't give a toss. Then I watched a current affairs show called *Spotlight*. They've got a couple of their staff stuck in a motorhome at Goose Bay.'

Lachlan scooped coffee from a tin. 'We know about them. And the assault victim they *supposedly* found in their garage this morning. The little one apparently whacked him in the pub last night. We'll talk to them – but they're really a low priority compared to the bodies. What did they say to make you call?'

'They linked their assault victim to the shootings. And they said he was a cop.'

'Christ!' Lachlan almost dropped the phone into the coffee. 'That's all we need right now.'

'There's more. The cross was cut off – and they couldn't reconnect. There was a loud rumble seconds before the screen went black.'

The boiling kettle was ignored. 'They were at a layby on the beach, close to the final checkpoint. There's been a lot of rain – more than 10 inches so far. Shit – I hope a slip hasn't wiped them out.'

'The producers tried to call their crew on both mobiles but got nothing. You might have luck with the checkpoint crew.'

The screaming kettle finally registered with Lachlan, he switched it off and sat down at the computer. 'We have contact numbers for the road guys. I'll call them. Thanks for the heads up, Flynn. I'll let Baz know what the Aussies are saying. It's going to make his day: four shot dead, one wounded, one assaulted – and there's a cyclone kicking shit out of the town. Does that program have a website?'

'You can watch a replay on Channel 5. The segment had only been going a few minutes when the lights went out.'

'Thanks mate. Gotta go.'

A mobile number for Derek Dobell didn't get beyond voice mail. He left a message and called Civil Defence headquarters. They had already received several reports of slips around Goose Bay, but there was nothing they could do until daylight. The cell towers along the coast must have been damaged.

The next mission was to notify Baz McCullers and the Blenheim detective about the Australian story. Lachlan decided it would be wise to view it first, rather than get roasted for adding to the headaches without all the information.

The website was easy to find. The presenter was handsome and professional, opening the program and seamlessly introducing his colleagues sheltering from the cyclone. He segued from vision of nature's battering to the other drama confronting Kaikōura: multiple shootings. Lachlan was surprised the isolated reporters had obtained those details.

He paused the replay for a moment to finish making the coffee. He picked up a pen and notebook, ready to listen for gems that might help the investigation. Next came a package about the man in the motorhome garage. They didn't say how he suffered his serious injuries, or why he was placed in their rental. The item finished with the road crew driving the victim away from the sodden layby.

The presenter returned to camera with a split screen of the women at Goose Bay. Lachlan knew this was what Flynn wanted him to see. He turned up the volume.

'Joining me now from Goose Bay, south of Kaikōura, are reporter

Kim Prescott and production assistant, Jo Trescowthick. That was a horrifying experience to find the injured man – but we now know there is much more to the story.'

'Yes Richard. We need to say there was a confrontation between Jo and the man in the pub last night. She slapped him – but did not cause the life-threatening injuries you saw in our report. The man was surprised; but was able to walk away. He was fine when he left the hotel.'

'Jo, we understand there is a long and tragic story involved. Can you explain what motivated the incident?'

'That man killed my stepbrother in a hit-and-run incident in Kaikōura two years ago. He fled, leaving Byron to die alone at Jimmy Armers beach.'

'I understand he surrendered to police the next day and pleaded guilty at the first opportunity?'

'He did. But there was something fishy about it. My family hired a private investigator. He was convicted in the court as Troy Michaels. There is no record that man existed.'

'What happened then?'

'Our investigator tapped into the old boys police network. We have evidence that he graduated from the police college at Porirua a decade ago. He was still in the force at the time he killed my stepbrother.'

'The man was gaoled for four years–'

'Supposedly.'

'You don't believe that to be the case, Jo. It has been two years since Byron's death, he might have been paroled early for good behaviour?'

'As I said – if he ever went to prison.'

'Did your investigator find evidence of a coverup, a special deal for one of their own?'

'No. We could never establish that.'

'Okay, let's move forward. You have learned there is a connection to the incident today where four people were found dead in a Kaikōura villa. Kim, I believe you have more information?'

'Yes Richard. The man we know as Troy Michaels was seen acting suspiciously in the town in the past few days. According to my contact, Michaels was covertly following a local fisherman, a man called Gordie Tulloch. The bodies were found at Tulloch's home – he is reported to be among the victims.'

'Okay Kim, you believe Troy Michaels might be an undercover operative, and that the assault which almost killed him is connected to the shootings at Mr Tulloch's home today?'

'Yes. The injuries he suffered were not caused by Jo.'

'Has your contact been able to provide any reason for the fallout at Mr Tulloch's home? Were illegal substances involved?'

The reporter never had a chance to answer. Lachlan watched both women turn to their left as a roaring, grinding sound overwhelmed their audio. Their professional faces gave way to terror seconds before the screen went black.

It was obvious what had happened; a slip on the coast road had taken out the cell phone site. Did it smash into the motorhome as well? Were the two women buried under a mountain of mud and shingle?

'Arghhhh! Can this day get any worse?'

Lachlan had vital information to update the shooting investigation, but lives might be at risk. The frustration was not being able to do anything – the road to Goose Bay was closed. There was no chance of getting a chopper up until morning. The Aussies were on their own.

MELBOURNE

There was no contact from either Kim or Jo in the hours following the program. Kiwi news services were filled with reports of damage and flooding along the west coast of both islands between Buller and Taranaki. There was a mention about two Australian journalists whose television broadcast from the middle of the storm was interrupted. There was no follow up story. Mac and Curly called stumps at 11pm.

All the beer and wine in the *Spotlight* and News fridges had been drunk. The senior producers didn't quaff it alone, half the news department and all the current affairs team lingered for updates on their colleagues. Ken Withers and Dugal Cameron had even sniffed out Ciaran O'Malley's secret stash of Jameson's. They left an inch in the bottom for the news chief of staff, before adjourning to the *Rising Sun Hotel* in South Melbourne. The alcohol kept the mood upbeat; Kim and Jo had survived more serious scrapes.

Mac stretched his shoulders and arms. His ear was sore from the fruitless phone calls. 'Remember the days before mobile phones Curly?'

'Yeah. Out of sight from head office, out of mind.' He shuffled a laptop and notepad into his shoulder bag. 'Check in each morning and night, make sure you come back with the story was the rule.'

'If anything did go wrong with a remote crew, quite often it was resolved by the time the bosses learned about it.'

'Or the problem was hidden so they wouldn't find out.'

Mac snorted. 'Too many times that happened.'

'I'm sure they're okay Mac. They're in the middle of a cyclone – we were lucky to get a Skype call through to them at all. We would never have considered that a possibility 20 years ago.'

'The most we could hope for was crappy hand-held video footage and the next day damage. Now, we expect to be in the eye of the storm.' Mac paused in the doorway. 'Imagine if we had this technology before Cyclone Tracy hit Darwin in '74?'

Curly nudged his boss towards the exit where an Uber driver waited. 'Fossickers would still be finding cameras halfway to Alice Springs.'

FEBRUARY 21

Fluffy white clouds stretched across the horizon. The turbulent seas had subsided, returning to a greenish tinge. Waves slapped onto the shingle and rocks, but without the ferocity of the previous day and night. The sun had ushered away the remnants of Cyclone Gita.

Mason Barnard had been at the heliport since before dawn, his craft ready to fly at first light. The only delay was the wait for an emergency response planner. David Greenway's arrival was delayed by a growing list of slips along the coast. They all needed to be inspected and assessed.

The helicopter was directed to start the mission a few kilometres south of Peketa. The first evidence of Gita's legacy was found moments after lift-off. Massive scars filled the ranges, at the base of each slip was a mound of rock, scrub and slush. In several places the debris included the contents of homes. It should not have been surprising; the cyclone dumped more than 200 mm of water along the coast.

The recently reopened railway had been smothered at multiple sites. So too was the highway which ran a few metres from the tracks. The Alpine Pacific Tourist Route was closed again for trains, trucks, cars and campers. Every new pile of rocks confirmed their worst fears: this was going to take weeks to clear.

'Can we set down at the checkpoint before Goose Bay.' Greenway held a map full of notes.

'We'll know in a few seconds.' Mason directed his craft between Panau Island and the ranges.

'You heard they lost contact with the road crew and TV news team at the height of the cyclone?'

'Yeah.'

'Apparently they're a couple of Australian TV journos stranded at the layby in a motorhome.'

'That will be a hell of a story – if they survived.' Mason banked closer. He knew the area well, but now there was a new landmark to guide him: Gita's biggest tear in the hillside.

'That doesn't look good,' Greenway recorded the damage.

The checkpoint shed, fence, barriers, water tanks and vehicles were gone; buried under a river of sludge. Fragments of the portaloos glinted in the sunlight. Dark patches indicated where the sewage was dumped. In the distance, Mason could see a similar gouge in the ranges, bookending the site. Higher up the range a line between the two scars caught his eye. He wanted to check it immediately. It wouldn't be wise to land beneath a hillside that could slide at any moment.

'Look at that!' Greenway pointed to the centre of the clearing. A white motorhome stood 20 metres from the debris. The four people beside it waving wildly at the chopper was the best sight of the day.

'Two journos, two road crew?'

'Yep.' Mason thumbed the radio to pass on the good news. 'I'll scoot low to give them a thumbs up. But first, we need to check that ridge line.'

Mason couldn't avoid pinging the motorhome with gravel when he set the chopper down 50 metres away five minutes later. It was the safest option. He didn't want to spend long on the ground; the inspection revealed a large fracture in the hillside between the two slips. Greenway hopped out of the chopper.

The four refugees waited at the rear of the motorhome to avoid the draft.

'Hi guys. I'm David. Looks like you had a lucky escape.'

The older member of the roadcrew, a woman in her 40s, responded. 'We were saved by the media.'

'How?'

'We lent the girls a laptop to use for their TV program. They invited us to watch the show in the motorhome. If we hadn't done that,' she pointed at the rockpile that covered their base. 'We'd be under that.'

'Wow! You used up a chunk of luck – and you're going to need some more.' Greenway gestured to the hillside. 'The land up there has slumped several metres. It could tumble down at any time. We need to get everyone out of here.'

'How many can you take?' Kim asked. She was still recording.

'Three, but no bags. Sorry about that ladies. Lives are more important. It's not far around to Peketa. We'll get you sorted from there.'

'I'll stay. I need some vision of our rescue from the ground.'

Jo laughed. 'Don't bother arguing with her guys.' She looked at the ruined checkpoint. 'These roadies drank all my wine last night – I need to find a bottle shop.'

Jo ducked into the motorhome while the road crew buckled themselves into the chopper. She emerged in several layers of tee-shirts and a sweatshirt. Spare knickers poked from the pockets of her jeans. Kim struggled to hold the camera steady as her resourceful friend waddled to the rescue flight.

FEBRUARY 25

There wasn't much for Jo to pack for the flight home to Melbourne. Even less for Kim, she felt too guilty to pad herself with clothes like the Michelin Man for her chopper rescue. She wouldn't miss anything that was left behind. Declan could donate it to charity – whenever he was able to recue Kwozzimoto from Goose Bay. They felt sorry for him; the current estimate was two weeks before a tow truck could reach the layby. The Fiat dealer had even worse news in Christchurch – he could not repair the transmission until late-march.

Their Air New Zealand departure was mid-afternoon, which left them five hours to fill after room checkout at 10 o'clock. They had spent Friday and Saturday night at *The Heritage*, an elegant stone 19th century government building converted to a hotel in the heart of the city. It was a few metres from the carcass of the cathedral destroyed in the earthquake.

The travellers were fortunate to leave on schedule. The police in Kaikōura had dithered for a day and half about Jo's confrontation with Troy Michaels, but his condition had improved rapidly on Thursday. Constable Naismith had arrived at their hotel that evening to announce Jo would not be charged. Troy Michaels corroborated her story from his Christchurch hospital bed.

Michaels told detectives he had been caught off-guard by Gordie Tulloch beside the motorhome. Jo's swipe had caused little damage; the serious injuries had been caused in the frenzied attack by the fisherman.

Then came a surprise; the disgraced policeman wanted to speak to Jo. She immediately rejected the olive branch. Kim watched that dismissal niggle at her friend. She held her tongue, until the final day.

'We've got hours to fill – and we don't want to sit at the airport. Why don't you go talk to him? Listen to what he wants to say. It's obviously something he needs to get off his chest. You can listen and respond – or not.'

'Why should I?

Kim placed her day pack on a table. 'Because I think you really want to know what happened at Jimmy Armers Beach – from start to finish. Was he on a police job when it happened? Did he ever go to prison – or was there a cover up and he was cut loose by the police? Did he know you chased him in Auckland? What was he doing in Kaikōura? Is he involved in the diamond smuggling trade?'

Word about the probable cause of the shootout at Gordie Tulloch's home had leaked on Friday. It surprised the whole country.

Jo sat with arms folded on the sofa. 'You're the journalist. *You* want to know that.'

'Okay. Yes, I do. But I think, underneath it all, you and your family deserve some answers.' Jo sat quietly. Kim pressed her case. 'I can come with you – clear the room of scalpels and other dangerous objects.'

The half-wattage glare confirmed Kim's victory.

Christchurch Hospital was on the edge of everything important: the city, the Avon River and Hagley Park. A 20-minute walk from Cathedral Square took them past businesses still emerging from the rubble. Kim's suggestion to go via the national memorial to quake victims on the riverbank was vetoed.

Jo's emotions were already swirling. They'd reached the hospital before she'd decided whether to include Kim in whatever discussion – shouting match – she was going to have with Troy Michaels. The meeting could provide the answers to questions that had gnawed at her psyche for two years. A natural disaster and fate had given her friend a rare insight into the family history, so perhaps Kim deserved an explanation as well.

She watched Kim charm the receptionists for information on Troy Michaels. The stressed-out reporter who'd boarded the flight in Melbourne had been through more adversity. Yet, she was calmer, stronger; back to the confident reporter ready to hunt down exclusives. Kim had her shit together again.

Mac and Curly had been happy to hear that assessment when they were reconnected with the outside world at Peketa. Almost as much as learning Jo and Kim hadn't been swept away by Cyclone Gita. Ten messages from them filled her voice mail before it shut down. Secretly she was chuffed most of the crew had tried as well; there were five anxious calls from Ken Withers. She tapped a scornful response, chastising Kenny for doubting her survival skills. It was deleted, replaced by another about Aotearoa having too many wineries to get herself washed out to sea.

Kim ushered Jo to the elevator. 'He's been moved to a private room on the second floor. He's recovering, but tired. The doctors will only allow you five minutes.'

'That should be enough for us to tell him he's a gutless prick.'

'Us?'

'Yes. You should be there – otherwise you'd nag me for details all the way home.' They exited the lift into a subdued corridor.

'Do I need to find a cop to handcuff you?'

'I can still stab him with a syringe.'

'Fair point. Wait until I leave – Mac needs one of us back at work tomorrow.'

'To keep him on his toes?'

'If they've healed.'

The door to the private room was open. A curtain shielded the bed; the greenery of Hagley park was bathed in sunshine. It was bucolic, but not settling for Jo's nerves. A nurse with a tray of soiled bandages emerged from behind the curtain.

'Hello. I was told he had visitors. He's sore and tired – but okay for a few minutes. Try not to upset him.'

Jo felt Kim's hand on her arm. *Me? Not upset him!*

'We understand,' Kim said. 'We have a plane to catch. It will only be a few minutes. He wanted to speak to us.'

Kim pulled the curtain back. Byron's killer was propped on three pillows, arms by his side, with two black eyes, a scarred nose and a head swathed in bandages. There was nothing threatening about him.

'Hi. I didn't think you were going to come.'

Jo was aware that Kim had stepped to the end of the bed. It created space for Jo to communicate, close enough to thwart an onslaught.

There was no sympathy for the injured man, but neither did she want to inflict more damage. It was time for answers.

'I'm Jo Trescowthick. Byron was my... my stepbrother.' Jo couldn't break eye contact. The battered face and several days stubble made it hard to label him a callous, evil bastard. He looked – haunted. 'I'm here and the doctors have only allowed us a few minutes. What can you say that can ease our family pain?'

She saw him wince, unsure if it was from his injuries, or anguish. He shifted on the pillows, pushing himself higher.

'You deserve the truth – the honesty that my bosses denied you.'

Jo swallowed. 'Who are they?'

'The police. I was an undercover cop when – when I killed your brother.'

'You were on an operation?'

'Yes.'

'What happened?'

He gestured to a seat on his right. 'Please, sit down. Don't worry about the doctors or nurses. I've wanted to share this for two years.'

Kim sat in a chair near the window, holding her mobile phone in her hand; the voice recorder app was running before they entered the room.

Troy reached for a glass of water from the cabinet. Voices filtered down the corridor. Jo settled into the seat; a daypack gripped tightly on her knees.

'My real name is Heath Michel. I was assigned to an anti-terrorist squad for a Kaikōura job. I was a watcher, generally my missions were short.' He gestured to himself. 'As a pakeha, I could never infiltrate gangs or other suspect groups. But I was a good observer, able to track targets without raising suspicion and report on secret meetings. And other stuff.'

Jo nodded. Kim recorded.

'Legally I can't reveal who my targets were, or what they were doing. For all I know, the investigation could be ongoing. But their rendezvous that February night put me on the road to Jimmy Armers Beach.'

'Just when Byron was leaving the pub.' Jo's cheeks burned. 'Did you see him?'

'Not until the last second.'

'I know the road narrows – but he should have been obvious. He wasn't drunk,' Jo said.

'I didn't have my headlights on.'

'Christ!' Kim's shock reminded the other two there was a witness to the confession.

Jo clenched the daypack tightly, fighting the urge to lash out. She shook her head at Kim. Hitting Troy – Heath – would definitely get her arrested. Worse, she might not learn the rest of the story.

'Why were you driving without fucking lights?'

'I was on the phone to my supervisor as I drove. They ordered me to stay dark; to give no indication to the subjects that were being followed. There's only one road into Jimmy Armers and the seal colony. Any approach by car at night can't be missed.'

Jo's shoulders slumped. *Under orders.*

'I was in a hybrid vehicle as well – running electric to limit the noise.'

Tears trickled both cheeks. 'Byron wouldn't have heard you over the surf … you couldn't see him … until you hit.'

'No.'

Jo couldn't talk. What a bizarre and horrible way to die. She raised her eyes to Kim, beseeching her to ask the next hardest question.'

Kim sat up straighter. 'No operation should take precedence in those circumstances. A man had been run down. Why didn't you stop?'

'I did.'

'You stopped?' Jo stared at the patient.

'Yes. Immediately. I told my boss that I had struck someone. I left the phone in the car while I checked.' Heath winced again. 'I'm sorry. There was no pulse – he died instantly. There was nothing I could do.'

'Why did you drive away?'

'I was ordered to. My boss said the operation was too sensitive – he'd been working on it for a long time. I was instructed to return to Christchurch.'

Kim was just as incensed as her friend. 'That was so wrong. What an incredibly bad judgement call.'

'That's an understatement.'

Jo was dazed. She left the rest of the interrogation to Kim.

'What happened when you returned to Christchurch?'

'The shit hit the fan. The big bosses knew the supervisor fucked up. They couldn't send me back to Kaikōura because everything was bound to unravel eventually.'

Kim stood, moved closer to the bed. She wanted to ensure the next audio was crystal clear on the recorder.

'So, they arranged a charade? You were told to confess, but never reveal you were a cop. The guilty plea, the quick sentence – it worked for the grieving family who didn't live in New Zealand. Their only glimpse of you was shrouded in a hoody in a prison video link. *Troy Michaels* went to prison – but Heath Michel walked free.'

'Yes. It was a dirty deal – but it saved red faces. Heads rolled, quietly. Two of my bosses were encouraged to take early retirement.'

'You were too young for that – what happened to you?'

'They buried me in the basement at headquarters – an administrative job guaranteed to drive me crazy.'

'Or leave?'

'Yes.'

Jo sat quietly. She finally had the answers. Byron couldn't have been saved. The man in the bed killed him, but he was a victim as well, a pawn in a public relations game to save reputations. She couldn't forgive him, not yet. But she didn't hate him anymore.

'Do you know you might not be banged up in here if I had caught up with you in Auckland last week?'

'What do you mean? I haven't been to Auckland for three years.'

'But I saw you running through Wynyard Quarter on the first Saturday we arrived. You ran across the drawbridge before I could stop you.'

Heath nodded gently. 'My brother. We're not twins, but close enough for many people to mistake us. He lives in a Viaduct apartment.'

'Oh. That could have been embarrassing then.' Jo stood.

The nurse returned. 'You're well over your allocated time with Mr Michel.'

Kim wasn't ready to depart. 'I have a couple of final questions.'

Heath looked at the nurse. 'I'm fine Jackie. The ladies are on their way to the airport.'

She tsked and swept out of the room.

Heath shrugged. 'You want to know why I was following Gordie Tulloch?'

'Yes. Did you go over to the dark side?'

Heath swallowed more water through a straw.

'I was good at my job. But those skills are useless in the real world. Except for a certain element of society.'

'Criminals.'

Heath nodded slightly. A painful expression indicated it was a bad move.

'They offered a lot of money?'

'Yep. I had a mortgage, no job prospects and no self-esteem. I reasoned that all I was doing was watching people – reporting on movements, meetings, contacts. The same as I did with the cops. I didn't go in to bang heads or rip off anyone – that was left to the Bruisers.'

'Who are in a morgue.'

'I'm lucky not to be there too.'

Jo stood. She'd heard enough and wanted to get home to Australia. Kim wasn't quite finished. 'What's going to happen to you? Have the detectives been in yet?'

'No. Just the bigwigs. I've been told to keep my mouth shut and I'll be all right. No charges.'

Kim held up the phone. 'You know I've recorded every word.'

'Yes. Do what you like. I'm finished with dirty deals.'

FEBRUARY 26

KAIKŌURA

Betty Quayle was going to miss her friendly witch. Of course, the octogenarian never used that moniker while Saffron Fernsby was in residence. Now, it didn't matter, the Oxford don had left Saturday and was booked to fly out of Christchurch yesterday. The departure was rather abrupt, considering the relaxed meanderings of the previous 12 months. Saffy loved meeting people, hearing their stories and studying Aotearoa.

Maybe the exit was hastened by the events of the past week: the cyclone, multiple shootings, a vicious assault. The coast road was still closed, the town economy was under pressure again. Perhaps a witch understood that the energy had been sucked from the town.

The flat had been left spic and span, nothing to clean before advertising for a new tenant. Saffy's parting gift should appeal to newcomers. The rockery was inspired by Māori symbols and created from debris that Saffy found during her stay. Betty loved the elaborate swirls and feature pieces. She pushed open the sliding door for a closer look.

'Hi Mrs Quayle.'

Spike Maloney stood on the pavement near the gate. His mate was wounded in the shootout. That was shocking. How could he get mixed up with diamond smugglers?

'I was wondering if Saffron was around?'

'You're too late Spike. She left on the weekend. I think there has been too much drama for an old Oxford professor.

Consternation replaced Spike's smile.

'Did you want to say farewell?'

Spike thrust hands into his jeans. He kicked a stone on the footpath.

'Um. I've just been to see Wiremu. He dropped a pack into your garden the other night.'

'When he was shot?'

'Um, yeah. Well after. He was on his way home. And he thinks – well, he's pretty sure, it fell in there.'

'Well Spike, I can assure you there's no backpack in Saffron's shingle and driftwood design.'

'Do you know if Saffron picked it up? She might have put it in a cupboard and forgot to tell you when she left.'

'There's nothing.' Betty waved a hand at the rocks. 'Apart from this lovely display.'

'That was a sudden goodbye. Did she say where she's going?'

'New York.'

'I thought she was on a study tour of Pacific islands and cultures?'

'Yes, it was a surprise. She was supposed to be going to Fiji. But then changed her booking – a cousin in Manhattan begged her to visit. He's a fancy jeweller.'

Spike's head dropped; another bluestone chip was booted towards the road. It pinged off the ute. He walked away without saying goodbye.

Betty sniffed at the bad manners. To be expected from the young. He could have learned much from a lady like Saffron Fernsby. She had been a tenant, yet she endeared herself with her charm, caring nature, manners.

'The world would be a better place if we had more people like Saffron.'

The kettle boiled in the kitchen, time for a cup of Earl Grey. She stopped in the doorway for another glance at Saffron's display. Betty admired people who could turn beach detritus into art. Saffron must have fossicked a long time for the handful of small centre pieces. It was like glittering gravel.

The End

STEPHEN JOHNSON

Stephen is an Australian-born writer, TV producer, kayaker and traveller who now plots crime fiction from his garret overlooking the Tamaki River in Auckland.

His debut novel *Tugga's Mob* was inspired by three seasons working as a tour guide on double-decker buses around Europe in the 1980s. Set in Australia and New Zealand, it was a finalist in the 2020 Ngaio Marsh Awards for Best First Novel.

Boxed, the second book in the *Melbourne Spotlight* series, follows the Aussie television crew as they unravel a series of interconnected crimes in Victoria.

In *Kaikōura Rendevous*, Jo and Kim, two of the *Melbourne Spotlight* crew encounter more bodies and drama on what is supposed to be a relaxing motorhome adventure in New Zealand.

Stephen is also the author of *Peace Stick* (2022).

www.ingramcontent.com/pod-product-compliance
Lightning Source LLC
Chambersburg PA
CBHW022350020726
47500CB00002B/213